The Fire Soul

ALSO BY MARION BLACKWOOD

Marion Blackwood has written lots of books across multiple series, and new books are constantly added to her catalogue. To see the most recently updated list of books, please visit: www.marionblackwood.com

CONTENT WARNINGS

The *Court of Elves* series contains violence, morally questionable actions, and later books in the series also contain some more detailed sexual content. If you have specific triggers, you can find the full list of content warnings at: www.marionblackwood.com/content-warnings

THE FIRE SOUL
COURT OF ELVES: BOOK FOUR

MARION BLACKWOOD

Copyright © 2022 by Marion Blackwood

All rights reserved. No part of this book may be reproduced in any form or by any electronic or mechanical means, including information storage and retrieval systems, without permission in writing from the publisher, except by reviewers, who may quote brief passages in a review. For more information, contact info@marionblackwood.com

First edition

ISBN 978-91-987259-6-4 (hardcover)
ISBN 978-91-987258-5-8 (paperback)
ISBN 978-91-987258-4-1 (ebook)

Editing by Julia Gibbs
Cover design by Claire Holt with
Luminescence Covers (www.luminescencecovers.com)

This is a work of fiction. Names, characters, places, and incidents either are the product of the author's imagination or are used fictitiously. Any resemblance to actual persons, living or dead, events, or locales is entirely coincidental.

www.marionblackwood.com

*For everyone who knows what it feels like
when the world is trying to break you*

CHAPTER 1

He threw a sword at me. It clattered metallically as it bounced across the red stones before coming to a halt in front of my feet. Fire danced in the shallow pool by the wall and joined the hissing torches in painting the room and its two inhabitants in the color of flames. I stared at the Prince of Fire. He jerked his chin.

"Pick it up."

Not moving a muscle, I simply continued watching him.

Steel sang into the air as Volkan Flameshield drew his own sword and spun it in his hand while watching me with yellow eyes that looked almost red in the firelight. His face split into a wide smile as he met my gaze.

"I'm making you a deal. If you can beat me," he began as he raised his sword and pointed it at my throat, "I'll take that collar off you and give you your freedom."

Indecision flitted through me. I had chosen, more or less willingly, to come here so that I could play out my undercover traitor scheme, but for that plan to work, I needed to keep

Volkan in the dark about my true motives. And that meant pretending to want my freedom more than anything.

Still keeping my eyes on Prince Volkan, I slowly bent to pick up the sword. I wasn't going to go all out, but I wasn't going to hide the fact that I knew my way around a blade either, so I straightened and crouched into an attack position.

Yellow eyes flicked up and down my body, assessing my stance, before Volkan met my gaze again. He arched a pale brow. I simply gave him a quick rise and fall of my eyebrows in reply, as if to say that being able to walk through walls hadn't been the only secret I had been keeping from him.

A malicious grin spread across his lips. Raising his free hand, he twitched two fingers at me.

I attacked.

The sword he had given me was of low quality and much shorter than the one that was still waiting for me inside my room in Mordren's castle. Not to mention that there was only one blade when I usually fought two-handed with both a sword and a knife. But it would have to do.

Metal clanged through the red stone room as Volkan slammed his blade into mine to stop my attack. I flicked my wrist, sending the sword sliding off mine, before whirling around and swinging it at his side again.

His fist connected with my wrist. Dull pain echoed through my hand as the force of the hit shoved my sword arm off course before the strike could land. I dove forward as silver flashed in the corner of my eye.

Volkan's sword whizzed through the air above me as I rolled across the rough stone floor. My black dress bunched around my legs but I ignored it and shot to my feet once I was outside his range. Leaping forward, I launched another assault.

He met my sword blow for blow until a feigned thrust made him jump backwards to escape. I pressed the advantage.

Zigzagging across the stones, I jabbed at him with my short sword but he managed to duck each strike. Black fabric fluttered around me as I twisted and threw my sword lower instead.

It sailed straight through his legs.

I blinked. Trailing to a halt in the middle of the room, I stared at Prince Volkan. He was standing right before me. Completely unharmed. Slowly, I reached out and poked at him with my sword again.

The tip moved through him as if he was nothing but a mirage. Which, of course, was exactly what it was. Prince Volkan was using his powers on me to make me see whatever he wanted.

Dread flitted through me. I hadn't even noticed when he switched from the real world to this fake one.

Derisive laughter echoed around me. Biting back a startled curse, I tried to pin down which direction the sound had come from but it was impossible because it came from everywhere.

The image of Prince Volkan grinned at me. And then it multiplied. Elves with long blond hair and yellow eyes appeared one after the other until the room was filled with identical copies of the prince. Flames painted dancing shadows over his face.

Lifting his sword, he spun it in his hand. The muscles of his arm flexed beneath the sleeveless red and gold tunic he wore. My eyes darted back and forth across the army around me.

They took a step forward.

Panic crackled through me unbidden. Whipping my head

from side to side, I tried to figure out which one of the apparitions was the real one but there was no difference between them.

The ring of princes closed in. I raised my sword.

Cold steel appeared against my neck. It was such a jarring sensation that I let out an involuntary gasp. Glancing down, I found a sword positioned across my throat from behind. The sharp edge bit into my skin. I swallowed. This one was real.

The grinning elves around me disappeared into thin air.

Volkan's muscled body pressed into mine from behind. With one hand keeping my upper arm in a firm grip and the other holding a blade to my throat, he leaned forward and placed his lips against my ear.

"Drop your sword."

After lowering my arm, I let the blade slip from my fingers. Metallic clanking filled the room once more as the sword hit the stone floor.

Volkan remained pressed against me from behind for another few seconds before stepping back. He kept the sharp edge at my neck as he moved around me. When he reached my discarded weapon, he kicked it across the floor. Steel scraped against stone as it slid through the room before clattering to a halt against the wall. I kept my eyes on the Prince of Fire.

Having completed his half circle, he drew himself up to his full height in front of me while keeping the point of his sword pressed against the base of my throat. "On your knees."

Still holding his gaze, I slowly lowered myself to my knees.

"From this day forward, you will address me as 'sir' when you speak to me," Prince Volkan announced.

I continued watching him in silence. Something flickered in his eyes. And then he struck.

Pulling the sword back, he swung it with impossible speed straight towards my head. Sheer terror pulsed through me as I realized that I would never be able to duck before the blade took my head right off my shoulders.

My mouth dropped open in a scream.

The sword whizzed through the air.

And then passed right through me.

Sucking in a desperate breath, I could do nothing but stare at the scene around me. The blade that should have been completing its arc to my right after taking my head off was back in its original place. Another fake vision. My head was still attached to my shoulders and Prince Volkan was still holding the point pressed against the base of my throat.

Another shuddering gasp racked my frame and something wet slid down my cheeks. Tears.

Above me, Volkan Flameshield was grinning. "I will enjoy breaking you."

I forced down the panic that still bounced around inside me after the terrible vision he had planted across my eyes, and drew a deep breath in an effort to gather my scattered wits.

"From this day forward, you will address me as 'sir' when you speak to me," he repeated.

Dropping my gaze, I bowed my head. "Yes, sir."

"You're learning. Good." He placed the sword underneath my chin, forcing my head back up so that I met his eyes again. "You will wear whatever I tell you to, say whatever I want, and do whatever I command."

"Yes, sir."

"You will not so much as breathe unless I allow it." A mass of sword-wielding copies once more appeared around him for a few seconds before disappearing again. "Don't worry, soon I will have broken you and then you will do all of this willingly. But until then…" Moving the blade downwards, he pushed it under my slave collar and lifted it slightly. "…this will make you do it. For now, I have set your range to the castle. If you try to leave without my permission, this collar will make it feel as if your body is on fire. Am I making myself clear?"

"Yes, sir."

"And since you apparently do have skills with a blade, I should probably also mention that if you were to kill me while wearing this collar…" Flames danced in his eyes. "Then your body actually *will* catch fire. Clear?"

"Yes, sir."

He withdrew the sword. The gold collar around my neck produced a soft thud as it fell back down and came to a rest against my collarbones again.

"Idra!" he bellowed.

A moment later, the door opened to reveal a female elf wearing tight-fitting leather armor. Her shoulder-length white hair shifted slightly as she came to a halt just inside the door. She looked to be only a few years older than me, but as with all elves, physical appearances were deceiving. Based on her facial features and body, she appeared to be in her mid-twenties. However, her dark eyes told a completely different story.

"Sir?" she asked.

"Take her."

Idra's emotionless black eyes slid to me. "Let's go."

I glanced up at Prince Volkan. He jerked his chin. By the door, Idra was already turning and striding back into the hall so I scrambled to my feet and hurried after her.

Wall-mounted torches hissed around me and cast the long

corridor in the same flickering red light as the room I had just left.

Since I didn't know where we were going, I stayed a step behind Idra Souldrinker as she marched down the stone passageway.

My heart thumped in my chest. Between the lethal elf leading me towards an unknown fate, the vision of Volkan decapitating me, and his promise to break me soon, I couldn't shake the feeling of dread that spread through my entire body.

I was a spy and a traitor and I had taken Eilan's place willingly, not only to save him, but also so that I could destroy the Prince of Fire. But after experiencing the crippling terror that his magic could bring, I couldn't help worrying that I had made a mistake in coming here.

With nervous anxiety flitting through my stomach, I cast a glance over my shoulder at the now closed door behind me where Volkan Flameshield was enjoying his victory.

He would stop at nothing to get what he wanted. And neither would I. He would do everything in his power to break me and turn me into a willing slave that he could use against Mordren. And I would do everything in my power to screw him over at every turn.

All I could do was hope that I'd be able to betray him before he broke me.

CHAPTER 2

*I*t could barely be described as clothes. I glanced down at the shimmering golden fabric that didn't leave nearly enough to the imagination. With a plunging neckline, an open back, and a skirt that bordered dangerously close to being see-through, the dress made me feel incredibly exposed. Fluffing out my long red curls, I arranged my hair around my shoulders so that it would cover more of my bare skin. At least I was allowed to wear clothes on my upper body, I reminded myself as I passed two male elves who were only dressed in gold-trimmed loincloths.

After Prince Volkan had handed me off to Idra, I had spent the rest of the day being transformed into the servant that the prince wanted me to be. The change in wardrobe had been a reluctant but quick affair. The explanation of rules and thorough tour of the palace, however... It had taken a lot of effort not to cackle like a villain as Idra completed my mental map of the entire castle. Little had she known that she was giving weapons to a traitor spy when she showed me around and filled me in on all the rules and protocols.

Night had fallen over the world when Idra was at last finished. She had sent me away with the parting advice to be ready to move at any time, day or night, for whatever Prince Volkan needed. But one question she had not been able to answer was *what* exactly that might be. Or what my role here would be.

My mind was spinning with both schemes and questions as I pushed down the handle and strode into the room I had been given. It looked exactly the same as Evander's room. One small bed with a nightstand and a candle next to it. And one trunk, containing the clothes that I was supposed to wear now, at the foot of the bed.

Closing the door behind me, I simply remained standing there right inside the threshold for a while. Staring at the tiny room before me.

It was strange to think that I had woken up in Mordren's luxurious bed back in the Court of Shadows just this morning. That I had watched Eilan in his shapeshifter disguise fight Prince Volkan on the sands of the arena earlier today. That I had left my friends behind in that pale stone room only hours ago. It felt as though weeks had passed since then.

Their devastated faces flashed through my mind. I wondered what they were doing now. How they were doing. I hadn't been able to explain my plan to them since Volkan had been in the room with us, but I hoped that Mordren's own scheming mind would pick up the threads of my plot.

A pang of sadness hit me. It was followed by a wave of worry. What if Mordren hadn't understood what I was doing? What if he was planning on doing something stupid to get me out? Drumming my fingers against my thigh, I flicked my eyes over my meager possessions. I needed to find a way to contact him. But how? It wasn't as though I could simply write him a letter.

I blinked.

Or could I?

Turning slowly, I stared at the red wall on my right. It would require me to trust someone I knew that I shouldn't be trusting. But then again, we had colluded before and he hadn't given me up then. I sucked my teeth. All things considered, I decided that it was worth the risk.

Slinking out through the door again, I made my way down to the end of the corridor. Torches flickered along the red stone walls, but other than that, the hallway was empty. Since it was late at night, most people should be back in their rooms by now, but I still kept a wary eye on the hall around me as I snuck forward.

When I reached my target, I paused outside for a moment. After taking another second to reconfirm that this was my best option, I raised my hand and knocked. My heart pattered in my chest as I waited.

At last, the door swung open to reveal an elf with short brown hair and dark green eyes.

Evander stumbled a step back and blinked at me. "Kenna?"

"Can I come in?"

"What are you…" He trailed off as his eyes locked on the gold collar around my throat. Then his gaze snapped back up to my face. "No."

"Yeah, I'm afraid so." I nodded towards his room again. "So, can I come in?"

He stepped aside wordlessly and then closed the door behind me as I passed him and took up position next to his nightstand. For a while, we only stood there. Staring at each other. Then he sucked in a long breath and raked a hand through his hair.

"How?" he asked.

"We had a plan. Turns out it was a trap." I shrugged. "So now I'm here."

"I hadn't heard from you in a while. I thought that meant things were going well."

"They were. Like I said, it was a trap. We didn't see it coming."

He frowned. "We?"

"Mordren and I." Lifting one shoulder, I gave him another casual shrug. "We."

"You were working *with* Mordren Darkbringer." His frown deepened. "You weren't trying to take him down too."

It wasn't really a question, so I didn't bother replying. Instead, I just shrugged again. Something flashed across Evander's face, but then he closed his eyes and blew out a long breath. When he opened them again, the expression was gone.

"And then he made you take the fall when things went wrong," Evander scoffed and shook his head. "Why am I not surprised?"

I opened my mouth to tell him that it hadn't gone down like that at all, but before I could, he pressed on.

"I'm so sorry that this happened to you." His eyes were filled with genuine concern as he searched my face. "I'm guessing you've had your first session in the breaking room with Prince Volkan?"

"The breaking room?" I furrowed my brows. "That's what it's called?"

He gestured vaguely towards the other bedrooms lining the corridor. "That's what we call it, anyway." Taking a step closer, he reached out as if to put a hand on my arm but then let it drop again. "Are you okay?"

"I'm fine." I crossed my arms over my chest but didn't back away. "And I'm still going to take Volkan down, so there's nothing to worry about. But I need something from you."

"Anything."

"Do you still have that traveling book I gave you?"

"Yes?"

"I need it back."

Evander blinked at me. "What for?"

"To communicate with the outside."

He narrowed his eyes. "You mean communicate with Mordren."

"So what if I do?"

"He's using you."

"If he is, then let me worry about it." Raising my eyebrows, I held out a hand expectantly. "Are you going to give me the book or not?"

The candle on the nightstand spluttered and threw shifting shadows over the room as we stared each other down in silence. At last, Evander blew out a forceful breath and stalked over to his bed. After lifting up the mattress, he withdrew the small leather-bound book I had given him weeks ago, and shoved it into my hands.

"Here. But trust me when I tell you that the Prince of Shadows won't get you out. He would never risk losing face in front of anyone, let alone Prince Volkan, just to save some girl he was banging."

Irritation crackled through me. "Some girl he was banging? Is that what you think of me?"

"No!" He looked genuinely horrified. "That's what *he*

thinks of you." When he saw me about to protest, his face took on a look of pity and concern. "Oh, Kenna. Please don't tell me that you thought it was love. Mordren Darkbringer isn't capable of that. Everyone knows it. All he has ever done since taking up the mantle of Prince of Shadows is to gather more and more power. At any cost. He has used people, *females*, before in the same way. And when push comes to shove, he always lets them hang while he slips away unscathed."

Oppressive silence fell over the room. I watched those green eyes brimming with concern for another few seconds before turning around.

"Thanks for the traveling book," I said as I threw open the door and stalked out.

"Kenna," Evander protested behind me as he followed me into the corridor.

Without turning around, I just gave him a wave with the back of my hand. "I need to sleep. We'll continue this conversation in the morning."

I had no intention of continuing that conversation in the morning, or at any other point in time, for that matter, but I needed him to back off. Thankfully, he appeared to take my word for it because he called out an affirmation and then presumably went back into his room. I wasn't looking in that direction, but a door clicked shut behind me so I assumed that was what he had done.

Restless irritation was still bouncing around inside me when I reached my own room. It felt as though I could no longer get through a single conversation with Evander without getting angry about one thing or another. I knew that he cared about me, and that he was saying things like that because of some misguided notion to protect me, but sometimes I wondered if he even knew how rude everything that came out of his mouth sounded.

Shoving the uncomfortable feeling out of my mind, I bent down to hide the traveling book underneath my mattress as well. Since there was barely anything in my room, it was the only logical hiding place.

There was a knock at the door.

I jumped at the sound. Wiping the guilty look off my face, I quickly smoothened down the sheets and then hurried over to the door. After casting a glance behind me to make sure that the traveling book was well hidden, I pushed it open.

A male elf in the red and gold armor of Volkan's court stared down at me. "Prince Volkan requests your presence."

"Now?" I managed while blinking at him in surprise.

It was late at night. What could he possibly want with me at this hour?

"Yes. Follow me."

My pulse thrummed in my ears. Too nervous to speak, I simply nodded in reply and stepped out into the corridor. The door swung shut behind me with an ominous click. Satisfied with my actions, the guard spun on his heel and started down the hallway.

With my heart thumping wildly in my chest, I followed him through the torchlit halls and towards my first ever mission for the Prince of Fire.

Blood rushed in my ears and my heart slammed against my ribs as I realized where we were going. Long rectangular pools of fire lined the wide hallway we followed before ending at a massive stone door carved in intricate patterns resembling flames. Swallowing against my suddenly parched mouth, I stared up at the gigantic door as the guard pounded on it.

"Sir, she's here," he called through the red stone.

"Send her in," came the answer from inside.

Drawing open the heavy door, the guard motioned towards the gap. "You heard him."

I remained frozen in place. The guard let out a soft sigh and raised a hand to give me a gentle push. Panic fluttered its poisonous wings through my stomach as I stumbled across the threshold and into Prince Volkan's bedroom.

The Prince of Fire was sitting on his neatly made bed, unlacing his boots. His long blond hair fell around his face as he leaned down and tugged the final boot off before chucking it towards the wall.

Behind me, the stone door shut with an unnaturally loud bang. Or perhaps it was just because the silence in my head was so deafening.

Please don't tell me that he...

Prince Volkan straightened and rose from the bed. In one fluid motion, he grabbed the edge of his red and gold tunic and pulled it over his head.

All blood drained from my face.

No.

The rich fabric fluttered through the air as Volkan tossed his tunic on top of a chair nearby. After watching it settle on the backrest, he turned towards me. Firelight from the pools of flame in his room danced over his muscled stomach and chest.

I flinched back a step.

Prince Volkan frowned at me for a second. Then he scoffed. Waving a hand in front of his face, he barked a cold laugh.

"Oh don't flatter yourself," he said, his voice equal parts

amusement and disgust. "I don't want anything that Mordren has already sullied."

It took a while for his words to sink in. *I don't want anything that Mordren has already sullied.* My mind turned the statement over and over in my head until it finally translated into one simple fact. Volkan was not going to demand that I sleep with him.

Relief so intense that I actually let out a small gasp coursed through me.

Malice gleamed in Volkan's eyes as he closed the distance between us and stared down into my face.

I wasn't sure whether he wanted me to look him in the eye or drop my gaze to the floor, so I did neither and remained staring straight ahead. I could see his muscles shift and his skin stretch around a scar on his chest as he reached out and placed a hand around my jaw. With a firm grip, he forced my head up so that I met his eyes.

"For some reason, Mordren has claimed you as his own and he is very protective, and *possessive*, about his things. I don't want to fuck anything that Mordren has already dirtied, but he doesn't know that. So play along." He tightened his grip on my chin. "Do you understand?"

"I understand, sir."

"Good." Letting go of my chin, he strode over to his desk instead. "Idra told me that you asked what your role here will be, so let me answer that for you. Your role is to be a weapon."

Paper rustled into the silence as the Prince of Fire started rummaging through the stacks of documents on his desk. I watched him in silence. When I didn't answer, he looked up and met my gaze. A villainous smile stretched his lips.

"I am going to use you as a weapon against Mordren. With you by my side, he won't be able to concentrate on anything other than the fact that *I* own you now. His mind will be filled with nightmares about my hands on your body, your lips on mine, and my orders in your ear. And you will play along."

Since I could read the implied threat in his voice, I dipped my chin in deference. "Yes, sir."

He chuckled and lifted an official-looking document from the pile on his desk. "I will use you to throw Mordren off his game. Starting tomorrow."

"What happens tomorrow?" When he arched an eyebrow at me, I quickly added, "Sir."

The Prince of Fire looked like someone who had received the greatest gift in the whole world as he grinned back at me. "Tomorrow, Mordren will be punished by the king for attempting to kill me in my tournament."

My heart leaped into my throat. I hadn't even thought about that. I had been so wrapped up in taking Eilan's place that I hadn't even considered that Mordren would be punished for this by the king as well. And of course he would. He had tried to kill a fellow prince and steal his court.

"So be ready to leave at dawn," Volkan finished. "Because I will be there to watch him get punished and you will be there as well, with *me*, to make it even worse."

"Yes, sir."

He jerked his chin. "Dismissed."

Cold dread washed over me as I bowed and then slipped back out to the waiting guard. Mordren would be punished by the king tomorrow.

And I would have to be there to watch.

CHAPTER 3

The cold light of dawn filtered in through the tall windows and painted the white castle in bleak hues. As if the sun itself knew that this would not be a day of joy. My pulse thrummed in my ears as I trailed behind Volkan Flameshield on the way to King Aldrich's throne room.

Mordren had tried to kill a fellow prince. I didn't know what the punishment for that was, but it couldn't be good. And on top of that already dangerous situation was the fact that I was here with Volkan. As his slave. I had seen Mordren's expression in that room before we left. He had been about one second away from leveling the entire arena, because Prince Volkan knew exactly which buttons to push to make Mordren lose his temper.

My thin golden skirt swished around my legs as we closed the distance to the open doors ahead. I needed to talk to Mordren. To tell him my plan. To tell him that everything would be alright. Writing in the traveling book had only solved half of that problem, because its twin was waiting securely inside a jacket pocket that Mordren would never be able to find. I needed to somehow get that information to him. But right now, all I could do was hope that he wouldn't do anything stupid.

Silence swept over the throne room like a crashing wave. It wasn't every day Mordren Darkbringer got caught, so the news had traveled fast, and by now all the princes already knew what had happened. Or at least a version of it. I studied the room from beneath my lashes as I followed Volkan into the vast hall.

Mordren was standing closest to the throne and he was joined by Eilan as well as Hadeon and Ellyda. All four of them snapped their gaze to me as soon as we entered. I gave them an almost imperceptible nod to let them know that I was alright. On the other side of the room were two other groups. Rayan Floodbender stood watching us with concerned violet eyes, while the Prince of Trees merely frowned from his place among his own people. Between them and Mordren was a fourth group.

Stone rumbled throughout the castle.

"You sold her to Volkan?" Edric Mountaincleaver growled, drawing out each word, as he dragged his gaze from our procession to Mordren.

Next to him, Ymas was looking at me with sad eyes. We hadn't exactly been friends when I lived in the Court of Stone, but we had always respected each other and he had even helped me when I was on the run. The blond half-elf on Edric's other side, however, flicked her turquoise eyes from my face to the slave collar at my throat and I swore I could see a small smile play over her lips. I ignored Monette's smug look and instead shifted my gaze to the target of Prince Edric's words.

Mordren's silver eyes flashed. "Of course not. He took her without my consent."

"Now, now," Prince Volkan tutted as we came to a halt between the two furious groups. "That is not entirely true, now is it?"

"Then what happened?" the Prince of Stone demanded.

"She joined my service willingly." With his yellow eyes fixed on Mordren, Volkan reached up and drew a possessive hand up my throat and then under my chin. "Isn't that right, Kenna?"

Across the pale white floor, Mordren ground his teeth together so hard that I could see the muscles of his jaw twitch. While clenching and unclenching his right hand, he looked like he was ready to stalk across the room and stab Volkan with one of the knives I knew he had hidden in his clothes. But thankfully, before that could happen, Ellyda brushed a discreet hand down his arm. Mordren forced out a slow breath while I shifted my gaze to Volkan.

"Yes, sir," I said in an emotionless voice.

"How convincing," Prince Edric snapped. "Look at her. She's only saying that because she's afraid of you."

Volkan flicked a dismissive hand in his direction but didn't take his eyes off Mordren. "I'm not the one people should be afraid of. After all, little Mordren here is the one who tried to have *me* assassinated."

"I have–"

A trumpet blast echoed through the high-ceilinged hall. Clothes rustled as everyone turned towards the door behind the throne and bowed to the king who strode out. Before sinking into a curtsey, I managed to catch Eilan's eyes and mouth: *after*. He gave me a small nod while bowing as well.

"Never did I think that you would act this way," King

Aldrich said without preamble as he came to a halt at the edge of the dais. "Not here. And certainly not now. So soon after Princess Syrene's plot and while we are faced with a politically dangerous situation involving the High Elves."

Only the soft whisper of cloth on stone disturbed the heavy silence that fell across the throne room as everyone straightened again. I shifted my gaze between the king and Mordren. Aldrich Spiritsinger looked more disappointed than angry. His normally twinkling brown eyes were somber and the lines on his face seemed somehow more prominent than they had been at the ball two weeks ago. With graceful movements, he swept his long white hair over his shoulder and locked eyes with the Prince of Shadows, who was keeping a neutral mask on his face.

"Mordren Darkbringer."

He dipped his chin in deference. "My king."

"You attempted to kill Volkan Flameshield and steal his court."

It hadn't been a question, but everyone expected Mordren to answer anyway. To confirm his guilt. Instead, the Prince of Shadows held the king's gaze with steady eyes.

"No, my king."

A few gasps rose from around the hall and were quickly followed by confused murmuring. I kept my face carefully blank as I watched the exchange.

"No?" King Aldrich said. "An entire arena heard you proclaim that Volkan had died by your hand, and you have the nerve to tell me that wasn't true?"

"With all due respect, my king, you have drawn a conclusion based on inadequate information." The murmurs throughout the throne room turned shocked but Mordren pressed on. "Yes, it is true that I spoke in such a way at the time when I thought Volkan was dead. But I am not the one who supposedly killed him, am I?"

"No, but you sent Julian Bladesinger to do the deed for you," Volkan snapped before the king could respond. "That still makes you guilty, little prince."

"Did I?" He arched a dark eyebrow at the Prince of Fire. "Then by all means, produce this Julian Bladesinger and have him confirm that I hired him to do this wicked deed."

"I can't, because I gave him back to you."

"No, you did not." Mordren spread his arms. "Ask anyone. The whole arena saw you drag him off with a slave collar around his throat. So the fact that you refuse to present him now and have him give testimony only serves to strengthen my case that this is an attempt by you to drag my name through the dirt. Again."

It took great effort not to grin. Of course Volkan couldn't produce Julian Bladesinger. Because Julian Bladesinger didn't exist. But the only people in this room who knew that were me and the four scheming liars from the Court of Shadows.

"Mordren," King Aldrich interrupted before the Prince of Fire could spit out his furious retort. "The fact still remains that you took credit for the deed."

"I did. I will freely admit that. When I saw Volkan fall, I genuinely believe that he was dead so I decided to take advantage of the situation and add to my own reputation. I knew that Julian Bladesinger would ultimately get the throne, but it would add to my own name if people secretly whispered in the shadows that I was the one responsible for it." Mordren lifted his shoulders in a casual shrug. "It was a power play. As simple as that."

"Lies," Prince Volkan growled.

"Then get Julian Bladesinger in here and have him tell you

whether I had anything to do with him or his fight." A smirk slid home on Mordren's lips. "But you can't, can you? Because you know that he will only corroborate my story."

"No, I can't because I don't have him."

"Of course not. Because you had him killed as soon as you realized that he would ruin your great plan."

"Oh you have some nerve—"

"Enough!" Stone rumbled under our feet as King Aldrich sent his power pulsing through the mountain palace. His eyes were hard as he shifted them between the two arguing princes until they both lowered their chins. "Volkan, can you get this Julian Bladesinger here to confirm your side of the story?"

"He's—"

"Yes or no?"

Prince Volkan ground his teeth together before finally pressing out, "No, my king."

Aldrich's gaze slid to the Prince of Shadows. "Mordren, can you get this Julian Bladesinger here to confirm your side of the story?"

"No, my king."

"Then we are at an impasse."

Irritation flashed over Volkan's face as he threw an arm out in Mordren's direction. "Just get the Orb of Verity here and make him talk with that!"

"And who is going to bear the cost of that?" King Aldrich raised his eyebrows. "You?"

"No, but—"

"Then the answer is no." Sadness swirled in his eyes. "Gaven still hasn't woken up from when he paid the price of using the Orb of Verity to confirm Princess Syrene's assassination plot against me. All magic comes with a price, and I refuse to let another innocent pay it just to satisfy the needs of princes and kings."

"So he gets off free?" Volkan's outraged voice rang through the white stone hall and made several elves from the Court of Water flinch. "Mordren tries to kill me and steal my court, and there's no punishment?"

Deafening silence followed his outburst as everyone held their breath, waiting to see what the king would do. Aldrich seemed on the verge of reprimanding the Prince of Fire for daring to raise his voice in such a manner to his king. Holding Volkan's gaze, he stared him down until the prince dipped his chin in deference. The throne room blew out a collective sigh of relief.

"I didn't say that," King Aldrich announced into the quiet room.

Mordren snapped his head up but before he could speak, the king met his gaze and continued in a calm voice.

"Mordren Darkbringer, while Volkan cannot prove that you were involved in the events of yesterday afternoon, the fact still remains that you tried to influence another court's succession. And actions have consequences." Aldrich paused, eyes locked on the Prince of Shadows, before continuing. "I hereby declare that you will have a chaperone."

"What?"

"From now on, Remus," the king motioned for a male elf with short blond hair who approached from his place by the wall, "will accompany you everywhere you go to make sure that nothing similar happens again."

"For how long?"

A flash of anger shot across Aldrich's features. Marble rumbled around us in response to it. "Until I say otherwise."

He slashed a hand through the air. "Until you have earned back my trust or until the Court of Fire is satisfied."

Shock and incredulity bounced around in Mordren's eyes as he stared back at his king. "You can't be serious."

"Oh I am very serious." King Aldrich's face looked to have been carved from the mountain beneath us as he held his stare. "And I am warning you, Mordren. One more act of aggression against the Court of Fire and I will strip you of your title."

Gasps echoed through the white hall. All around us, the other princes and their attendants were whipping their heads between the king and the Darkbringer prince. Mordren looked like someone had slapped him. Next to me, Volkan was grinning like a fiend.

"Now, stop behaving like children fighting over toys and start focusing on what's truly important." This time, the king's brown eyes swept across every group gathered in his hall. "The High Elves are gaining influence over the common people. I am doing what I can on my end, but I want the situation monitored in every court from your perspective as well. Am I making myself clear?"

It took a few moments for the shift in conversation to settle among the other princes, but then they all bowed and spoke in unison.

"Yes, my king."

He flicked his hand and strode away. "Dismissed."

No one moved. Every eye in the room tracked the king's movements as he stalked across the dais and then disappeared through the same door he had arrived through. Once it had clicked shut behind him, the spell broke.

Intense murmuring spread like wildfire through the white stone hall. The attendants who had arrived with their princes hid their mouths behind their hands and whispered hurried comments to each other while darting glances at Mordren and Volkan. Those two, on the other hand, only had eyes for each other. Murder and malice shone on both their faces as they stared each other down from across the shining floor.

Eilan leaned forward and whispered something in Mordren's ear. His silver eyes flicked to me. And then he was prowling across the room.

Prince Rayan saw the calamity about to happen and set off across the floor as well. His attendants hurried after him.

"I never thought you would stoop to this level," Mordren said as he closed the distance to the Prince of Fire. "But I guess I should not be surprised."

"Likewise, little prince," Volkan said. "I never thought you'd dare to lie to the king like that. But you did. And now you got off with a slap on the wrist." A sneer twisted his face. "A chaperone? You should have been forced to get down on your knees before me and beg my forgiveness."

Mordren's voice was a cold midnight wind. "I would burn my own court to the ground before I ever got down on my knees before you."

As he got closer, he didn't stop but instead plowed straight for Volkan as if to trample him. Or force him to retreat. Before that could happen, Idra stepped forward and blocked the way. In response, Hadeon shouldered past and squared up against her. She looked back at him with a blank expression on her face but the whole room crackled with tension.

"Please," Prince Rayan said as he weaved through the others to separate the fight about to happen. "Not here. Take a deep breath."

Everyone ignored him.

"How dare you?" A voice cut instead through the bubbling

threats like a knife. Ellyda's violet eyes were cold and sharp as ice as she strode up to Volkan and snapped, "How dare you speak about my prince in such a way?"

Prince Volkan had always been interested in Ellyda, so when she got in his face like that, all his attention snapped right to her. And with Idra occupied by Hadeon, Mordren managed to slink to the side and grab my arm without either of them noticing. Understanding flickered in Rayan's eyes. Sidestepping the glaring couples, he smoothly blocked Volkan's view of us for a few precious moments.

"I will get you out," Mordren promised in a frantic whisper, his hand still wrapped tightly around my arm.

"No." I looked up at him with calm eyes. "It will start a war."

"Then I will start a war!"

"And you will be stripped of your title."

"I don't care," he hissed.

Placing my hand over his, I gave it a gentle squeeze. "I do. And besides, I have a plan."

To my left, Prince Rayan cleared his throat. We were out of time.

"Check the traveling book," I whispered as I removed his hand from my arm and slid back towards Volkan. "Two pockets from the right, five pockets down."

His eyes were wild. Fury and fear flashed and mingled until they formed a terrible storm in the otherwise glittering silver, but we both knew that I was right. Going to war with Volkan was not an option.

"I will get you out," Mordren breathed, so softly that I almost missed it.

But I was already back by Prince Volkan's side so I just

dropped my gaze and pretended that I had simply been swept away by the crowd for a few seconds.

"As fun as this has been, I do have other things to…" Volkan hooked a finger under my golden collar and pulled me closer, "…*do* today."

Lightning crackled in Mordren's eyes again. "Watch your back. Because the moment you let your guard down, I will be there to stab a knife in it."

"Careful now." A vicious grin spread across his mouth. "Wouldn't want your new babysitter to hear that, now would you?"

I stumbled forward when Volkan yanked me along by the collar as he brushed past the fuming Court of Shadows. Idra stared Hadeon down for another few seconds before following as well.

Fury hung like storm clouds around my friends, but they couldn't do anything other than watch us leave. My heart thumped in my chest. Mordren would have a chaperone. That would complicate my plan quite a bit since I couldn't rely on his help as much as I had planned. But I had schemed my way out of trickier situations before.

Flicking my gaze around the throne room, I modified my plan slightly to fit the new circumstances. It would take more effort, but I could make it work. I glanced back towards where Mordren was standing.

At least now, I had a solid line of communication with the outside.

It was a start.

CHAPTER 4

*A*nxious silence spread across the throne room like a sweeping wave. Gripping the pitcher of wine tightly in my hands, I tried to resist the urge to get down on my knees as two tall figures strode into the red stone palace.

Fire glinted off bronze breastplates as High Commander Anron and Captain Vendir made their way through the pools of flame set into the floor and approached the raised throne at the end of the hall. The petitioner who had been addressing the Prince of Fire swallowed and flicked nervous eyes between his prince and the two newcomers. His left knee buckled slightly. While straightening again, he snapped his gaze back to Volkan Flameshield and waved a hand in front of his face as if to say that what he had been asking about wasn't important. After a deep bow, he hurried out of the path of the approaching High Elves.

"Prince Volkan," High Commander Anron said in a pleasant voice as he and his captain came to a halt before the throne. "I came to congratulate you on a most spectacular display in the arena the other day."

Surprise flickered in Volkan's eyes, but he inclined his head. "I thank you."

From my place by the wall, I could see Volkan's expression but not those of the High Elves so I started edging further down the room, towards the raised throne. Since my job was to be a weapon against Mordren, Prince Volkan had simply dumped me in the throne room today while he handled petitioners, in case Mordren decided to make an appearance. Standing there in the low-cut golden dress, with my only task being holding a wine pitcher and looking pretty, was incredibly boring. But it gave me the opportunity to overhear conversations like these.

"I hope you received proper compensation for it," Anron continued.

A smirk played over Volkan's lips. "In part. And the rest is underway."

Evander glanced at me as I sidled up to him. He was standing close to the wall and was holding a large fan set onto a golden pole. Wariness flashed in his eyes as he shifted his gaze between me and Volkan, but he said nothing.

"Would you care to speak privately?" the High Commander asked.

Now that I could see his face as well, I caught the scheming look in his sharp blue eyes as he smiled at the Prince of Fire. Volkan replicated the gesture.

"I would indeed."

Clothes whispered against stone as he pushed himself up from his sturdy red throne and started down the steps.

"Where will they go?" I whispered to Evander while still keeping my eyes locked on Volkan.

Evander considered for a moment and then breathed back,

"There's a private meeting room through that doorway over there. First door on the right."

Following the slight shift of his fan, I found which doorway he meant. It was a wide arch set into the back wall, to the right of the throne. Realization sparkled inside me. I knew which meeting room he was referring to. Back when I had been spying for Prince Edric, I had visited that room several times. With varying degrees of success. But at least I knew how to get in.

"Cover for me," I said as I started moving towards the back wall.

Evander kept his expression blank and focused on the room before him, but he gave me a small nod. Still holding on to the metal pitcher, I drifted over to my target and then leaned back against the cool red stones. The rest of the room was watching the Prince of Fire and the two High Elves as they moved towards the open doorway on the other side. After one final glance to make sure that no one was looking in my direction, I took a step backwards and phased through the wall.

A torchlit corridor greeted me on the other side. Moving as fast as I could without spilling the wine, I hurried towards the end of the hallway. It emptied out in the hall that Volkan and the others would be heading to, but since I didn't want to risk being spotted, I leaped through the wall to my left before I reached it. A wide room full of chairs and other pieces of furniture waited inside.

Red liquid sloshed precariously as I weaved through the packed storage room. I glanced at an empty pot as I slunk past a stack of tables. The wine was becoming cumbersome to lug around but I couldn't leave the pitcher behind either.

Making a split-second decision, I screeched to a halt and

poured the wine into the waiting pot. With a much lighter load, and no fear of leaving a dripping trail of red behind me, I lowered the now empty pitcher and ran across the room with it dangling from my fingers.

The sound of a door closing echoed into the hallway as I phased through the next wall. They were already inside. Taking off at a run, I sprinted around the corner and approached the meeting room from the other side. Torches hissed in annoyance as the draft I left in my wake made them splutter. I called up my mental map while moving into position. Since I had been in that room before, I knew where to enter so that I would remain unseen.

Silk brushed against my skin. And then I materialized in the darkened corner by the back wall. The urge to kneel hit me like a blow to the chest.

"...wasn't sure before, but now I am," High Commander Anron said.

Hidden in the shadows between two stone bookcases at the back of the room, I glanced around the corner and took in the view before me.

The meeting room was on the smaller side, but was luxuriously furnished with expensive-looking couches and armchairs clustered around a low stone table. Bookshelves and statues lined the walls while a fire burned brightly in a grand hearth. Since it was already warm in the Court of Fire at this time of year, the flames made the room even hotter. Captain Vendir, who stood behind Anron's armchair and closest to the fireplace, adjusted his bronze armor slightly while beads of sweat gathered at his brow.

Volkan, on the other hand, appeared entirely unaffected by the heat as he watched the High Commander from the seat opposite him. "Oh?"

"Yes." Anron swept his brown hair back over his shoulder and leaned forward with his elbows on his knees. "We do indeed seem to view the world in a similar way."

"I am glad to hear that."

"As am I. It is rare for me to find someone who shares my way of... handling things. Handling *people*."

Prince Volkan inclined his head but said nothing, waiting for the High Elf to continue. Flames crackled in the fireplace behind Anron as the two of them only considered each other in silence for a while. Captain Vendir drew a discreet hand from his temple and through his long blond hair in order to wipe away the bead of sweat trickling down his skin, but his observant brown eyes were locked on the Prince of Fire. From my spot in the shadows, I barely dared breathe as I waited for someone to speak. I couldn't stay long, otherwise my absence might be noticed, but I had to hear this.

Still leaning forward with his elbows on his knees, the High Commander steepled his fingers. "If I may be so bold... I have plans back home and I would be in a much better position of carrying them out if you were the ruler of this continent."

Surprise and pleasure flickered in Volkan's eyes for a moment before he hid it again behind a composed mask. Smoothening an invisible crease in his dark red tunic, he leaned back in his seat. "What kind of plans?"

"Oh, I intend to make a play for power." A wicked smile spread over his lips. "What if I were to back you up in this fight and help you become king of this continent, and then you provide me with some assistance once I make my move?"

"I would say that sounds like an excellent arrangement."

The sharp glint in his eyes told me that Volkan hadn't yet decided whether he was going to fulfill his end of the bargain since that would come after he had gotten what he wanted. But the High Commander, apparently oblivious, only flashed him a satisfied smile.

My heart thumped nervously in my chest. The High Elves were going to help Volkan Flameshield take over the continent. I already knew that Anron's long-term scheme somehow involved Volkan, but I hadn't even considered that *making him king* was part of the plan. This was beyond bad.

"Fantastic," High Commander Anron said as he leaned back in his chair as well. "So, how do we make you rule?"

"We need to make sure that I get chosen as the next King of Elves." He ran a hand over his jaw. "Which means that we need to make the other princes look bad. Make them look weak. Incompetent. That way, Aldrich will have no choice but to pick me."

"So, we need to cut off their power source?"

"Yes."

"And how do we do that?"

Stone scraped against stone as Volkan pushed back his armchair and stood up. "Hold on, let me just get the map and I will show you…"

My heart leaped into my throat. He was getting a map from the bookshelves. From my hiding place.

Not hesitating a second, I threw myself back through the wall and phased into the corridor outside. With my pulse still smattering in my ears, I ran back towards the throne room. That had been close. But at least I had heard the most important parts. And I had gotten out in time.

Jumping through another wall, I made it back into the storage room I had passed through earlier and then phased into the corridor behind the throne room. Since I was no longer in the very conspicuous hallway next to

Volkan's meeting room, I finally dared to breathe a sigh of relief.

Slowing to a walk, I rounded the corner that would take me back towards my final exit point in the wall.

Black eyes stared me down.

I screeched to a halt and blinked at the white-haired elf who had been coming around the corner from the other side.

"What are you doing here?" Idra Souldrinker took a step towards me.

On instinct, I retreated a step in response. "I was supposed to get more wine, but I don't know where to go."

Her hand shot out. Panic pulsed through me when her fingers closed around the edge of the metal pitcher in my hand, but then relief followed it as I remembered that I had emptied it back in that storage room earlier. So at least one part of my lie was believable.

She tipped the container towards her and cast a quick look inside. When she had confirmed that it was indeed empty, she slid her gaze to me but kept her firm grip on the pitcher. Narrowing her eyes, she studied my face. Looking for traces of lies.

Keeping my expression somewhere between innocent and scared, I simply remained standing there.

At last, she let go of the metal container and jerked her chin in the direction she had come from. "It's that way."

I dipped my chin. "Thank you."

Taking a step to the side, I made as if to slip past her but her arm shot out, blocking my way, before I could get away.

"Tonight, you will attend me in the training room."

The comment took me completely by surprise, so for a moment I only blinked at her in stunned silence. Idra, however, seemed to take that as reluctance to follow her orders. She cocked her head, her silken hair brushing the top of her shoulders with the movement.

"Problem?" she said, her eyes boring into mine.

Snapping out of it, I shook my head. "No. Sorry. Yes, of course I will attend you in the training room."

Idra stared me down for another few seconds before finally saying, "Good."

Without another word, she dropped her arm and jerked her chin, informing me that I could now leave. I gave her a parting nod and then hurried away.

Only once I had rounded the next corner did I let out the long breath I had been holding. I had no idea why Idra wanted me in the training room tonight, but that was a problem for later. Right now, I had to make it back into the throne room before Prince Volkan realized that I had been gone for a while. And then I had some scheming to do.

High Commander Anron's plan involved making Volkan king. I couldn't let that happen. So there was one thing I had to do. One thing I had to start right now before it was already too late.

I had to mess with the Prince of Fire. Mess with everything he did. I had to ruin his and Anron's budding friendship and make them turn on each other. And I had to do it all before the High Commander could manage to make Volkan Flameshield the King of Elves. Or else everyone I cared about would suffer.

CHAPTER 5

Terror hung like poisonous mist over the room. I cast a quick glance at the four male elves standing in a neat row next to me. They remained motionless, but their eyes tracked the movements of the couple before us. Shifting my attention back in that direction as well, I studied the fifth fight of the night.

Idra advanced across the padded floor. The black-haired elf, Hilver, retreated in response, keeping a good two strides between them. Light from the torches flickered over the multitude of scars across Idra's entire body, but the blank expression on her face never changed. While still backing away, Hilver flicked his gaze to the practice dummies on his right.

She struck.

Using his second of inattention, Idra flashed across the floor. With a lightning-fast blow, she slammed the heel of her hand into his stomach. Hilver doubled over, gasping, as his breath was driven from his lungs but Idra's hand shot out again. Wrapping her fingers around his throat, she forced his head back up while she squeezed.

Panic darted around Hilver's pale blue eyes as he tried to break her grip on his throat. One of his knees buckled. A dull thud sounded into the dead silent training room as his kneecap hit the floor. Idra, keeping her death grip on his windpipe, stepped in closer.

The row of elves beside me held their breath. Fear pushed out the panic in Hilver's eyes and he raised his hands in surrender. For a moment, Idra only continued staring down at him. The cloud of terror hanging over the room grew so thick I could practically smell it on all the males in the room.

Then she let go.

As soon as Idra released his throat, Hilver collapsed to his hands and knees, and sucked in desperate gasps. No one else moved. Once he had managed to get some air back in his lungs, he scrambled back to his place in line. Right next to me.

Idra turned towards the six of us. All five males beside me flinched in response, but Idra's gaze locked on me.

"You." She twitched her fingers. "Let's go."

Different plans swirled in my mind. I didn't particularly relish the idea of letting her beat me up unchallenged, but at the same time, I didn't want to get stuck on training duty every night. If I was to have any chance of succeeding in my mission to take down Prince Volkan, I couldn't afford to waste time on anything else.

Making a decision, I squared up against Idra.

She frowned at the poor stance I had opted for, but didn't comment. Instead, she just twitched her fingers again.

I attacked.

Swinging widely, I made a terrible attempt to hit her with

my right fist while also leaving my flank wide open for a counterstrike. Just as I had predicted, she went for it. Pain shot through my body as her hand connected with the side of my ribs. Gasping in a breath, I stumbled to the side and threw out my other arm in a lame effort to defend myself. Idra watched me through narrowed eyes but allowed me to straighten again.

She struck.

Her hand came flashing over my head as I ducked the blow and twisted to the side. In my mind, I groaned in annoyance. I should have let that strike hit. But I had seen it coming too late and my body had acted on instinct. As Idra feigned another blow and then followed it up with a second strike, I realized how difficult it was to pretend to be bad at fighting. At least when fighting someone who was this fast.

The instincts that my War Dancer father had instilled in me when I was a child were screaming at me to leap out of the way, to twist, or to block, and I had to actively remind myself I shouldn't be moving like that.

Forcing my body to remain in place, I ducked Idra's feigned strike and let the second one land. I sucked in another desperate breath as her hand connected with my stomach but Idra was already spinning around me.

My knees buckled as she slammed her leg into them from behind.

Instead of diving forward with the motion, as I normally would have, I let myself crash down face first on the ground. The hit jarred my bones but I rolled over on the ground and raised my arm to block the hit that should be coming. My hand slammed back into the ground as Idra kicked aside my raised arm before she straddled my chest.

With one foot trapping my wrist to the floor, she crouched

down over me and placed her open hand right below my throat. Her impassive gaze met mine.

Behind her toned shoulders, the five males were holding their breath once more.

I looked up into Idra's black eyes, trying to see whether I had managed to fool her or not, but they betrayed nothing of her emotions. Hoping that I had at least accomplished my mission, I slowly moved my one free hand a little further from my body and then tapped it against the floor in a sign of submission.

She moved her scarred hand higher. Her warm fingers closed around my throat. And then she started to squeeze.

Confusion blew through my mind. What was she doing? I had already tapped out so there was no need to keep proving that she had won. The only thing I could think of was that she was trying to provoke me into showing her my true skills. To make me afraid enough that I actually fought back.

Still holding her gaze with steady eyes, I just tapped my hand against the floor again.

This time, I swore I could detect a flicker of confusion in her dark eyes. She stopped squeezing. After searching my face for another few seconds, she drew her eyebrows down in a scowl and then straightened.

I sucked in a deep breath as the pressure on my throat disappeared.

Stalking away from me, Idra flicked a hand in the direction of the exit. "Dismissed."

After blowing out a soft sigh, I struggled to my feet and started towards the door. When none of the male elves moved, Idra snapped her gaze to them.

"That means you too."

They lurched into motion. Without a second look back, they scrambled after me and hurried out the door.

Only hissing torches broke the silence as the six of us made our way back towards our rooms. I flicked my gaze between the males, trying to figure out if they were friends or just people who tolerated each other. But none of them looked at the others. They only cast nervous glances over their shoulders.

Just when I had come to the conclusion that they probably didn't like each other and weren't talking because of that, we rounded a corner and the whole group heaved a collective sigh of relief.

"I don't know how much more of this I can take," Hilver said, as if the corner somehow marked the point of where Idra could no longer hear them.

"Same," muttered the blond elf next to him.

Hilver turned his pale blue eyes to me. "You're lucky you're a terrible fighter. She probably won't call you back a second time." Drawing a hand over the long black hair he had tied up in a bun, he shook his head. "I wish I had pretended to be bad my first time. Then maybe I would've been spared this torture."

I arched an eyebrow at him. "Torture? What do you mean?"

"You know what she can do, right? She can kill anyone with a single touch and we," he swept his arms wide to encompass the other four elves walking alongside us, "have to help her train basically every night. We can't win. All we can do is fight and then tap out in submission and hope that she doesn't decide to kill us anyway."

"It's terrifying," the blond elf added with a shake of his head. "Constantly hoping that she doesn't have a bad day that ends with her using her death magic on us just because she can."

Hilver shook his head as well. "I would do anything to get out of this training duty."

The other four murmured their agreement. Keeping my mouth shut, I watched the fear and hopelessness on their faces.

At least I had been able to trick them into thinking that I didn't know how to fight.

I could only hope that I had managed to fool Idra too.

CHAPTER 6

"Come with me." An elf clad in the gold and red armor of the Court of Fire prowled up to me and jerked his chin. "Your presence has been requested."

Glancing down at the water pitcher in my hand, I opened my mouth to ask if I should bring it, but before I could get any sound out, the guard cut me off.

"Leave it." He jerked his chin again. "Let's go."

A soft clink sounded as I placed the pitcher on the floor and then straightened again. Brushing my hands over the thin golden dress I was wearing, I followed the guard across the throne room.

No courtiers or petitioners filled the room today, which meant that the only people inside were slaves or guards. I flicked my eyes over the firelit hall.

Surprise flitted through me.

Across the red floor, another guard was leading Evander in the same direction as we were heading. And from the other side, there was a third guard who was marching yet another elf towards us as well. What was Volkan up to now?

Our footsteps echoed against the stone walls as the three guards led us through the open doorway to the right of the throne and into the empty corridor beyond. Prince Volkan had retreated to the private meeting chamber with High Commander Anron a while ago, but it still didn't explain why they wanted to see us three.

"Do you know what's going on?" Evander whispered on my left.

"Quiet," the guard in the middle snapped.

On my other side, the third slave flinched. She was thin and wary-looking, with hair so dark it was more blue than black and eyes the color of a storm-swept sea. The gold collar around her throat hung heavy above a low-cut blue dress that matched her eyes.

She kept her eyes fixed on the guard's back while I twisted slightly towards Evander and shook my head in response to his question.

The guards stopped outside the private meeting chamber that I had managed to eavesdrop in last time, and then the one in the middle raised his fist to knock.

"Enter," came the reply a second later.

While the guard pushed down the handle and opened the door, the other two stepped aside and motioned for us to go inside. The three of us exchanged a glance. Then I shrugged and strode into the meeting room. Evander and the blue-eyed elf followed me.

"Kenna," Prince Volkan said as I approached the armchairs where he and Anron were seated. This time, Captain Vendir was also sitting down, but at the back of the room. Volkan slid his eyes to the elves behind me. "Evander. Viviane."

Coming to a halt before the low table that separated the two armchairs, I bowed my head. "Sir."

Evander and the elf with blueish black hair, Viviane, murmured the same greeting as they stopped on either side of me.

High Commander Anron watched us with sharp blue eyes. I fought against the usual urge to kneel in his presence as I kept my eyes on the floor until Volkan twitched his fingers, motioning for us to straighten. Bright light from the midday sun fell across their faces as Volkan and Anron watched us in silence for a few moments.

"Shouldn't there be a fourth one?" Anron asked at last, his gaze sweeping across our faces.

"Yes, ideally there should be. But it doesn't matter." Prince Volkan grinned and nodded towards me. "Because she is connected to both the Court of Stone and the Court of Shadows. Which means that we still have one from every court."

It took great effort to keep the frown from my face. He was right. I did possess knowledge about both of those courts, and Evander was from the Court of Trees, which meant that Viviane was from the Court of Water. But what did he want from us?

As if he could read my mind, Volkan turned calculating eyes on the three of us. "What is the source of your previous prince's power?"

The High Commander, and the blond captain at the back of the room, watched us intently. My mind was spinning. Should I lie? Studying Volkan's face, I could almost read the anticipation swirling in his eyes. No. He knew.

If my assessment of Volkan was correct, he already knew the answer and was testing us to see if we would dare to disobey him by lying.

"Viviane?" he prompted.

After flicking her eyes between the powerful elves before her, she cleared her throat. "Prince Rayan's power comes from the fact that he is a very organized and levelheaded person."

A scream tore from Viviane's throat. It bounced between the red stone walls as she dropped to her knees and pressed her hands to her head. I stared in mute horror but didn't dare intervene as she started sobbing on the floor.

"I'm sorry, I'm sorry, I'm sorry," she pleaded while rocking back and forth. "Please, I'm sorry."

Cold dread filled my stomach. This was what Volkan did with all his slaves in that torture room. He tried to find the one thing that would break them. That would make them surrender to him just so they would never have to see it again. And he had clearly been able to find the one thing that Viviane couldn't bear to see. Fear flitted through me. I had to finish my mission before Volkan figured out the one thing that I knew would break me.

Anron sat forward in his armchair. Interest shone across his whole face as he watched the slender female beg on the floor.

At last, Prince Volkan pulled back his magic and stopped whatever nightmarish scenes he was making her see. "Do not lie to me."

"Yes, sir," she gasped. "No, sir. I'm sorry, sir."

"Stand up."

Viviane pushed herself off the floor. She swayed slightly as she straightened and wiped the lingering tears from her cheeks.

"Now, I will ask again. What is the source of Rayan's power?"

Drawing in a shuddering breath, she answered, "He cares

about people. His power in the Court of Water comes from the fact that he actually cares about everyone in his court."

A satisfied smile spread across Volkan's mouth as he turned to the High Commander and motioned towards the shaking elf before them. *So, my assessment had been correct. He already knew the answer and was now only using us to prove it to Anron.*

The High Elf inclined his head in acknowledgement.

Shifting his gaze to me, Volkan raised his eyebrows in silent question.

"Prince Edric has power and support from his court because he's hardworking, does his job well, and because people know that they can count on him to do the right thing," I said in an even tone.

Since Prince Volkan technically already knew this, I wasn't betraying Edric's trust by sharing it.

Anron met Volkan's gaze and nodded again. The Prince of Fire turned back to me and waved his hand expectantly.

"And Mordren?" he said.

"Prince Mordren's power is based on fear."

"Elaborate."

I had to once more remind myself that Volkan already knew all of this, before I did as he commanded. "No one wants to challenge Prince Mordren because they all know that he is too dangerous to cross and that it will end with them on their knees, begging him for mercy."

Annoyance flickered in Volkan's eyes at the mention of Mordren's usual victories, but Anron looked satisfied with the answer, so the Prince of Fire just shifted his attention to Evander.

"And Iwdael?"

"Prince Iwdael makes people feel good about themselves,"

Evander said. "That is why they like him and support him. He always makes sure that his people feel appreciated and that they're having a good time."

Logs popped and fire crackled from the hearth behind us as the two powerful elves considered us. The swelling heat inside the room made me want to move out of the range of the fireplace and the bright sunlight streaming in through the windows, but I forced myself to remain standing where I was.

"Who do you want to start with?" High Commander Anron said, finally breaking the silence that had settled.

"I think Rayan has gotten a bit too comfortable in his water palace," Prince Volkan replied. His sleeveless tunic of dark red shifted against his muscled chest as he turned towards the High Elf. "And besides, that might give you a bit more room to breathe too."

"That would be a most desirable side effect."

His yellow eyes locked on Viviane again. "Rayan grants people's petitions for financial aid every month, correct?"

"Yes," she replied.

"When is the next one?"

"In two days."

"Do you know where he keeps the lists of those who have applied for aid?"

Sadness and regret swirled in her storm-swept eyes, and for a moment, it looked like she was going to deny it. But then she dropped her gaze and whispered, "Yes."

"Good." He turned to me. "Kenna, since you can walk through walls, you will break into the castle to change those lists."

Evander whipped his head towards me. *Shit.* I had managed to hide my power from him for so long, but now he knew. And this wasn't exactly how I had wanted him to find out about it either.

"You will erase the names of all the people from poor families," Volkan continued. "So when he announces the aid he is giving, it will look like he only cares about the rich families in his court." Raising a hand, he pointed between me and Viviane. "You'll take her with you so that she can show you where the lists are and who the poor people are."

"I can't," I said.

Prince Volkan sat forward. "I don't think you heard me."

In the other armchair, Anron was watching us with curious eyes again while his captain only stared blankly at us from the back of the room.

"No, I mean, I literally can't." Keeping my eyes soft, I lifted my shoulders in a helpless shrug. "It's one of the limitations of my power. Only I can walk through walls. I can't take anyone else with me."

I thoroughly disliked telling people about how my power worked, but since he would find out that only I could walk through the walls as soon as we started this mission anyway, I didn't really have any other choice than to tell him. And besides, I had to make sure that I was sent on this mission alone.

Volkan clicked his tongue in irritation. We all waited in silence while he finished making up his mind. When he at last waved a dismissive hand through the air, I had to suppress a victorious grin.

"Fine," he said. "Viviane, you will give Kenna all the information she needs beforehand and then she will sneak in on her own."

"Yes, sir," we answered in unison.

"I want it done tonight."

"Yes, sir."

He nodded. "Dismissed."

We all bowed low before disappearing back out the door again. As soon as we stepped into the cool dark corridor, I breathed a sigh of relief to be out of that infernally hot room. As the guards fell in beside us and escorted us back to the throne room, I couldn't help thinking that it had to be deliberate. Prince Volkan must have the fire going in that room on purpose. To throw the High Elves off their game a little and to make sure that he would be the one in control. It was rather impressive.

While I might hate the Prince of Fire with every part of my soul, I couldn't deny that he was intelligent. And intelligent people were dangerous.

Glancing at the thin elf from the Court of Water, I started piecing together a plot in my head.

If I was to outsmart Volkan tonight, I would have to be really clever. Or this scheme would never work.

CHAPTER 7

*A*djusting the mattress before me, I straightened and brushed my hands over the set of clothes I had been given earlier that evening. Since sneaking into a heavily guarded castle would be next to impossible while wearing a sparkling golden dress, Prince Volkan had allowed me to own a pair of black pants, a long-sleeved shirt in the same material, and a pair of soft leather boots that were to only be used on missions like this.

An image of my jacket and blades flashed through my mind. I missed them, and I wished that I could have worn them too, but this would have to do for now. Soon, after my mission was complete, I would be free again and then I could wear whatever I wanted once more. Shoving the uncomfortable feelings aside, I moved towards the door.

The sun had set long ago, and it was almost time for me to leave now. I had planned everything that could be planned. Now, all I could do was hope that it would be enough.

Stone scraped against stone as the door to my room was

yanked open. I blinked in surprise as Evander stalked across the threshold.

"You're magically gifted," he announced.

His tone made me cross my arms in annoyance. "And you have apparently forgotten how to knock."

"Like you're one to talk. You who have broken into my room in the middle of the night while I was sleeping." He scoffed. "At least now I guess I know how you did it."

"Is there something you want to say to me?"

"Yes." Since he had come straight from the throne room, he was still wearing only the white and gold-trimmed loincloth. Drawing himself up to his full height, he crossed his arms over his toned chest and glared at me. "We worked together for weeks. We *slept* together. And not once did you think to tell me that you can walk through walls."

Drawing my eyebrows down, I returned the scowl. "Seeing as you betrayed me and locked me in a basement after we had done all that, I'm pretty sure I made the right call."

"What about after that?" he challenged. "When I agreed to help you take down Mordren and Volkan? What about now? You've been here for three days now. *We've been here* together for three days now. And you still didn't think to tell me?"

"Why would I?"

"Because we're working together towards the same goal. Freedom."

"So?"

He shot me another challenging look. "You still don't trust me? Even after I warned you about the attack? And covered for you in the throne room yesterday?"

We had barely begun this conversation and I was already fed up with it. Shaking my head, I shouldered past him and made for the door. "I have to go."

"Don't–"

I whirled towards him. "Unless you want to explain to Prince Volkan why I'm late?"

When he didn't immediately reply, I spun on my heel and stalked away without another word. Irritation still burned through me as I made my way towards the front gate. I didn't owe Evander anything. Just because we now had a common goal didn't mean I had to spill all my secrets to him. And with our history, it baffled me that he had even considered that likely.

A small voice in my head reminded me that I had found a way to trust Mordren despite everything that he had done to me, and I to him, but I didn't want to hear it so I shoved it out of my mind.

Dull thuds echoed into the silent corridor as I moved along the hall. The door to the training room was open so I cast a glance inside as I passed. Idra was sparring with the blond elf that I had spoken to briefly, and as always, he was thoroughly outmatched.

The next elf in line to spar was Hilver. He apparently heard me coming because he cast a quick glance at the door right as I looked inside as well. Pleading blue eyes met me for a few seconds before he swallowed and turned back to the fight before him. Fear hung over the whole room. Again.

Tearing my gaze from the desperate elves inside, I continued down the corridor and towards my own dangerous mission.

Guards stood waiting just inside the gigantic doors at the front of the castle. I trailed to a halt on the floor in front of them and waited for the Prince of Fire.

When Volkan at last came striding towards me, I was more

nervous than I wanted to admit. He flicked a disapproving glance up and down my body.

"Only for missions like this."

"Yes, sir."

He jerked his chin. "Let's go."

Warm night winds caressed my face as I stepped outside the castle walls for the first time in two days. Drawing a deep breath, I relished the feeling of fresh air in my lungs. Glittering stars watched from the darkened heavens as the Prince of Fire and I made our way towards the wrought metal gates.

The guards on duty bowed to their prince and then opened the gates before us. I had barely gotten a glimpse of the empty courtyard outside before Volkan had thrown an arm around my waist and worldwalked us away.

I swallowed the nausea climbing up my throat as we reappeared in another empty courtyard made of stone. The winds here were colder than the ones in the Court of Fire, but it still wasn't as cold as it should have been at this time of year. Staggering away from Volkan, I swept my gaze over the buildings around us.

The Court of Water was also located in a warmer climate, so it felt more like spring rather than winter. That also meant that the water didn't freeze here. A merry trickling came from the wall beside us where a thin sheen of water ran down the stones, but it was almost drowned out by the rushing sound that came from further up ahead.

I had barely reoriented myself when Volkan grabbed my arm and yanked me along.

"Viviane said that it wouldn't take more than an hour to get inside, erase the names and get out," he said. "So that's the time frame you have."

"Yes, sir," I answered even though I wanted to point out that Viviane knew nothing of how I planned to get inside.

We rounded the corner and the tall defensive walls around the castle became visible. Great waterfalls rushed down over them. Trying to hold the dread and anxiety at bay, I followed Prince Volkan in silence until he pulled us to a halt in an alley close to the palace.

A group was gathered farther down. Squinting against the darkness, I could just barely make out a dozen or so elves who were kneeling on the cobblestones. They were a mix of male and female elves and their attention was focused away from the castle. Volkan seemed reluctant to let them see him, however, so he remained standing out of sight.

"I have set your range to the castle grounds and a short distance outside the walls," he said to me. "So you can move freely inside while completing your mission. If you try to run, or if you're not back within the hour, the magic of that collar will be activated. And then what happens?"

Looking up, I met his eyes that shone a pale yellow in the silvery moonlight. "Then the magic will make it feel like my body is on fire."

"Correct. And then you will truly wish that you were dead." He let go of my arm. "Complete the mission. Don't try anything. And don't get spotted. If you do that, you might just survive to see tomorrow. Am I making myself clear?"

"Yes, sir."

He jerked his chin towards the palace. "One hour."

After bowing my head, I turned and disappeared down the street.

The group of elves up ahead were still on their knees, but they had now raised their arms towards the sky. I adopted a casual pace and glanced at them from the corner of my eye as I passed them on the other side of the street.

Stars glittered in their eyes as they stared up into the heavens with faces full of burning fervor.

"We give thanks to the winds," a male elf at the front said as he stretched his arms upwards. "We give thanks to the sky. We give thanks to all the forces of the world that have finally brought them here. That have finally brought our gods here."

It took every bit of my self-control not to screech to a halt. Gods? The elven race did not believe in gods. They worshipped the spirits of their ancestors.

The group of elves bowed down and pressed their foreheads to the ground before straightening and raising their arms towards the heavens again. "Honored High Elves, shine your light of wisdom down on us."

My blood froze.

They were worshipping the High Elves. As if they were gods. *Our* gods. It took everything I had to keep walking. With cold dread spreading through my veins, I left the kneeling elves behind and continued towards the palace.

It might only be a small group right now, but if this belief that the High Elves were gods was allowed to take root, then we would have more than one life-threatening problem on our hands.

Volkan Flameshield and High Commander Anron were using each other to get what they wanted. And if either of them actually got it, we would all be doomed. The freezing dread turned into a flaming sense of urgency as I cast another glance behind me at the bowing citizens.

My plan had to work.

CHAPTER 8

*O*nly the sound of softly trickling water filled the hallways as I snuck through the darkened castle. Since we were far into the night, all the occupants were already asleep, but I still kept my eyes sharp as I phased through a pale stone wall and made my way towards my target.

As with every palace in every court, I had been there at one point or another when I worked as a spy for Prince Edric. But there were always some sections that I had never been able to enter. Until now.

Viviane, who had previously worked in the castle, knew the whole structure like the back of her hand so she had been able to draw up a map that contained everything I needed to know. With that information swirling in my head, I could easily find the secret passageways that no one else should know about.

Stopping in front of a small fountain, I studied the wall on the other side. It was nothing special. Tall and carved with decorative patterns, just like all the other walls in the palace. But according to Viviane's map, this was it.

I glanced towards the end of the corridor. Only the occasional creaking of leather and whisper of clothes betrayed the mass of guards waiting on the other side.

The entrance to the secret passageway was heavily guarded by a host of Prince Rayan's best soldiers. No one got in or out without their permission. Well, almost no one.

With a small smile on my lips, I skirted around the fountain and strode straight into the wall.

Oppressive darkness fell across my eyes. After turning to the right, I put one hand on the cold stone wall and then started forwards. Even though I couldn't see anything, I knew where the pathway would take me, so I just kept my fingers trailing along the wall to make sure that I was heading in the right direction.

When my other hand at last brushed something solid right in front of me, I paused to run through my plan. I desperately wished that I had some kind of weapon in case things went sideways, but there was nothing I could do about that now, so in the end I just sucked in a bracing breath and stepped through the door.

Silvery light from the moon shone in through the panorama of glass windows along the outer wall. For a moment, I just stared at the view beyond. The tall windows opened up to a balcony made of pale stone, and beyond that was the ocean. Glittering stars were reflected in the vast dark blue water and the bright moon painted a river of silver across it. It looked like a flowing blanket woven from waves and starlight. And it was breathtaking.

Tearing my gaze from the stunning vista beyond, I moved farther into the room.

Two people were asleep in the luxurious bed by the inner wall. I swallowed. My heart pattered in my chest as I hoped that what I was about to do wouldn't end up getting me killed. Backing away two more steps, just to be on the safe side, I raised my hands.

"Prince Rayan."

Chaos erupted.

Blue silk fluttered through the room as the Prince of Water and his wife flew up from the bed. Landing in a crouch, Rayan drew his hands through the air in big sweeping gestures. Water from the pool by the windows rose in response to it. While a tidal wave surged upwards, Princess Lilane rolled over the mattress and landed next to her husband. Shards of ice, sharp and pointed like blades, materialized and filled the space between me and them.

Keeping my hands raised, I opened my mouth to explain myself. But before I could, the mass of water crashed into me. The force of it sent me flying backwards and I hit the wall behind me hard enough to break my ribs. Crashing down on the stone floor, I sucked in a desperate gasp. White hot pain pulsed through my whole chest as I pushed myself up on my knees. I barely managed to throw my arms up over my head before a mass of ice blades surrounded me.

"Please," I gasped out through the pain and dizziness. "Don't."

A cold sharp edge pressed against the side of my neck, tightly enough to draw blood, and for a few seconds I thought I had made my last ever mistake, but then the pressure eased up.

"Kenna?" Prince Rayan said. Stunned shock filled his voice. "What in the spirits' name is the meaning of this?"

Still on my knees, I finally lowered my arms and glanced

up at him. Both he and Princess Lilane were standing behind the curtains of ice blades that the princess was holding between us, and they looked equally surprised.

"I'm here as a friend." Spreading my arms, I showed them my empty hands. "I don't have any weapons."

They exchanged a glance but kept their magic up. When neither of them said anything, I pressed on.

"Prince Volkan is making another play for power, to become the next King of Elves after Aldrich, so he's now targeting all the other princes." I nodded towards Rayan. "All of you. He's trying to make you look weak and incompetent. To make you lose your support and power."

Rayan's dark brows creased but he only continued watching me, listening to my explanation.

"He sent me here to screw you over." Moving slowly, I reached into my pocket and pulled out the list I had stolen a few minutes before I entered the secret passageway. After unfolding it, I held it up for them to see. "Prince Volkan wanted me to erase all the names of the poor people on this list, leaving only the rich families, so that your court would think you didn't care as much about the common people."

Terrible anger flashed in Rayan's purple eyes. "He tried to do *what?*"

"But I didn't want that to happen." I shook the document in my hand to emphasize that I could have easily just erased the names instead of bringing it to them. "So that's why I'm here."

The two dark-haired royals exchanged another glance. And then the ice daggers finally disappeared. While Lilane made her weapons disappear, Prince Rayan returned the mass of water that had been swirling behind him to the pool by the window again. Not sure what to do, I stayed on my knees by the wall.

Once all the water was back in its proper place, Rayan approached me. I held out the document, thinking that he wanted it back, but he took my hand instead and pulled me up.

A gasp ripped from my lips.

"What's wrong?" he said, concern flashing over his face.

Straightening, I cleared my throat, but that only made me wince in pain again. "I think you broke some of my ribs when you flung me into the wall."

"Oh, by the spirits." Genuine regret swirled in his eyes as he held my gaze. "I'm sorry."

"It's fine. I did break into your room in the middle of the night without warning."

Lilane let out a soft laugh from my other side. "Yes, you did give us quite the scare."

"Come." Prince Rayan motioned towards a cluster of chairs by the windows. "I will heal you while you explain what it is that Volkan is expecting, and what we should do about it."

After taking off my shirt so that Rayan could fix my broken ribs, I sank down on a chair and once more explained what the Prince of Fire had wanted me to do. It became easier to breathe every second as Rayan poured his magic into my body.

"But if we just act as if the list had never been tampered with, won't you get punished?" Princess Lilane asked once I had finished.

"Yes."

"No." She met her husband's gaze over my shoulder. "Rayan, we can't let him hurt her for this."

"I agree," he said from where he was working on the back

of my ribcage. "What about if we pretend to have fallen for it, but then someone comes running with a spare list at the last second? Then he will think that you did your job and that we just got lucky."

"That could work." I drew in a deep breath now that all my ribs were whole again, and then put on my shirt and stood up. "I have to get back before Prince Volkan activates my collar." When both of them opened their mouth, I held up a hand. "It would hurt, that's all you need to know."

"Wait," Rayan said and grabbed my arm before I could leave. He drew a hand over the side of my neck, healing the cut from the ice blade. "Thank you. For risking all of this for us. I wish I could..." His eyes lingered on the collar around my throat for a second, but then he shook his head and met my gaze again. "I'm in your debt. If you ever need anything, just say the word."

I inclined my head in acknowledgement. Princess Lilane gave my arm a gentle squeeze as she and her husband led me towards the door. The real door. Not the secret one that they still had no idea that I knew about.

Armor rustled into the silence as the guards stirred when Prince Rayan opened the door. Surprise darted from face to face as their gaze fell on me. Before any of them could ask about it, their prince spoke up.

"Make sure she gets out safely," Rayan said. "But don't let anyone see you."

Confusion still swirled in their eyes, but they only bowed while two of them stepped up to escort me out. I glanced back at the two royals. They gave me a nod.

I replicated the gesture and then followed the guards as they led me towards an exit.

Thankfully, they followed their prince's orders and

showed me to a side exit that let me disappear back into the city without any prying eyes noticing that I had been accompanied by guards. Temperate winds blew across the pale stones as I darted towards the nearest alley.

Staying well away from the group of praying elves I had seen before, I made my way back towards the Prince of Fire. The night lay dark and still around me. I cast a glance over my shoulder to make sure that no one was following me as I neared the end of a narrow alley.

A hand slammed over my mouth and I was yanked to the side.

CHAPTER 9

Strong fingers kept my mouth firmly shut and prevented the scream that had tried to rip from my throat while I stumbled into the corner of someone's back porch. A wall of darkness shot up and blocked the view from the street.

My heart fluttered in my chest as I stared up into a pair of glittering silver eyes. Mordren slowly took his hand from my mouth.

"You got my message," I said, thinking back to the quick note I had scrawled in the traveling book before I left.

"Of course I did." Light from the moon fell across his dark hair and painted it with silver streaks. He searched my face. "Are you okay?"

Since I had been escorted out by the guards, I had a little more time before I had to be back. Craning my neck, I glanced at the clock tower that was just barely visible above the wall of shadows Mordren had summoned to shield us from view. We had a few minutes at least.

I met his gaze again and nodded. "Yes, I am."

He looked thoroughly unconvinced. After looking me up and down, presumably in search of injuries, he locked eyes with me again. "I meant what I said earlier. If you want me to get you out, I will get you out. No matter the consequences."

"I know." Raising my hand, I drew my fingers over his cheek and gave him a sad smile. "I know. But I need to be inside Volkan's court for this to work."

"Then what do you want me to do? Just say the word and I will do it."

The guilt and pain that burned in his eyes as he looked down at the slave collar around my neck made my heart ache. It also made me want to slap him. It wasn't his fault that I was here. I had chosen to enter the Court of Fire entirely on my own. Because I had a plan. A solid plan. And the thought of him blaming himself for a choice I made sent a flash of irritation through me.

"I want you to stop looking at me like that," I snapped. "Stop looking at me like I'm a victim."

"But what Volkan is doing–"

"Is nothing I can't handle. He's not forcing me to sleep with him, if that's what you're worried about. In fact, the only reason he isn't doing that is because of you." When confusion flashed over Mordren's face, I elaborated. "Volkan doesn't want, and this is a direct quote, *anything that Mordren has already sullied*. And the little visions he casts over me when he tries to break me, I can handle. So enough with the self-blaming."

The small kernel of relief I had seen in his eyes when I told him that Volkan wasn't touching me disappeared under another way of guilt. "But you're still a slave."

"I was a slave when you first met me and you didn't look at

me like this back then," I sniped back, my anger surfacing again. "So why are you suddenly doing it now?"

"Because this time it's *my fault*."

"Oh get over yourself!" I gave his chest a shove. "Not everything is about you. You might think that no one can make a single decision without your involvement, but let me burst that bubble for you. The world does not revolve around you."

He stumbled back from the shove but it was my words that made him stare at me as if I had slapped him. "That's not what I meant."

"I don't care. And I don't have time for your useless, self-centered moping. So get the hell out of my way." Taking a step forward, I started pushing past him.

As if on instinct, his arm shot up and he put his hand to my chest, shoving me back against the wall. "You can leave when I say you can leave."

The command in his voice vibrated through the shadows around us. It took a second for Mordren to realize what he had done, and once he had, he yanked his hand back and retreated a step before looking at me. An apologetic look flashed over his face as he opened his mouth to say something, but then he stopped when he noticed the wide grin that had spread across my lips.

"That's more like it." The wicked smile on my mouth grew as I winked at him. "I want you to fight with me, flirt with me, scheme with me, talk to me, threaten me, kiss me. You asked me what I wanted you to do. I want you to treat me the way you have always treated me and not as if I'm suddenly made of glass."

Mordren blinked at me in shock. Then a soft laugh escaped his lips when he realized that I had baited him on purpose in order to make him snap out of his misplaced guilt. Dragging a hand through his hair, he shook his head. The haunted look in his eyes didn't disappear completely, but it lessened somewhat at least. He drew a deep breath, which made it look like he was surfacing from a stormy dark sea for the first time in days. I watched with a growing smirk on my lips as at least some of his usual confident swagger returned.

"Well?" I prompted in a teasing voice, trying to pull him that final bit back to his old self. "Aren't you going to lecture me for starting a scheme like this without telling you or something?"

Surprise flitted across his face. For a moment, he only blinked at me as if trying to figure out if I was serious. I raised my eyebrows expectantly. His eyes darted to the side briefly, but then a bossy expression of smug arrogance slid home on his features.

"If that is what you want, then…" He took a step forward, forcing me to back up against the wall. Bracing one hand against the stones next to my head, he leaned down and leveled a stare dripping with authority on me. "… allow me to remind you that you technically still worked for me when you made the decision to join Volkan's court. And I thought I made it perfectly clear that you will ask my permission before you decide to go rogue."

"That you did."

"And still you disobeyed me."

"Yep."

His dark hair rippled as he cocked his head. "When you are free again, there will be consequences for that insubordination."

"There you are. Finally." I grinned at him. "Now, I might actually believe that you have some faith in my skills."

Mordren raked his eyes over my body. "Oh, my infuriating little blackmailer, I thought you already knew by now. If there is one thing I will never doubt, it is your ability to scheme."

"Good." Grabbing the front of his shirt, I pulled his face closer to mine. "Now, we only have about two minutes before I have to go. Are you going to kiss me already or do you intend to make me beg for it?"

"That depends." He drew his hand up my throat before taking my jaw in a firm grip. His eyes sparkled as he smirked down at me. "Do you want me to?"

My dark laugh danced across his mouth before I pulled his lips to mine. Dragging my fingers through his silken black hair, I pushed him harder against me until I could feel his lethal muscles shifting against mine. With one hand still braced on the wall next to my head, he kept the other wrapped around my throat, pushing my chin up with his thumb.

A wave of pleasure rolled over me as Mordren's lips ravaged mine. I raked my fingers down his back and then over his ribs while I let myself get lost in his confident touch for a few moments. But an urgent voice soon whispered in the back of my mind. I had to get back.

With great reluctance, I broke off the kiss and pulled back. Breathless, I rested the back of my head against the cold stone wall behind me while staring up into those glittering silver eyes.

"Volkan tried to mess with Prince Rayan tonight," I said, my voice suddenly serious again. "He will come for you too. And every time you and Volkan are in the same room, he will use me against you. Use me to rattle you. To throw you off your game." Reaching up, I traced soft fingers over his sharp cheekbone and then down along his jaw. "You can't let it get to you."

Mordren placed his hand over mine. "Easier said than done."

I brushed my lips over his one last time and then ducked under his arm. Backing away towards the street, I gave him a sad smile. "I know. But you have to try. I'll see you soon."

"Yes, you will."

With a small smile, I tore my gaze from his handsome face and disappeared through the shadow wall and back onto the street.

While the world-ending guilt in Mordren's eyes was now gone, and while he seemed to have accepted that he wasn't the reason that I was a slave again, I couldn't shake the feeling that things between us still weren't back to normal. There was still something off about him. About the way he acted. But I couldn't quite put my finger on what it was.

However, I could spare neither time nor energy on figuring it out, because I would need every scrap of it for the dangerous plot I was currently in the middle of. Our relationship troubles would have to wait.

Taking off at a run, I pushed the lingering thoughts of Mordren from my mind and instead concentrated on my scheme again as I hurried towards where the Prince of Fire was waiting for me.

All in all, this night was a success. I had gotten to talk to Mordren, alone, for a few moments and the mission in Rayan's court had gone more or less according to plan. Give or take a few broken ribs. I had managed to warn the Prince of Water about Volkan's treachery in time to prevent it from doing serious damage to Rayan's reputation, and also gained his favor. Volkan Flameshield thought he could manipulate himself onto the throne, but he had no idea that the true manipulator was the girl he had let walk right through the front door and into the heart of his court.

He would have to work a lot harder than that to pull off his scheme when he had an opponent like me.

CHAPTER 10

*S*urprised murmuring spread through the throne room. I kept my eyes downcast as I trailed behind Volkan Flameshield while we made our way into the castle in the Court of Water. Idra flicked her impassive eyes over the crowd in search of threats, but Volkan looked more like a particularly malicious child who was waiting for his turn to bully someone.

Nobles from the Court of Water frowned as the foreign prince strode through the groups and took up position at the back of the room, but no one dared question what he was doing there. I came to a halt behind Volkan's left shoulder, while Idra drew herself up on his other side, and I had to keep my head slightly bowed to prevent people from seeing the villainous smile on my lips. In a few minutes, Volkan would realize that his plan had failed.

A cheer went up. I flicked my gaze towards the raised dais on the other side of the room and found a black-haired elf in a beautiful purple silk shirt striding onto the platform. Rayan Floodbender smiled at the crowd before him, and the midday sunlight that fell in through the windows made his violet eyes sparkle like gems.

"Welcome, ladies and gentlemen, men and women, elves and humans." He came to a halt at the edge of the dais and inclined his head. "I'm glad to see you all here. As always, we will begin with those of you who have applied for financial aid." A dazzling smile spread over his lips as he winked at the audience. "So that you can all get started with your new business ventures as soon as possible."

Genuine mirth and laughter spread through the crowd. Next to me, Volkan let out a derisive snort. Keeping my face a carefully constructed mask, I watched as Prince Rayan unfolded a document. The sneer disappeared from Volkan's face, and he leaned forwards slightly as a wide grin took its place.

"The following people have applied for financial aid to start new businesses and have been granted it," the Prince of Water began.

Volkan's yellow eyes gleamed as he listened to the prince read the names of noble families. When Rayan nodded and lowered the paper again, a confused murmur swept through the gathered crowd like wildfire. From the group of farmers next to us, the surprise was quickly turning sour as they muttered that maybe their prince didn't consider them as important as the nobles. The grin on Volkan's lips widened. I kept my face blank.

"My prince," a fair-haired elf called as he hurried up on the platform.

Another document flapped in the air in front of the blond elf as he skidded to a halt next to the prince. After bowing deeply, he leaned in and whispered something in Rayan's ear while gesturing towards the paper in his hand. Then he bowed again. And again. With an apologetic look on his face, he backed away while the Prince of Water faced his court once more.

"My dear citizens," Prince Rayan began and spread his hands in a helpless gesture. "I must profusely apologize. There appears to have been some sort of administrative error with the applications. The document I was given listed only some of the people who had applied for financial aid, and my scribes only noticed the error just now." He waved the paper in his hands. "They have assured me that their back-up list holds all the names, so if you applied for aid but did not hear your name earlier, please return tomorrow when I have been able to look through your application as well. Again, I deeply apologize for the confusion."

"Thank you, my prince," came the grateful voices of the farmers who had been angry only moments before. "No need to apologize. Mistakes happen. Anyone who's grown up on a farm knows that."

A ripple of laughter drifted through the crowd and banished the rest of the tension as more voices called out support and agreement. I transformed my face into a mask of shock and fear right as Volkan snapped his gaze to me. Fire flickered around his fingers.

"I erased the names on the list," I pressed out before he could speak. "I swear."

"Clearly not on all lists," he ground out.

"I'm sorry. I didn't know they kept a spare one. There was only one list in the room when I went there. Please, you have to believe me."

What I was saying was technically the truth. I didn't know if they kept a back-up list and there had only been one document in the room when I broke in to steal it. Keeping those truths at the front of my mind, I looked back at the Prince of Fire with wide eyes, hoping that he couldn't see the lies that were hidden behind them.

Volkan clicked his tongue in annoyance. While the flames licking his fingers disappeared, he whirled around and stalked away. Idra studied my face for another few seconds before following her prince. I cast a quick glance at Prince Rayan before doing the same.

His eyes swept over me without stopping, but a small smile played over his lips. I had to suppress a cackle.

Volkan's attempt to damage Prince Rayan's reputation had been successfully averted. My secret mission was off to a good start. Now I just had to make sure I finished it before the Prince of Fire figured out what I was doing. Or before he found a way to break me.

CHAPTER 11

Wolves the size of horses prowled around me. Holding my short sword up in front of me, I turned in a slow circle to keep them all in view. Vicious growling echoed through the room as the wolves bared their teeth at me. They moved closer.

A shadow fell in through the open door on the other side of the room, and a moment later, another beast prowled inside. This one was twice the size of the others. The alpha wolf.

My heart slammed against my ribs as I took in its massive form. Still keeping my blade raised, I backed away.

One quick snarl and the faint scrape of claws against stone was the only warning I got before the wolf behind me attacked. Since I'd been so focused on the new threat walking through the door, I barely had time to throw myself to the side before the leaping wolf flew across the floor and landed in the spot I had been occupying only moments before. Whirling around, I swung my sword in a wide arc to fend it off as it lunged towards me, its jaws snapping.

Low growling spread through the room as the other wolves tightened their circle. I started turning again, drawing the blade through the air before me to stop their advance. They paused. Moving slowly, they all turned to look at their alpha. He took a step forward.

All six of them leaped towards me.

Panic pulsed through my whole body as I threw myself backwards and then turned and sprinted towards the wall.

Gray fur flashed in front of me as one of the wolves skidded to a halt right in my path, blocking my way to the exit. Backpedaling furiously, I tried to escape its huge maw full of bloodstained teeth. In my hurry to get away, I slipped on the red stones and crashed back first onto the floor. With fear poisoning my limbs, I rolled over on my stomach and pushed myself up on my knees so that I could get up.

Blood dripped on the floor in front of me.

Still on my knees, I stared up into the massive face of the alpha wolf. The others had formed an unbreakable wall around me. Forcing air in and out of my lungs was getting more difficult by the second and the muscles in my arm throbbed as I held my sword in a death grip.

There were two voices in my head. The loudest one was screaming in panic because I was about to die. The other one sent the same sentence pulsing through my brain over and over again: *It's not real.*

It's not real. It's not real. It's not real.

The wolf growled again and moved closer. Blood fell from its red-stained maw and landed on the floor in muted drops.

It's not real. It's not real. It's not real.

The other beasts snarled, their jaws snapping a mere breath from my body.

It's not real. It's not real. It's not real.

Casting a hurried glance over my shoulder, I looked back at the elf seated on the raised dais.

Volkan Flameshield watched with a wide grin on his face as the wolves kept me trapped in the middle of the room.

I knew that it wasn't real. It couldn't be. This had to all be a vision that he was making me see. But the problem was that I didn't actually know that. When the door had opened and the bloodthirsty animals had come pouring through, it could have been because someone had let them in. And it could just as easily have been what the Prince of Fire wanted me to see. There was no way of knowing. Except to call his bluff.

Desperately hoping that I wasn't about to do something that would get me devoured by a creature of nightmares, I slowly pushed to my feet and leveled the sword at Volkan instead.

"They're not real," I declared. "So why don't you just come down and fight me instead."

"Aren't they?" Prince Volkan stood up and spread his arms. "But sure, if you want to add one more enemy to the fight then who am I to refuse?"

All the wolves turned to watch the Prince of Fire as he strode towards us with his sword in hand. When he got closer, they parted to let him through.

It's not real. It's not real. It's not real.

With my heart still slamming in my chest, I raised my chin and squared up against Volkan.

He lunged.

Steel whizzed through the air as he leaped towards me and swung his blade at my head. I sidestepped quickly and threw up my own sword to block it. The force of the hit vibrated through my arm but I flicked my wrist and sent his weapon sliding off mine. With a quick twirl, I moved to slam my sword towards his back.

The black wolf next to me attacked.

I jerked back on instinct, my blow falling short as I tried to evade the sharp teeth that clamped together in the spot my sword arm had been in earlier. In my attempt to fend off the wolf that had tried to take my arm off, I left my back completely unprotected against the other threat in the room.

Cold steel bit into my skin as Prince Volkan put his sword against my throat from behind. Using the sharpened edge, he forced me to take a step back until my back was pressed against his chest. My own sword hand hovered at chest level, but with my body trapped in this position, there wasn't a lot I could do to break his grip and win the fight.

With his blade still pressed tightly to my throat, Volkan leaned forward over my shoulder and growled a command in my ear. "Drop your sword."

Metal clanked against stone as I slowly moved my arm away from my chest and then threw my blade to the side of the room. The ring of wolves shifted and snarled. And then they vanished into thin air.

It wasn't real.

Prince Volkan shifted as well. With a few quick strides, he positioned himself in front of me instead and rested the point of his sword at the base of my throat.

"Kneel."

Holding his gaze, I lowered myself to my knees before him.

"You failed me."

I swallowed. "I didn't know that they kept a spare list. No one knew. I changed the list that was there. You saw it. He read from the list I had altered at first. How was I supposed to know that his scribes kept a back-up somewhere in another location?"

"*You* are supposed to make sure of that." The flames from the fire pits in the room burned in his eyes. "If you want to avoid punishment, then *you* are supposed to make sure of things like that."

My pulse leaped into a smattering staccato at the word 'punishment' but I forced myself to remain calm. "Yes, sir. I will make sure next time."

"Yes, you will. Because next time you will already know the price of failure."

Red and orange light flickered over the stone walls of the breaking room as fire from the flame pools leaped up and started towards us. Four burning lines slithered like snakes across the floor.

I snapped my gaze from the advancing fire and back up to Volkan. My mouth was suddenly very dry. "Sir?"

He held my gaze as the fiery snakes drew closer. "This, Kenna, is the price of failure."

The flames whooshed across the stones, drawing closer with each second. Panic blared inside my skull. Approaching from all four directions, the fire was almost upon me now. I desperately tried to escape, but Prince Volkan pushed the blade harder against the base of my throat, forcing me to stay on my knees.

My heart hammered in my chest.

"Please." The word was out before I could stop it. But my pride could survive the humiliation of begging. My skin, on the other hand, would not survive those flames. Meeting his burning yellow eyes with a pleading look, I held up my hands in submission. "Please, don't. I know the price of failure and I won't ever fail you again."

Volkan Flameshield said nothing.

The fire sped towards me.

"Please, sir. I'm begging you. Don't do this. I'll be better, I swear."

But nothing could stop the flames now. With panic and dread tearing through my chest, I threw up my arms in a futile attempt to protect myself from the fire as it crashed over me like flickering red waves.

The scream got stuck in my throat.

For a moment, I could do nothing but stare at the room around me while my mind tried to make sense of what had happened. The flames had definitely fallen over me, engulfing my body. But I had felt nothing. And now they were gone.

Clarity pushed its way past the blinding panic still bouncing around inside my skull. *It wasn't real.* It had been another one of Volkan's visions.

The Prince of Fire was still towering over me. Shifting his hand, he moved his sword up under my chin instead and forced me to tip my head back until I met his hard gaze again. "That is what will happen if you fail in your duties again. Understood?"

"Yes, sir," I managed to press out. When he only raised his eyebrows, I quickly added, "Thank you, sir."

After staring me down for another few seconds to make sure I truly understood that I had only been spared the flames tonight because of his mercy, he flicked his wrist and removed the blade from my throat before jerking his chin. "Dismissed."

My knees wobbled slightly as I struggled to my feet. It took all my self-control to manage a respectful bow before I hurried out of the breaking room.

These sessions were getting more intense every time and I hated how helpless I always felt in that room. I couldn't fight back fully. Partly because I didn't even know if what I was fighting was real, and partly because I couldn't fight at full strength because I didn't actually want to win my freedom. At least not yet.

But not being able to fight back with everything I had was slowly chipping away at my soul. And if I was going to survive long enough to succeed in my mission, I would need an outlet for those feelings of helplessness.

Adjusting my course, I started towards a room that would already be occupied at this time of night. I knew what I had to do. Even if it was going to be almost as dangerous as the breaking sessions with the Prince of Fire.

CHAPTER 12

Stone ground against stone as I shoved open the door and stalked inside. All six people in the room turned to look at me. Five of them blinked in surprise and flicked their gaze between me and the final elf in the room. Idra Souldrinker narrowed her eyes at me.

"You have not been summoned," she said, her voice cold and flat. "So you'd better have a very good reason for this interruption."

"I do."

I snatched up a sword and a dagger from one of the racks by the door. The five male elves who had been helping Idra train immediately scrambled backwards as I stalked forward. Something flickered in Idra's usually so impassive gaze.

Raising the sword, I pointed in the direction of the male elves. "I'm here to tell you that you can dismiss all of them from this duty."

Idra cocked her head. "And why is that?"

"Because what you really want is a proper sparring

partner. Someone who will truly give you a good workout session."

"And you're that person?"

"Try me and find out."

A dangerous expression gleamed in her eyes as she flicked her wrist, motioning for the five males to back up against the wall. They scrambled backwards until they were standing as far away from us as they could get. Idra considered me for a few seconds before sauntering over to another weapons rack and drawing a sword of her own. Ringing steel filled the silent training room.

She was wearing the tight-fitting black pants and short top that left most of her stomach and arms bare, as she usually did when training, and the light from the wall-mounted torches danced over her scarred skin.

The flimsy gold dress I was still wearing was not ideal for battle, but I would have to make do. Spinning the sword once in my hand, I advanced on the lethal elf before me. She darted forward.

I yanked up my sword to block hers while twisting with the motion and stabbing my knife towards the side of her chest. She barely managed to leap back in time before it flashed through the air right next to her ribs. Pressing the advantage, I feigned left with my blade and struck right. Idra saw it coming and blocked the hit. Sparks flew as she flicked her wrist, sending my sword sliding off hers.

With a forceful push, she shoved my blade wide and darted forward. Leaping back, I jabbed my knife towards her neck while drawing my sword back into position. She ducked and drove her blade upwards to catch me unawares. Having read her movements, I smacked my already moving sword into hers and knocked it off course. She threw a savage kick at the back of my knee as she danced aside.

Pain shot through my leg as my knee smacked into the ground. Behind me, I could feel Idra moving into position to end the fight with a blade to my neck so I twisted my upper body and swung my sword in a wide arc to force her back. She jumped backwards just in time.

Using the moment of grace, I shot to my feet and whirled around to face her. Her white hair brushed her collarbones as she zigzagged towards me.

Clanging metal filled the otherwise dead silent room as Idra and I continued pushing each other back and forth across the padded mats. My pulse beat steadily and my body thrummed with energy as I fought Idra with everything I had.

This was what I needed. After being forced to endure Volkan's overwhelming magical power that I couldn't fight back against, I needed a way to take back control. To feel like I was in charge of the situation again. And going all out in a sparring match provided that small break that allowed me to feel like I could breathe again.

Steel clattered as my knife flew from my hand and hit the wall before bouncing to a halt on the mat below. I threw my sword up to block against Idra's assault as she backed me across the room. With terrifying speed, she flicked her wrist and sent my blade cutting through the air instead while she took my legs out from underneath me.

Air exploded from my lungs as I slammed down back first on the ground. I yanked my sword up right as Idra flashed over me and placed the point of her own blade over my heart. Surprise flickered in her black eyes as she glanced down at the sword I had almost managed to press against the side of her ribs while she moved into position. In another impressive display of speed, she moved before I even knew what was happening, and kicked my arm sideways.

The back of my sword hand slammed into the mat. And a moment later, Idra's foot appeared on top of my arm, trapping it against the floor.

My chest heaved.

Lying on my back with Idra standing above me, I glanced from the sword waiting uselessly in my pinned hand to the blade she kept positioned above my heart.

Before I had even started this fight, I had known that I would lose. Idra Souldrinker was known for her ability to kill people with a single touch, which meant that developing her skills in close combat had probably been her sole focus all her life. Not to mention that she most likely had a few centuries of life experience on me. Taking all that into consideration, I knew that I would always be outclassed against her. But it didn't matter. Because when I was fighting her, I could give it my all and that was enough to keep the helplessness and desperation at bay. Even if I lost.

Idra stared me down. Holding her gaze, I moved my one free arm a bit further from my body and then tapped my hand against the floor in submission.

A wicked grin spread across her face, and in that moment, I realized that it was the first time I had seen her smile. Though to be honest, the smirk on her face could still hardly be classified as a smile. It looked a lot more threatening than mirthful.

"I knew you were faking it last time," she said.

A resigned huff of laughter escaped my lips. "I see. Why didn't you confront me about it?"

Ignoring my question, she dragged the point of her sword up my chest, across my throat, and then placed the flat of the blade under my chin. With a decisive push, she forced my head all the way back, exposing my throat. "Why did you fake being bad?"

With my head tipped back like that, I couldn't see her clearly, but I knew that she could read every expression on my face so I decided to go with the truth. "Because I didn't want to be forced to come here every night and help you train."

"And now?"

"And now, I've realized that I want to."

She stopped putting pressure on my chin, allowing me to tilt my head back down so that I could meet her gaze, while she moved the point of the sword to the base of my throat instead.

"How did you know?" I asked while looking up at her and holding her gaze. "That I was faking it last time?"

"Your reflexes gave you away. And you didn't panic when I wrapped my hand around your throat and squeezed. You only tapped out again." She pushed the point of her sword harder against my skin. "Just like you're not panicking now. You're trusting the rules of the sparring session. Trusting that if you tap out in submission, your opponent won't harm you. Only people who have been trained by real warriors do that." Sliding her gaze to the tense males by the wall, she threw them a contemptuous look. "Inexperienced people don't."

After casting one last look down at me, she finally took her sword from my throat and stepped back. Blowing out a long breath, I ran my hand over my throat to check for blood. When it came back clean, I instead rubbed the spot on my arm where Idra's foot had been. While I pushed myself back to my feet, Idra stalked a few steps closer to the five silent males. They flinched in unison at her sudden advance.

Stopping halfway across the room, Idra lifted her sword and pointed at them. "You're relieved of this duty. Don't bother coming back." Relief flooded their faces at her words, but if she saw it, she hid it well. Instead, she turned back to me and fixed me with a look that I couldn't quite interpret. "You will attend me instead."

I inclined my head in acknowledgement.

"Dismissed," she said.

After returning the two blades I had borrowed to the rack again, I followed the group of males as they exited the training room. They were practically skipping across the floor as we made our way down the corridor.

Once we had reached the spot that seemed to mark the end of Idra's range of hearing, Hilver turned to me. His pale blue eyes glittered in the torchlight.

"Thank you," he said, his voice full of sincerity. "I don't know why you did it, but thank you."

"You're welcome."

"When I said that I would do anything to get out of that training duty, I meant it." He spread his arms to motion at his friends. "*We* meant it. What can we do to pay you back?"

While still moving down the corridor, I flicked my gaze between the five elves around me. This had been the second reason for sparring with Idra tonight. It was mostly for my own sake, but having five people owe me a debt was an added bonus that I would badly need if I was to succeed in my mission.

As if it hadn't even occurred to me before then, I lifted my shoulder in a casual shrug. "You can owe me a favor."

"Done," Hilver said while the other four echoed the word in agreement.

A satisfied smirk spread across my lips as I turned down the hallway to my room. Now, I had an outlet for the awful feelings that Volkan instilled in me inside the breaking room, and I had five people who owed me a favor.

The Prince of Fire would not know what hit him.

CHAPTER 13

"Volkan, how good of you to join us," Edric Mountaincleaver muttered as the Prince of Fire sauntered into the room.

Keeping my eyes downcast, I trailed in after Volkan and Idra. The soft trickling of water grew fainter as I left the hallway and crossed the threshold into a very cozy lounge in the Court of Water.

Comfortable-looking couches and armchairs stood artfully arranged around a low table, and a well-stocked bar covered the entire length of one wall. On the other side of the room was a beautiful but shallow pool of crystal-clear water.

"I'm here on time, am I not?" Volkan Flameshield replied to Edric's annoyed comment.

"Barely."

As the Prince of Fire moved over to a large armchair and dropped onto the smooth cushions, I got a clear look at the other people in the room. Prince Edric was seated in another armchair across the table while the Prince of Trees had opted for an entire couch, and our host, Rayan Floodbender, lounged on the divan closest to the pool of water. The room was also filled with other elves, but my eyes went straight for the black-haired one seated on another couch.

Mordren Darkbringer snapped his gaze to me as I entered the room. I gave him a look that I hoped would remind him of my warning that Volkan was about to use me to rattle him. Since I had no way of telling if it worked, I simply broke eye contact and drifted over to the wall where most of the other attendants were standing.

The two dark-haired elves from the Court of Trees barely gave me a second look, but the two spies from the Court of Stone looked at me head-on.

"Kenna," Ymas said by way of greeting as I slid up next to him and Monette.

"Ymas," I replied, ignoring the blond half-elf next to him.

Monette didn't seem fazed by my lack of greeting. In fact, she seemed almost happy about something. Since I couldn't bring myself to care about what it was, I just shifted my gaze back to the room.

Idra had taken up position behind the back of Volkan's chair and was watching the room with sharp eyes until her gaze ground to a halt on another elf across the table. Red eyes stared right back at her. Hadeon was also standing behind the back of his prince's couch, studying the room in case a threat presented itself. Now that one had, both Idra and Hadeon barely took their eyes off one another for more than a few seconds. I shifted my attention to the person sitting next to Mordren.

While Eilan was nowhere to be seen, Ellyda appeared to have accompanied the Prince of Shadows instead. Curled up against the armrest, she was staring at a spot by the wall as if the secrets of the universe were written there.

Neither of them had acknowledged my presence when I entered, which was good. Doing that would give Volkan too much power. I suppressed a satisfied smile. At least they would be clearheaded when Volkan decided to start using me against Mordren.

Clothes rustled into the silence as all five princes shot to their feet and bowed. We all followed suit. Well, everyone except Ellyda, who was still lost somewhere inside her own head.

A second later, the King of Elves strode into the lounge.

"I can only stay for a moment," King Aldrich announced as he sank down into one of the armchairs. "But we have a matter we need to discuss, which is why I asked you to meet me here."

Prince Rayan snapped his fingers while everyone sat back down again. Glass clinked as the servants positioned throughout the room began pouring drinks and handing them out to the elven royals.

"I have just returned from my journey through the Court of Water," King Aldrich said as he waved off the servant trying to give him a glass. "And there is a bad feeling in the air. The spirits are restless. Worried."

While it wasn't an official magical ability, Aldrich had always been known as someone who could feel the presence of the elven spirits. Sometimes even communicate with them. Hence the name, Aldrich Spiritsinger.

When both Edric and Iwdael opened their mouths to ask more about it, the king held up his hand to stop them. "But that is not why I asked you here. Anron has invited us to his camp in three days' time. What we need to decide is if we are going to attend."

Golden light from the setting sun filtered in through the windows and painted the pale stone room in a warm glow. The water in the pool glittered as a few soft ripples went through it but only the faint creaking of leather armor broke the silence while the princes considered. At last, Mordren spoke up.

"I think we should attend. It would be a great opportunity to study them and gather information about their military capabilities."

Prince Edric nodded. "Agreed."

"And besides," Rayan added, "it might be interpreted as an insult if we were to refuse."

"That was my reasoning as well," King Aldrich confirmed. Smoothing down his long white hair, he swept his gaze over the room. "That only leaves the question of who should attend."

"I think continuing to deny them easy access to you, my king, is a good strategy," the Prince of Stone said. "In case they do decide to try something."

Aldrich moved his gaze from face to face, but the others only nodded. Seated in his armchair, Prince Volkan was suspiciously quiet. Worry gnawed at my bones. It was at times like these that I started second-guessing my decision to keep Volkan's involvement with Anron a secret from the other princes. I had considered telling Prince Rayan about it when I broke into his bedroom, but had decided against it. If the information somehow got back to Volkan, he would know that I was the one who had tipped them off and if that ever happened, I didn't think I would live to see another sunrise. Mordren knew, of course. But he was in on my plan. And besides, he was much more invested in my survival than the king and the other princes were.

"Then it is settled," King Aldrich announced. "All five of you will attend this visit to the High Elves' camp in three days, and then you will come straight to my castle and report your findings. Clear?"

"Yes, my king," they replied in unison.

Wood creaked softly as the king pushed himself up from the pale blue armchair and started towards the door. "I'll leave you to work out the details."

With an unceremonious wave with the back of his hand, the King of Elves strode out the door and left the elven princes alone.

Silence descended on the room for a few seconds. Then the Prince of Trees drank loudly from his glass before raising it in the air before him.

"Well, I hope they'll have good food at least," he said, his voice sounding completely unbothered.

A surprised chuckle escaped Rayan's lips while the Prince of Stone only shook his head at Iwdael and muttered something under his breath. After taking a sip of wine from the glass he had been handed, Mordren leaned forward and rested his elbows on his knees.

"We need to agree on a plan before we enter their camp." His silver eyes swept through the crowd. "We need to make sure that we pay attention to everything, so it would make sense to divide it into parts."

"Kenna."

I had been looking at Mordren so the sharp command caught me a bit off guard. Shifting my attention back to Volkan, I found him jerking his chin at me.

"Bring me some more wine," he said.

Prince Rayan raised a hand to motion at a servant close to me. "Oh, no need. I can have my people do that."

"No offense, Rayan," Volkan said with a tone that suggested that he didn't care if he took offense or not. "But I don't trust your people." Locking eyes with me again, he snapped his fingers and pointed to his glass. "Get a move on."

Picking up a decanter of wine, I carefully weaved between the pieces of furniture before coming to a halt next to the Prince of Fire. With a neutral mask on my face, I poured red wine into his glass. Once I was finished, I started back towards the wall, but before I could take so much as a step, a strong hand shot out and grabbed my arm. With a firm tug, Volkan pulled me back until I sat on top of the armrest next to him.

His yellow eyes were locked on Mordren as he reached out and rested a casual hand on my thigh. "So, little prince, what were you saying about the plan?"

Mordren's hand tightened around his glass. I cast a quick glance at Remus, the blond elf who was his chaperone and who was lurking by the opposite wall, before returning my attention to the situation before me.

"I think it's a great idea to focus on different things," Prince Rayan picked up smoothly when the silence stretched a little too long. "So that we don't miss anything."

"I agree," Edric filled in. "But we all need to pay attention to everything around us as well. We can't rely on one person to give us all the information about one thing since they could... *miss* something."

Volkan began tracing circles on my thigh just above my knee. "Do you not trust the competency of your fellow princes, Edric?"

"No."

Prince Volkan huffed out a laugh and slid his gaze to Mordren while continuing to trace his finger over the golden fabric of my dress. "What do you think, Mordren?"

The Prince of Shadows was clamping his teeth together so hard that the muscles in his jaw flickered. I suppressed a groan. This was what I had warned him about. Staring straight at him, I silently begged him to pull himself together.

As if he had heard my thoughts, Mordren finally dragged his gaze from Volkan's hand and up to my eyes. I shot him a stern look. Forcing a breath into his lungs, he shifted his attention to the Prince of Fire.

"Yes, as I was saying," Mordren began. "I agree with Edric that we need to pay attention to everything, but we should also have main areas of focus."

Iwdael emptied his glass in one long gulp and signaled for another one while saying, "I can take supplies. Food and drink definitely fall within my area of expertise."

The comment thankfully shifted attention away from Volkan and Mordren's silent battle and the tension eased up slightly as the princes began dividing different areas between themselves. Hadeon cast a quick glance at me when no one was looking, and I managed an almost imperceptible nod to inform him that I was okay. He slid his eyes back to Idra right as Prince Rayan switched topic.

"There is also another troubling aspect." His violet eyes met each of theirs in turn. "I'm sure you must have noticed that small groups of our people have started worshipping the High Elves as if they were gods."

"Yes," Mordren confirmed. "I have noticed that as well. We need to put a stop to it immediately."

Liquid sloshed against stone. I started in surprise as I glanced down to find that Volkan had spilled some of his wine on his shoes. A malicious glint crept into his eyes as he turned to me and pointed to the floor.

"Clean it up." Grabbing a napkin from the table, he threw it at me. "Now."

If I hadn't worked as a spy for so many years and learned quite well to control my facial expressions, I would have rolled my eyes in exasperation. Instead, I simply slid down from the armrest and dropped to my knees before the Prince of Fire.

Wood scraped against stone. Casting a glance over my shoulder, I found that Mordren had shot to his feet and taken a threatening step towards us. Volkan remained in his seat but turned his head to look pointedly at the chaperone by the wall.

Shadows flickered around Mordren's fingers. "Listen carefully, for I will only say this once."

I glared at Mordren, but he wasn't looking at me. His murderous stare was fixed on Volkan. Still on my knees, I hurriedly cleaned up the spilled wine while a lazy smirk spread across Volkan's mouth.

"Say what, little prince?" he baited.

"Prince Mordren," Remus said in warning.

The Prince of Shadows either didn't hear or didn't care because he took another step towards Volkan. I finished mopping up the wine and began pushing myself up, but Volkan's hand on my shoulder forced me back down on my knees. Lightning flashed in Mordren's eyes as he opened his mouth. Dread spread through my veins. Whatever was about to happen would not end well.

"Have you noticed that they all wear black bracelets?"

The whole room started in surprise. Clothes rustled and leather creaked as everyone turned towards the source of the voice. Ellyda Steelsinger dragged her gaze from the wall she had been staring at. Her eyes went in and out of focus several times before they finally cleared enough to look at each of the princes in turn.

"It seems to be their way of recognizing one another," she continued as if an entire room wasn't staring at her in bewilderment. "So if we see someone wearing a black bracelet, odds are that they belong to the fanatics who worship the High Elves as gods."

I held my breath. Flicking my gaze from face to face, I waited to see what would happen next.

"I hadn't noticed that," Prince Rayan said. Genuine surprise, and something else, swirled in his eyes. "Great observation. Pay extra attention to those who wear those bracelets then, and we might be able to stop this cult from spreading."

The others nodded in agreement as the tension drained from the room. Inwardly, I heaved a relieved sigh. Leave it to Ellyda to stay level-headed and pull a disastrous situation back from the brink of ruin. I glanced at her as I climbed to my feet and hurried back to my previous place by the wall before Volkan could recover. She didn't look at me but a small smile tugged at the edge of her lips.

After depositing the pitcher of wine on the table by the wall, I returned to my position next to Ymas and Monette. Gradually, the conversation started back up as Mordren sat down and the princes fell back into their discussion about the High Elves and the small groups of fanatics that were surfacing.

Leaning back against the cold stone wall, I let out a sigh. That had been close.

Something turquoise moved in the corner of my eye. Turning my head, I saw Monette slide past Ymas so that she was standing next to me instead. Ymas shot her a disapproving look but didn't stop her.

I furrowed my brows in confusion as Monette sidled up to me, and for a moment, I thought she would express her sympathies for my situation. Or maybe just remind me that she knew what it was like. However, that particular assumption was promptly drowned and beheaded as she leaned closer to me and spoke in a whisper.

"See?" In a move that, from the outside, looked like she was just sweeping her long blond hair back behind her shoulder, she brushed a discreet hand over the gold collar around my throat. "This is what happens to people who reach for too much. I've always told you that ambition is not a good thing."

"Really?" I cut her a disinterested stare. "You haven't talked to me in months and the best you can do is, 'I told you so'?"

Monette scoffed. "Now I truly know that I made the right decision the day I told Prince Edric about your plans. I have a comfortable life in his castle while you have to get down on your knees and wipe Prince Volkan's shoes in front of a whole room filled with the elite of society. Oh, how the mighty have fallen."

Irritation crackled through me at her words, but I knew that any explanation I could give would be thoroughly wasted on her so I just kept my mouth shut and continued watching the meeting.

What people like her would never understand is that if you want to get anywhere in life, you can't just stay in your comfortable bed. You have to actually put yourself out there. You have to make a plan. You have to gamble. You have to plot and scheme and be prepared to risk it all. And yes, sometimes you will lose. But if you want to win, you have to actually play the game.

CHAPTER 14

Heaving a deep sigh, I sank down on my bed and rested my arms above my head. It was game day in Volkan's tournament, and since Mordren wouldn't be attending the fight, Volkan had decided to leave me here. That meant I had a couple of hours to myself while both Idra and the Prince of Fire were away. I could barely believe that it had only been a week since Eilan had fought Volkan in that arena and I had agreed to come here in his stead.

A sharp knock sounded at my door. Narrowing my eyes, I glared at the slab of stone. I had come here because I needed to finish the half-formed plan that was swirling around the edges of my mind. The time before Volkan returned again was very limited, and I needed to make the most of it, so I was not happy about being disturbed.

Another knock sounded.

Suppressing an annoyed groan, I stalked over to the door and pushed it open.

Dark green eyes met me. "Hey."

"Hi."

Evander cast a hesitant glance over my shoulder, at my room beyond. "Can I come in?"

We hadn't really talked since our falling-out the other day, so for a moment I only frowned at him, but then I stepped aside and motioned for him to enter. Pulling the door shut behind him, I leaned back against it and crossed my arms. Evander hovered awkwardly in the middle of the narrow room.

"I'm sorry," he blurted out.

That was not what I had been expecting, so I just blinked at him in surprise.

"For how I acted when I found out about your powers," he clarified. "For what I said, and all that. It's just that, I was sure that you were like... That you didn't have any magical powers." Reaching up, he rubbed the back of his neck while an embarrassed look drifted over his face. "It's just a sore subject for me."

I frowned but uncrossed my arms and straightened from the door. "Why? I mean, after everything I didn't tell you about, why is *that* such a deal-breaker for you?"

"I just thought you were..." he repeated before trailing off and shrugging self-consciously.

Realization dawned. Flicking my eyes up and down his lean muscled body, I considered everything I knew about him before I opened my mouth again.

"Like you," I finished for him. Meeting his gaze again, I gave him a look of understanding. "You thought I didn't have any magical powers. Just like you."

"Yeah."

That one word sounded a lot heavier than it should have been. Far from all elves had magical powers, so it wasn't as if he was the only one. And besides, the majority of elves who did have powers had been born with something that was fairly low scale. If not downright useless. People like Mordren and Volkan, who possessed gifts of incredible power, were rare. After all, there was a reason why they were princes of a court and not shop clerks in some backwater part of town. But because people like Mordren and Volkan played such large roles in society, it was quite easy to forget that that was not the norm. No one looked down on those who had been born without magic, but based on the look on Evander's face and the tone of his voice, he appeared to be bothered by it.

Tilting my head, I studied him. "Why does that bother you so much?"

"Because..." He paced back and forth in front of the bed and raked his fingers through his short brown hair before finally stopping. Meeting my gaze, he threw his arms out. "Because I want what everyone else has. I want to have a comfortable life. I want to be able to wake up every day and not have to worry about anything."

"Not everyone has that," I pointed out.

My voice had come out sounding gentler than I had expected, but I couldn't seem to bring myself to be rude after I'd seen the look on his face. The yearning. I knew what it was like to desperately yearn for something too.

"I know," he replied with a humorless laugh. "Since I'm obviously one of them. But enough people do, and I've always thought that if they had that, why couldn't I have it too?" Lifting a hand, he absentmindedly rubbed his arm while staring at a spot on the red stone wall to his left. "But to wake up and not have to worry about anything, you need money or power. I have neither." He met my gaze again and shrugged. "That's why I jumped at the chance to work for Princess Syrene."

I nodded in understanding before moving forward. Edging past him in the narrow room, I gave his arm a quick squeeze before I dropped down on the bed. He took that as invitation and followed. The thin mattress shifted underneath me as Evander sank down beside me.

"A cushy position as a courtier spy." He flicked his eyes to me. "A job that basically just entailed flirting with gorgeous people while attending parties. All of my needs taken care of. Servants who prepare delicious food for me every day. Clothes and alcohol and everything I could wish for. Plus an enormous sum of money that I could set aside for the day when my services were no longer required. How could I pass that up?"

Since I had lived like that for years, I knew that it wasn't as glamorous as he made it out to be, but still I said, "I guess you couldn't."

"It was a dream come true for someone who grew up in a poor family on the outskirts of the forest where you had to do everything yourself. Those weeks in the castle, the way I lived back then, I want that again."

"I can imagine."

"I had it all." He let out a bitter laugh and gestured down at his bare chest and the white loincloth. "And now, I'm not even allowed to wear a shirt."

Brushing a hand over my thin golden dress, I huffed out a short laugh. "Yeah, I know the feeling." I snapped my eyes back to his when a sudden idea struck. "Wait, you said that you did everything yourselves back home. How much do you know about plants?"

Amusement danced over his handsome features as he looked back at me. "I grew up in a cabin in the forest, so quite a lot."

"Come with me." I shot to my feet and pulled Evander with me towards the door. "I need your help with something before Volkan gets back."

"Oh, okay."

He blinked but followed me willingly as I steered us out of my room and then turned down the hall in the direction of the kitchens. For a while, only our soft footsteps echoed against the red stone as we made our way through torchlit corridors. With all the nobles and courtiers in the arena to watch Volkan's fight, the castle was unusually quiet. I still kept a wary eye on our surroundings as we walked.

Evander seemed to be doing the same.

Turning my head slightly, I studied his face before finally asking the question I had been mulling over since he confirmed that he didn't possess any magical abilities. "Why did Prince Volkan offer you a deal? It wasn't until he saw that I could walk through walls that he decided he wanted me. Why did he want you?"

"Information." Evander blew out a long breath and grimaced. "Since I worked for Princess Syrene, I have a lot of information about the inner workings of the Court of Trees that ordinary citizens won't know about. That's why I don't really do anything other than stand in the throne room looking useless until he needs specific information, like a few days ago."

"Ah." I returned my gaze to the hallway before us as we turned a corner. "I'm guessing Viviane is the same?"

"I'm not sure if she's magically gifted too, but yeah, she serves the same function as me. Information, except about the Court of Water." He shook his head. "Prince Volkan must be ecstatic now that his set is complete. Between me, you, and

Viviane, he has someone with insider information about all the other courts."

"Yeah, which is why we have to sabotage his plans." I stopped in front of a set of glass doors close to the kitchen. "With this."

Evander frowned. "A greenhouse?"

"Correct."

Metal rattled as he pushed down the handle. "It's locked."

"Good thing that you now know someone who can walk through walls."

With a wicked smile flashing over my lips, I stepped right through the glass before turning and unlocking the door from the inside. Pushing it open, I found Evander looking at me with raised eyebrows.

"So that's how you got into the mausoleum," he mumbled under his breath as he crossed the threshold and then closed the door behind him. Looking up, he flicked his eyes between me and the space around us. "What exactly are we doing here again?"

Turning, I gazed out across the sea of green. Glass walls and a glass roof helped keep the temperature optimal for the leaf-clad inhabitants that stared back at us. Plants of every shape and size filled almost every available surface, except for the narrow pathways that ran through the green maze, and the whole room smelled of damp soil and herbs.

"Like I said, we're going to sabotage Prince Volkan's plans." With that wicked smile still on my lips, I turned back to Evander. "And here's how we're going to do it."

Evander's eyebrows climbed higher as I explained what I wanted to do, but in the end, he only nodded and moved deeper into the greenhouse. Leaves rustled faintly as he stroked a gentle hand over them while searching for what I needed.

"I'm sorry," he suddenly said.

Disappointment fluttered its cold wings in my chest. "You can't find anything that will work?"

"Oh, no." He whirled towards me and waved a hand in front of his face. "Not that. I'm sure there's something we can use." Turning his gaze back to the plants, he chewed his lip before continuing. "I'm sorry for what I said when I locked you in that mausoleum basement. Well, and for actually locking you in there too, I guess. But that was part of my job. Telling you that the sex had at least been good wasn't." He rubbed the back of his neck and glanced at me. "That was a really awful thing to say. And I'm sorry."

A cloud of fragrant air drifted over me as I ran my fingers through a cluster of lemon balm while I considered his words. He sounded sincere. And I had treated him pretty badly too when I manipulated him into falling for me.

"I'm sorry too," I said at last as I met his gaze. "Like you said, it was our job to betray each other, but what we made each other feel was still real. I'm sorry that I played with your feelings like that."

Evander held out his hand. I blinked at it while a smile spread across his lips.

"Hi, I'm Evander," he said, mischief glittering in his emerald eyes. "And I'm a double agent."

A baffled laugh slipped my lips. Pulling myself together, I reached out and took his hand. "Hi, I'm Kenna. And I'm a traitor spy."

His grin grew wider as he shook my hand. "Nice to meet you, Kenna." With that satisfied look still on his face, he withdrew and turned back towards the sea of green leaves before us. "Now, let's see if we can find that plant for you."

After giving him a nod, I followed him deeper into the soil- and herb-smelling maze.

What had happened today didn't mean I had forgotten about his betrayal, but it made me understand him better. After all, I had played him too. And if I could forgive Mordren for everything he had done to me, then maybe Evander deserved a second chance too. His words today didn't make up for everything. But it was a start.

CHAPTER 15

*A*fternoon winds swept across the landscape. White clouds covered the heavens and painted the otherwise bright ocean in muted hues. My golden dress fluttered around my legs as I descended the green hill and approached the camp below.

At the front of our procession marched the five elven princes of our lands. Backs straight and chins raised, they oozed confidence and power even though every step closer to the High Elves' camp amplified that terrible urge to kneel. I flicked my gaze over the other guards and attendants who had followed their prince. They were all staring at the group gathered on the sands below.

High Commander Anron stood at the head of a small squad of soldiers. Their bronze breastplates shone as if newly polished and they all bore neutral expressions on their faces. All except Anron. His face showed a friendly smile that I didn't believe for a second.

"Welcome, to our humble camp," he called as we drew close. Sharp blue eyes quickly scanned our faces before a slight frown creased his brow. "I was under the impression that King Aldrich would be attending too."

"I'm afraid the king is very busy at the moment," Prince Rayan replied and spread his arms to indicate the four elves beside him. "But we are overjoyed to be here."

Tension fell across the beach as everyone waited to see if the High Elves would challenge the statement or demand another meeting with the king present. Anron's long brown hair rippled behind him as a rogue breeze snatched it up. For a moment, he said nothing. Then the practiced smile slid home on his lips again.

"Of course." He inclined his head slightly. "And we are more than happy to have the five of you here. Please, let me give you a quick tour."

Armor clanked as the High Elf soldiers turned as one and then marched back to their posts while Anron steered our group towards the shoreline. Lifting one arm, he motioned towards the grassy banks on the other side. "As you can see, there is not much to show since we are not planning on staying. As soon as we have reached some sort of agreement on diplomatic ties we are returning to Valdanar."

"Valdanar?" Iwdael Vineweaver asked, his voice the epitome of innocent curiosity.

The High Commander smiled. "Our homeland."

"Ah, I see. Is it far?"

"On our air serpents? Not as far as it could have been," Anron answered vaguely before sweeping an arm towards the massive shapes moving before us. "Would you like to meet them?"

"Of course."

Sand trickled into my shoes as we crossed the beach and closed the distance to the winged serpents resting by the waterline. My heart thumped in my chest. They were even bigger up close and those sharp teeth could easily devour a person. If the talons didn't shred them first, that is.

Most of them looked to be sleeping, but a white one and a green one were... fighting? Playing? It was hard to tell.

High Commander Anron put two fingers to his lips and blew a series of short whistles. The white serpent snapped its head in his direction. And then it sprang forward.

Almost everyone in our group flinched back as the massive animal barreled straight for us. The only people who managed to remain standing resolutely were the five princes, along with Hadeon, Idra, and Ymas. I flicked my gaze towards Ellyda, who had taken a step back. Today, her violet eyes were clear and sharp, and she studied the air serpents with a scrutinizing gaze.

Great ruts appeared in the sand as the white serpent skidded to a halt a mere stride in front of Anron, who said a few words in a language I didn't understand. The animal turned its lethal head towards us. Pulling back its lips, it let out a rumbling snarl and flicked its tail across the ground.

Behind Ymas, Monette looked like she was about to throw up at the sight of it, and about half of the other attendants took another step back.

"He's not dangerous," the High Commander said with a small shrug, but his eyes gleamed. "Well, he can be. But all the air serpents follow our orders, so you have nothing to fear as long as we're here to command them not to attack you."

The implied threat did not go unnoticed. Even with his back to me, I could feel the annoyance rippling off Mordren's body.

"I see," Prince Rayan said diplomatically. "You have tamed them then?"

"They're bred in captivity."

"How... efficient."

"Very."

The winged serpent bared its teeth again, which made several from our group flinch once more. Narrowing my eyes, I watched the expression on Anron's face. I had a distinct feeling that this was a deliberate power play. Just like what Prince Volkan was doing with the fire in the meeting room. Calling the dangerous animal here and making it growl at us was intended to serve as a warning of what the High Elves could unleash on us if they wanted to.

"Well then," Anron said and motioned towards the large tent close to the banks. "Shall we eat and talk some more?"

Clanking metal, rustling fabric, and groaning wood echoed around us as we left the shoreline behind and made our way through the camp. The elves we passed seemed to be engaged in mundane activities. They didn't look like they were getting ready for an assault, but I still kept my eyes peeled.

A little in front of me, to my right, walked Hadeon and Ellyda. I watched their sharp gazes assess everything they saw as well. To my left, Idra was doing the same.

"They're all soldiers," Hadeon observed in a low voice.

Idra snapped her gaze to him. When he noticed the attention, he narrowed his eyes slightly but said nothing more. For a while, the two warriors only watched each other.

"Yes," Idra said at last. "Even the ones who pretend to be civilians are actually soldiers. I noticed that too." She flicked a quick glance towards Volkan, who was walking with the other princes out of earshot before finishing with, "How did you know?"

Hadeon considered her in silence for a few seconds before finally replying. "They all move like warriors."

Silence fell across the sands as the two of them studied one another again. Then Idra gave Hadeon a short nod before returning her attention to the camp around her. I was just about to sneak closer to Hadeon and Ellyda when a dark-haired elf that I assumed belonged to either the Court of Trees or the Court of Water sidled up to me.

"Are you alright?" he said.

I shot him a brief frown in confusion. "Sure."

"It's just that being in the presence of the High Elves can leave such a *void* in one's chest."

It took all of my self-control not to whip my head towards him. Instead, I simply kept my gaze locked on Idra's back while we continued walking. "True. But I can handle myself."

"That doesn't surprise me," Eilan said in the voice that belonged to his current disguise. "But it's always good to have friends."

"I already have friends. Though I have to admit that I'm pretty angry with one of them because he lets stuff bother him so easily. I wish someone would tell him that."

Eilan smiled blandly in a calculated show of mild disinterest. "Well, maybe someone will. If you want more friends, I would be happy to fill that void."

Stopping the chuckle in my throat took more effort than I wanted to admit, but we had finally reached the large tent in the middle so I forced a neutral mask on my face while Eilan slipped away.

The sides of the tent had been pulled open to let in the warm salt-tasting winds, and through them I could see a table that had been set for six. If Anron had been expecting the King of Elves, one of his men must have quickly rearranged the plates while we were looking at the air serpents.

A soft murmur spread through our group as everyone started shifting around so that they were placed behind their prince. I kept my eyes downcast and slid up next to Prince Volkan, just as he had instructed. He was already standing behind the chair next to Anron's seat so he had a few seconds to spare while the rest of the group was still busy moving into position.

Fixing Mordren with a smug look, he drew his hand up my arm. From where he was standing behind the chair opposite him, the Prince of Shadows only stared back at him with expressionless eyes. *Good.* Maybe he finally had managed to get himself under control.

Volkan dragged his hand up over my shoulder and over my collarbones. Across the table, Mordren tightened his grip on the back of his chair.

A vicious smile spread across Volkan's mouth as he moved his hand up my throat and then took my chin in a firm grip.

Turning my head, he leaned closer and whispered in my ear, "Look frightened."

As soon as Prince Volkan had found out about this dinner, he had informed me that he was bringing me and that I should do whatever he told me to in order to rattle Mordren. I had written that in the traveling book, so Mordren already knew, but it apparently didn't matter all that much because he still looked about ready to murder the Prince of Fire.

Suppressing an exasperated sigh, I transformed my face into a frightened mask.

Lightning flashed in Mordren's eyes. He opened his mouth to say gods and spirits know what, but before he could, a loud clanking noise filled the air. Volkan yanked his hand back and stared down at the table that someone had bumped into rather forcefully. I swept my arm out as if to steady myself, and then took a quick step back before the Prince of Fire could grab me again.

There was a small smile playing over Eilan's lips as he, still in his shapeshifter form, expertly weaved away from the table he had rattled without anyone noticing. I had to force myself not to return the grin as I took my position next to Idra.

"Please, have a seat," Anron said when everyone was finally in place.

Wood scraped against wood as the six of them pulled out their chairs and sat down. Since the planks that had been laid out to provide stability for the table didn't reach all that far out, the rest of us were standing on the shifting sands further behind. I discreetly twisted my foot and shook some sand from my shoes while Captain Vendir arrived with a pitcher of wine.

The blond captain looked to Anron, who nodded, and then began pouring wine into the six metal goblets on the table. Once he was done, he withdrew without a word and took up position behind his commander's shoulder.

High Commander Anron lifted his goblet. "To new opportunities."

There was a brief pause before the five princes echoed, "New opportunities."

I watched as the six of them took a long gulp before returning their goblets to the table. Metal thumped against wood. A second later, Anron snapped his fingers and signaled to the High Elves further out that it was time to serve dinner.

The spicy aroma of grilled fish drifted through the air as several soldiers approached with large trays.

Anron shifted his attention back to the table and cleared

his throat. "Now that we are all here, perhaps we should finally discuss what it is that we hope this new friendship will lead to. Tell me, what is something that you desire?"

"I was just about to ask you the same question," Mordren replied. "Since you are the one who sought us out, perhaps it..."

He trailed off as a terrible coughing sound started up from across the table. Prince Volkan thumped a fist against his chest.

"Volkan, really, this is..." The Prince of Shadows trailed off once more as Volkan coughed violently and sucked in a few desperate gasps.

Wood clattered as the Prince of Fire shot to his feet, making his chair topple backwards. Gripping the table so hard his knuckles turned white, Volkan struggled to suck air into his lungs. His face was turning a pale shade of blue.

The shock that had frozen everyone at the table finally snapped loose, and panicked voices filled the air while all the other princes shot to their feet.

"What is the meaning of this?" Edric Mountaincleaver demanded.

Iwdael turned to Prince Rayan while gesturing towards the choking Prince of Fire. "Help him."

Idra was already by her prince's side, but she could do nothing more than catch him as he collapsed. Lowering him gently to the floor, she snapped her gaze to Rayan as well. "He can't breathe."

For a brief moment, the Prince of Water looked like he would have preferred to keep it that way, but then he elbowed his way through the screaming courtiers and dropped down next to Volkan. Raising his arms, he closed his eyes and moved his hand over Volkan's spasming body.

"He's been poisoned," Rayan declared a few moments later.

"Poisoned?" Prince Edric snapped.

The boulders on the hill behind us rumbled and cracked as the Prince of Stone whirled towards Anron. Captain Vendir took a step forward while the rest of the High Elves closed in around us as well. Raising his hands, High Commander Anron made a placating gesture but I could see the hints of shock and panic in his eyes.

"Not by our hand," he said. "We invited you here as friends. What possible reason would we have for poisoning you?"

"That is what we want to know," Edric growled.

"It would serve absolutely no purpose."

"Unless your purpose was to kill us off?"

"No," Anron protested. "You are not listening. If I had tried to poison you, why are not all of you choking right now?"

Mordren slid his silver eyes to the High Commander. "Perhaps because you were only targeting Volkan."

The Prince of Fire sucked in a deep breath as Rayan's healing magic finally cleared his airways. The shock of betrayal danced in his eyes as he met Anron's gaze.

"You tried to poison me," he pressed out between ragged breaths.

While High Commander Anron began spluttering denials once more, I used my foot to grind a small glass vial deeper into the sand. With Evander's knowledge of plants, it had been easy to find an herb that was poisonous when pressed into sap. The convenient table bump orchestrated by Eilan had provided me with opportunity to pour a few drops into Volkan's cup while I pretended to stabilize myself. Then all I had to do was wait for the show to start. Since Rayan was here, I knew that the Prince of Fire was in no actual risk of dying. But an attempted poisoning was sure to put a strain on Volkan and Anron's relationship.

With everyone else focused on the chaos around them, I met Mordren's gaze from across the table and winked. His silver eyes sparkled. Drawing a hand over my mouth as if in shock, I wiped the smug smirk off my face before anyone else could see it.

How terribly inconvenient it must be for powerful elven princes when a scheming blackmailer spy poisoned their wine.

CHAPTER 16

Cold blue eyes stared down at me from the dais. I started slightly in surprise at the unexpected sight but continued forwards anyway. Coming to a halt in the middle of the room, I looked back at Prince Volkan while jerking my chin towards the other four people in the room.

"What's with the audience?" I asked.

A vicious smile spread across Volkan's face. "It took me a while to figure out who you really are and track down your family. But here they are. I thought they might like to see what has become of their daughter."

Metallic clanking filled the room as the Prince of Fire tossed the short sword towards me, making it bounce across the red stones before gliding to a halt in front of me. I glanced down at it before looking back up at the five people on the dais. Lord Elmer Beaufort draped an arm around Adeline's shoulders, but said nothing.

Volkan nodded towards the blade and then took a step off the raised platform. "Go ahead. Attack."

Bending down, I picked up the blade and spun it once in

my hand. It was the same bad sword he gave me every time he summoned me to the breaking room. I crouched into an attack position.

"Kenna, this is unseemly," my adoptive father said from behind Prince Volkan. "You are embarrassing us all with this behavior."

Ignoring him, I kept my eyes fixed on the Prince of Fire. Tall flames from the shallow pool by the wall made his blond hair and yellow eyes gleam like gold. I darted forward.

With a quick thrust, I aimed for the side of his stomach. He slammed down his own blade and blocked it while twisting to the side. Pain shot through my chest as his elbow took me in the ribs.

"Kenna, please," my mother said from the dais. "You're only making it worse. For yourself. And for us."

Instead of answering, I ducked Volkan's next swing and then leaped back to put some distance between us. Fire hissed from the flame pool to my left. I feigned right and then jabbed at my opponent's throat.

"This is absurd," Lord Elmer protested. "I know how terrible it must be for you to once more be a slave, but this is what life is like now. There is no point in trying to fight it. If you just accept your position, life will become so much easier. Don't you want that?"

I risked a glance at him. He still had one arm wrapped around Adeline's shoulders and he seemed very flustered. My mother watched me with concerned eyes while remaining under her husband's protective arm. To her right stood both of my half-siblings. Patricia and Elvin were watching the scene with passive expressions on their faces. I narrowed my eyes at all four of them.

The second of inattention cost me as I missed the boot

coming for the back of my leg. A dull thud sounded as my knee buckled and slammed into the floor. Rolling with the motion, I managed to get away. I swung my sword in a wide arc to give me some space while I jumped to my feet again.

"Kenna, stop this," Lord Beaufort suddenly snapped. "Right now."

Still continuing to ignore him, I went on the offensive. Darting forward, I executed a series of strikes towards Volkan's chest. He frowned slightly but parried my thrusts.

"If you don't stop this right now, I will disown you," Elmer threatened, his voice rising in anger. "Cease this foolishness and accept your lot in life, or I swear I will make sure that you will never see any of us or our money ever again."

I twisted and stabbed at Volkan's side. Metal clashed as he yanked down his own blade to meet it. Confusion swirled in his eyes. After casting a quick look at my family, he shook his head and then pressed forward.

Steel whooshed through the air as Prince Volkan came at me with everything he had. His curved sword slashed through the space I had just been in as I leaped backwards while trying to block. If he had looked confused before, it had quickly been replaced by anger.

Somewhere to my right, fire crackled as an entire column rose into the air. I whipped my head towards it.

The move left my back exposed.

A strong hand wrapped around my arm and yanked me back into a muscled chest while cold steel bit into my throat.

Prince Volkan leaned over my shoulder and placed his lips next to my ear. "How did you know?"

"Know what?"

His grip on my arm tightened as he pushed the blade

higher up under my chin. I could feel the muscles of his chest shift against my back.

"Don't play dumb with me," he growled in my ear. "Answer."

Fixing my gaze on the four blue-eyed humans on the dais, I blew out a short laugh before finally replying. "My family has already disowned me. In fact, they sold me into slavery years ago because they couldn't stand the sight of me. So I'm afraid your vision wasn't very convincing."

In the blink of an eye, the Beaufort family disappeared from the dais without a trace. But even with Prince Volkan's vision gone, he was still standing behind me with a sword to my throat. I carefully lifted my own blade higher up towards my chest.

"Is that so?" He forced my head back further while continuing to pour threats into my ear. "But don't you worry, I will find the thing that breaks you. And then you will be on your knees, begging to serve me willingly just so you won't have to see it again."

Shadows danced over the rough stone walls while I held my sword still and waited for Volkan to make his next move. When he realized that I wasn't going to answer, he scoffed and drew back slightly but kept his blade at my throat.

"Drop it."

Metallic clanking once more filled the otherwise silent room as I lowered my sword and let it fall to the floor. Steel scraped against stone as Volkan kicked it aside while he walked back around me so that we stood face to face.

"In four days, Edric is going to give a status report to the king," Volkan said. Holding the tip of his blade steady at the base of my throat, he locked eyes with me. "What are his routines when he prepares for a presentation like that?"

A sudden burst of worry flitted through my stomach. I had sworn to Prince Edric that I wouldn't reveal any of his secrets after I left his service. Telling Volkan that Edric's strength was his reliability hadn't been very compromising. Or even a secret. This was.

"Answer," the Prince of Fire demanded.

I hesitated. This went against everything I stood for. I might be a liar and a blackmailer and a spy, but if there was one thing I always did, it was to keep the secrets I had promised not to reveal.

Fire surged to life along Volkan's left arm. It spread quickly down his sleeveless arm and gathered in his free hand. Raising that flame-covered hand, he took a step towards me.

The heat from the fire washed over me as he drew his fingers over my arm, just short of actually touching. I could almost feel the flames lick my skin.

"You will answer." His hand moved over my shoulder and up towards the side of my face. "And if you lie, there will be consequences."

My heart thumped in my chest. I didn't want to break Prince Edric's trust like this, but there was no telling what Volkan would do if he got too angry. Mordren had said that Volkan liked pretty things and I knew that the Prince of Fire still wanted me to look beautiful. That was the only reason he was using mental torture inside this breaking room instead of just burning me until I gave in.

But I still had a plan. And I needed to be around Volkan to make sure that I could see it through. If I pushed him too far, if I was too defiant, he might restrict my freedom even more. Or worse, actually lock me up in here until he had figured out how to break me.

"He writes his notes in a special ledger," I pressed out.

Victory danced in Volkan's yellow eyes but he kept his burning hand close to my head. "Explain."

The heat from the flames continued soaking into my skin as I explained how and where Prince Edric wrote the reports that he prepared for King Aldrich. Edric would understand that the treachery was done under duress. He had to. I hoped.

At last, Volkan withdrew his hand and extinguished the flames covering his skin. With a flick of his wrist, he took the sword from my throat as well.

"You will change his notes," he announced. "So that when Edric presents his report, nothing will make sense."

"Yes, sir."

Malice seeped into his eyes. "And Kenna, if yet another one of my targets somehow manages to *find* his notes in time… Let's just say that you will find out exactly what I do to traitors."

I swallowed. "Yes, sir."

Satisfied with my answers, he jerked his chin towards the door. "Dismissed."

The sinking feeling of breaking someone's trust was replaced by anger as I moved towards the door. Not only had I been forced to fight Volkan with the intention of losing to keep my cover intact, I had also been made to share secrets that I should have kept. In addition to that, I now had to use those secrets and break into the Court of Stone to damage Edric's credibility in the eyes of the king. And as if that wasn't enough, I couldn't even warn him like I had done with Prince Rayan.

Staying passive like this was starting to really get to me. But if my plan was to succeed, I had to keep following Volkan's orders and I had to keep losing to him while he tried to break me.

Lost in my own thoughts, I crossed the threshold and stalked down the corridor outside without really looking where I was going.

A pair of feet suddenly appeared before me.

I had to jerk to a halt to avoid mowing the person down. Snapping my head up, I found Idra looking at me intently. Even though I had helped her train every night this past week, I still didn't know where we stood. She was often so cold. Distant. But sometimes, I thought I could see a spark in her eyes that might suggest that she actually enjoyed our workout sessions together. Since I wasn't sure how to behave, I cleared my throat a bit self-consciously.

"Did you want to spar with me?" I asked.

Idra looked back at me in silence for a few seconds. Then her gaze slid to the door to the breaking room behind me before once more settling on my face. "Do you need to let out some anger?"

Her question took me by surprise, so my answer was out before I could stop to think about it. "Yes."

She nodded. "Then let's spar."

CHAPTER 17

My chest heaved. Slamming down my sword, I blocked Idra's attack while jabbing at her ribs with my knife. She read it easily and twisted aside. The knife cut the air next to her while she rammed the hilt of her blade down on my wrist.

Pain crackled up my arm.

The move sent my sword way out of position and I was forced to leap backwards as both of Idra's blades descended on me. Excitement shone in her dark eyes.

We had been at it for the better part of an hour. Idra had had the upper hand the whole time but she had pulled back before she could strike the winning blow in order to keep the fight going. My muscles shook with exertion and my body begged for a reprieve. But in a good way.

Silver blades became a blur before me as Idra pushed me back across the padded mats. It was all I could do to avoid the forceful strikes, let alone deliver any of my own. She was backing me into a corner, I knew that. But there was also nothing I could do to stop her.

With a soft thud, my back connected with the wall. A moment later, Idra slammed the sword from my right hand in a fluid move that had her own blade racing for my throat afterwards.

Sharp steel pressed into the heated skin of my throat. I sucked in ragged breaths as I looked down at my other hand. *Damn. Almost.*

Idra followed my gaze.

The knife in my left hand was hovering a short distance from her unprotected stomach. I had almost managed to get it against her ribs before her sword froze my movements. Almost.

"Good," Idra said. A small smile blew across her lips as she locked eyes with me and pushed her sword harder against my throat. "But not good enough."

Huffing out a laugh, I let go of the knife and then tapped my hand against the wall. She stepped back. I flashed her a smile and shook my head before bending down to pick up the blades I had dropped.

"You look a lot less angry," she observed as I returned my weapons to the rack.

"Yeah." I let out a long sigh before turning to face her. "I feel a lot less angry."

She placed her twin swords on another weapons rack before nodding. "What brought it on?"

Only the soft hiss of the torches burning brightly along the walls broke the stillness as I considered in silence for a moment before answering. Idra didn't press me. She simply started her stretching routine on the other side of the room.

"I had to break someone's trust."

She looked up at that but didn't comment. I drifted closer

to her and began stretching my muscles as well before elaborating.

"When I bought my freedom from the Prince of Stone, I promised him that I wouldn't betray any of his secrets. Prince Volkan made me break that."

"I see."

"It's kind of ridiculous." I shook my head. "I've done much worse things to people, but this somehow makes me feel… like an awful person."

Idra straightened and started on her arm muscles. "If it makes you feel better, he often does that. To Viviane. To Evander. Not just to you."

"He's made you betray someone's secrets too?"

"No." When I raised my eyebrows in confusion, she just lifted her toned shoulders in a shrug. "There was no one left whose trust I could break."

The expression on her face was neutral. Casual. Slightly passive. The way it usually was. But I couldn't help feeling like there was much more to the story than that.

My leg muscles sighed in relief as I straightened and got started with my arms as well. For a while, silence reigned in the training hall. Staring at a spot on the wall, I thought about what Idra might have been through in her life but I hadn't quite worked up the courage to ask about it yet.

Clothes whispered next to me as Idra changed position again.

"Does it ever get any easier?" I asked. When she only frowned at me in response, I clarified. "To obey Prince Volkan without question?"

"No."

Even though it wasn't the answer I had wanted to hear, I almost smiled at that. Idra never minced words. She got straight to the point and said exactly what she wanted to say, without trying to sugarcoat it or spin some half-truth. I realized that I liked that about her.

Perhaps it was because of that small revelation that I suddenly found myself asking, "Who were you before you worked for Volkan?"

She snapped her gaze to me. An entire storm of emotions roared in her black eyes but I couldn't decipher any of them. The intensity of it was enough to make me blink in surprise but before I could open my mouth to say anything, it was gone. Sucked out as if by a strong wind. Only black eyes, as dark and still as death, remained as she stared me down.

"Get out," she said, her voice cold enough to give me frostbite.

"I'm—"

She took a step towards me and raised her arm in a threatening gesture. "I said, get out."

Confusion and irritation mingled inside my chest. I had only just started to feel like we'd become friendly, and then I had to go and ruin it. And I didn't even know why that simple question had brought on such a strong reaction.

Kicking myself for ruining the small amount of goodwill I had built up, I gave Idra a respectful nod and said, "I'm sorry."

Before she could bite my head off again, I turned and walked back out into the corridor.

The wall-mounted torches hissed at me in mockery as I made my way back to my room. I really should have just kept my mouth shut. Idra was an incredibly powerful ally to have, and she would have been able to help me a lot, but now I might have just ruined that chance with one careless question.

Shaking my head, I turned the next corner.

Idra clearly hated to talk about her past. I would have to

keep that in mind and hope that I could rebuild her trust while we trained. But for now, I had other problems. Like the fact that I had to break into the Court of Stone and ruin Prince Edric's reputation in front of the king. This was going to be painful to watch.

CHAPTER 18

*D*read and guilt spread through my veins like poison. Standing behind Volkan's back, I watched from under lowered lashes as Prince Edric read the report to the silent throne room. The king, as well as the other princes, were all frowning at him in confusion.

"And in the Court of Stone, we have found two people worshipping the High Elves," Prince Edric said.

"Two?" King Aldrich stared at him in disbelief.

Edric frowned down at his paper. "I mean, two... hundred?"

"Are you asking me or telling me?"

"Uhm..." The Prince of Stone flicked his gaze around the room, desperation swirling in his gray eyes. "I'll just move on to the High Elves and the situation at their camp. We have estimated that they only have supplies for another two weeks."

"What?" Prince Iwdael interrupted. His long brown hair rippled down his back as he shook his head. "No, that's not at all what I said."

"Then how long?"

"I don't remember! I gave the numbers to you to summarize into your report, so I don't know exactly but I do know that it was a lot more than two weeks."

"Uhm..." Edric repeated while his eyes darted around the room again. "There must have been some kind of misunderstanding. I will look into those numbers again. In the meantime, I assessed their soldiers and the High Elves appeared to have..." He squinted at his paper. "No, this can't be right. I'm sure I wrote..."

"Edric," the king said. His voice was hard and his gaze unflinching as he stared down at the Prince of Stone. "This is highly disappointing. We are in a uniquely dangerous situation, and you cannot even be bothered to make sure your report is in order before you present it."

A wave of guilt crashed over me again. The report had been in order. Prince Edric had double-checked it last night before he had gone to bed, the way he always did to make sure that everything was ready. It was impossible to remember every single number in a report that detailed, but he always went through it anyway. And then an awful little traitor spy had snuck into his study and changed all the numbers. I truly hated myself in that moment.

"Perhaps it is time that someone else took over that responsibility," King Aldrich continued. "If you cannot be trusted to take this seriously."

"N-no, my king," Prince Edric stammered. "There has just been some sort of miscommunication somewhere. I will set things right, I swear it."

I had never seen him that flustered before. Usually, the Prince of Stone was composed and straightforward. Except when he was angry. But even then, there was always this air of control around him. Now, he looked worried and uncertain. It made sharp needles stab into my wicked heart.

"You'd better," the king warned. He held Edric's gaze for another few seconds before shifting it to sweep across the rest of the gathered audience. "I have been traveling through your courts. Ensuring people that the spirits are listening. That they're still there. Turning people away from the worshipping of these false gods. Some of them have listened and returned to the true path, but far too many hold on to those black bracelets and pray to the High Elves."

"We'll crack down hard on them, my king," Prince Edric said, desperate to restore Aldrich's faith in him.

But the king shook his head. "No. Forcing people to believe in something or to stop believing in something else is never a good idea. It only makes them cling harder to their beliefs. I will continue to travel through our lands, speaking with people. Many trust me in matters of faith. They know of my connection to the spirits. I will try to gently guide them back to our faith."

"What would you like us to do, my king?" Mordren asked into the silence that fell.

A weary sigh escaped King Aldrich's lips. "I don't know. You have all felt the High Elves' power. What it feels like to simply stand in their presence. It is no wonder that ordinary people have started to believe that they are gods. We cannot forbid people to worship what they believe in. But we also cannot let these High Elves accumulate any more power. You will have to figure out ways to limit the spread of this, without being too heavy-handed about it."

The five elven princes exchanged a glance.

"I know," Aldrich said and waved a hand in front of his face. "Easier said than done. But try." His brown eyes hardened as they locked on Prince Edric. "And you, get your head on properly and give me an accurate report next time."

"Yes, my king," Edric replied.

He probably wasn't showing anything on his face, but I could practically feel the smug satisfaction rippling off Volkan's body.

"Good." The King of Elves gave the silent throne room a nod. "Dismissed."

Clothes rustled as everyone bowed to the retreating king. Only when he had disappeared through the door behind the throne did a soft murmur start back up in the white marble hall.

Prince Volkan snapped his fingers at us. "Follow."

I cast a glance at Idra, who only kept her eyes on the rest of the gathered crowd, before hurrying to catch up with the Prince of Fire as he stalked across the throne room. There had been another tournament match yesterday, Volkan's fourth, and I would have thought that he'd gotten his fair share of confrontation from that already. But apparently not. My heart pattered nervously in my chest as Prince Volkan set his sights on Mordren.

"This was your doing, wasn't it?" Volkan called, loudly enough for the whole hall to overhear.

Mordren turned and arched a lazy eyebrow. "Excuse me?"

The other princes exchanged a glance across the shining marble floor and then started towards Mordren and Volkan as well. Pale morning sunlight from an overcast winter sky fell in through the windows and painted the room in patches of white and gray. I watched the light glint in Hadeon's red eyes as he stepped to the side and took up position between Mordren and Idra while Volkan stopped right in front of the

Prince of Shadows. Ellyda was nowhere to be seen, but Eilan stood firmly next to his brother.

"You did something to Edric's report, didn't you?" Prince Volkan accused.

Surprise flitted past in Mordren's silver eyes. And in mine as well. Mordren already knew that Volkan had made me change Prince Edric's notes because I had written to him in the traveling book and told him. But Volkan didn't know that. And it had never occurred to either of us that the Prince of Fire might actually try to pin his own crime on Mordren.

"Why in the spirits' name would I do that?"

Volkan raised his eyebrows in a show of incredulity. "As a play for power of course. Making Edric look incompetent in front of King Aldrich in order to advance your own position as his heir. It wouldn't be the first time you did something like that."

Oh he was good. I had to give him that.

Edric had come to a halt next to them and was now looking from face to face. He narrowed his eyes as he fixed his attention on Mordren. "Is it true?"

The Prince of Shadows kept his eyes locked on Volkan for a moment. Then he let out a derisive snort. Tilting his head, Mordren slid his gaze to Edric while a cold smile graced his lips. The gesture was the epitome of lazy arrogance, but underneath it all was a sharp edge of danger that made Ymas take a step forward to block the Darkbringer prince's access to Edric.

"If I wanted to discredit you," Mordren said, his lethal gaze locked on the Prince of Stone, "there are much worse secrets that I could use. Would you not agree?"

Some of the color drained from Edric's face and Ymas

edged another step forward. Mordren only raised his eyebrows expectantly.

"Agreed," Prince Edric grudgingly admitted.

Mordren slid his gaze back to Volkan. "Since you were so quick to cast blame on someone else, perhaps it was you who did it."

"Me?" Prince Volkan scoffed. "I'm much more direct than that. If I wanted to challenge someone, I would do it to their face. Everyone knows that you are the sneaky one, always scheming in the shadows."

"That's not quite true," Rayan Floodbender interjected from my other side. "You are not above being sneaky, Volkan."

"Give me one example."

Rayan's eyes darted to me for a second. He couldn't tell the others about what Prince Volkan had tried to do to him without putting me in danger.

When the silence stretched on a little too long, Volkan barked a short laugh. "I thought so. Now, let's get back to the real threat to our safety." A malicious smirk tugged at his lips as he turned back to the Prince of Shadows. "Mordren, prove to us that you were not behind this."

"I do not need to prove anything to you."

"Spoken like a guilty person."

Rage darkened Mordren's eyes as he took a step closer. Idra flashed forward, blocking his way, which made Hadeon move as well. Idra's hand hovered in front of the warrior's chest where he stood between her and Mordren.

"I suggest you back off," Idra said, her eyes locked on Hadeon.

"You first," he growled back at her.

On their right, Eilan let out a deliberate chuckle as he

looked back at Volkan. "Wow, you really are scared of my brother."

Irritation crackled across Volkan's face. Flicking a hand, he ordered Idra to withdraw. She took a step back but kept her impassive gaze on Hadeon. As soon as they were out of the way, Mordren continued towards the Prince of Fire.

"What are you going to do, little prince?" Volkan taunted while spreading his arms. "Attack me? Then do it. Prove to everyone here that you are the real threat to our lands."

Mordren stopped only a breath away from him. They were roughly the same height so for a moment, the two princes only stared at each other while the rest of the throne room held their breath. Then Mordren cocked his head. His night-black hair rippled over his sharp suit with the movement.

"I would advise you not to start something you cannot finish," Mordren said, his voice cold and flat. "Or you might find yourself in a position you would rather avoid."

"Is that a threat?"

"Stop this," Rayan said from a few strides away. "Mordren could not have done anything to Edric's report." Lifting a hand, he motioned towards the blond elf standing a short distance behind them. "He has a chaperone monitoring his movements, remember?"

Nodding, Prince Edric muttered something in agreement. But the two lethal elves weren't listening.

"I do not need to make threats," Mordren said in response to Volkan's question. A predatory smile spread across his lips. "I think you and I both know exactly what I am capable of."

"Careful now." Volkan kept his eyes locked on Mordren while reaching towards me and curling his fingers around my collar. I let out a small yelp as he yanked me closer to him.

"You wouldn't want to make me angry, or else I might decide to take it out on my slaves when I get home."

Mordren's eyes flicked to me. I shot him a pointed stare in the hopes that he would remember to act unaffected and not let these obvious attempts get to him. Relief fluttered in my chest when Mordren apparently interpreted my look correctly.

He simply lifted his shoulders in a casual shrug and replied, "Why should I care what you do with your slaves?"

"Do you not?" Small flames flickered over Volkan's fingers as he tightened his grip on my collar. "Then perhaps you would like a demonstration?"

"Wow, this is getting incredibly boring," Iwdael Vineweaver suddenly announced. "I think I need to throw a party tonight to cleanse myself of all your tedious vibes."

A surprised laugh slipped past Rayan's lips. As I glanced towards the Prince of Trees, the mood around us lightened. The aggression drained away and disappeared into the smooth floor as a calm feeling took its place.

"He's right," Prince Edric grumbled. "We have much more important things to do than to fight amongst ourselves."

"Yes," Rayan filled in. "Like figuring out how to stop these religious fanatics from spreading."

The Prince of Fire scoffed as he let go of my collar and flicked his wrist in Mordren's direction. "Whenever you want to challenge me, I'm right here." A dangerous glint crept into his yellow eyes as he shifted his attention to Iwdael. "And you, get your mood-influencing shit away from me right now or you're going to get more than tedious vibes from me."

In a heartbeat, the calm and comforting feeling evaporated. I started in surprise. The change had been so small, so gradual, that I hadn't even realized that Prince

Iwdael had been using his powers of mood control to diffuse the situation.

While Volkan turned towards Idra, the Prince of Trees winked at the rest of us.

"Let's go," Prince Volkan said.

Spinning on his heel, he turned and stalked towards the doors. Idra tore her watchful gaze from Hadeon before following. With a small nod towards the other four princes, I did the same. Pale morning light illuminated the hall around me as I made my way back out of the castle with Prince Volkan and Idra.

Because of what I'd done to Edric, today had been a setback in my plan. Disappointment blew through me. I had been a traitor spy inside the Court of Fire for over two weeks now and the only two things I had managed to accomplish were to avert a plot against Prince Rayan and to make it seem like High Commander Anron had tried to poison Volkan. Not a lot of progress compared to the amount of time I'd had.

I would have to step up my game.

Narrowing my eyes, I watched the muscles shift underneath Volkan's dark red tunic while my mind turned over a couple of schemes in my head.

It was time to call in a favor.

CHAPTER 19

Volkan Flameshield strode across the throne room with confident steps. Word had arrived moments before that High Commander Anron was here for his scheduled dinner with the Prince of Fire. Firelight glinted off the gold threads in Volkan's sleeveless tunic as he reached the massive doors on the other side. I flicked my gaze towards the small group across the floor.

Pale blue eyes stared back at me. I dipped my chin in a discreet nod before returning my attention to the doors.

From the corner of my eye, I could barely make out a few elves disappearing into the corridor behind the throne. Anticipation bounced around inside me but I kept the neutral mask on my face as I stood by the wall, holding a feathered fan on a long golden pole.

A few minutes later, Prince Volkan reappeared, and this time he was not alone. High Commander Anron strolled across the red stone floor next to the Prince of Fire. Flames glinted off the polished bronze armor that the High Elf always wore. I idly wondered what Anron would look like in casual clothes.

"Kenna!"

My heart leaped into my throat at the sharp command from Prince Volkan. *Did he know? He couldn't possibly know.*

"Evander. Viviane," he continued. "Follow."

With blood rushing in my ears, I exchanged a look with Evander before setting the fan down and hurrying after the prince and his guest. This hadn't been part of the plan. I had to admit that I had wanted to see the result for myself, but I had assumed it would be the aftermath. Not the immediate reaction.

When I fell in next to him, Evander cast me a sharp look as if to say, *do you think he knows?*

I lifted my shoulders in an almost imperceptible shrug. On Evander's other side, Viviane stayed silent and kept her eyes on Volkan's back.

Torches spluttered along the walls as we strode past, creating a draft. With my heart still beating its nervous rhythm, I paused as the Prince of Fire stopped in front of the door to a private dining room and motioned for the High Commander to step through. Anron inclined his head in acknowledgement before pushing the handle down and moving inside.

Prince Volkan followed, with the three of us close behind.

We had barely made it inside the room and closed the door before a dark voice split the silence.

"What is the meaning of this?" High Commander Anron demanded.

"What is the meaning of what?" Volkan replied as he stepped up next to him.

I swept my gaze across the room. It was a relatively small

space, meant for private conversations rather than grand receptions. A table for eight took up most of the floor space in the middle of the room but only two places had been set. The ones on each end of the smooth stone table. Shining plates and sparkling glass goblets gleamed in the firelight and a series of candles burned brightly along the middle of the tabletop. A carved stone chair stood proudly waiting on one end, and on the other... only a pillow rested on the floor. As if the other person was supposed to kneel in front of the table while eating.

"Is this meant to be some kind of insult for the supposed poisoning?" Anron said, his voice cold.

Volkan blinked at the scene before him in surprise. "What? No."

"Do you actually expect me to sit on my knees in front of that table while you sit in your chair?"

"Of course not."

"Then why did you have the table set in this way?"

"I didn't."

"You are a fool if you expect me to believe that you didn't check this room before you came to greet me."

Volkan whipped his head towards Anron, his yellow eyes flashing. "Are you calling me a fool?"

"Do not take that tone with me." The High Commander drew himself up to his full height and looked down on Volkan as if he were a child. "I will not stand for these kinds of insults."

"You don't speak to me like that," Prince Volkan growled back.

The force hit me like a blow to the chest. Ever since I got close to Anron, the urge to kneel had been present around me. But now, it was as if he removed the damper on his power.

Fear and awe screamed inside me and I had to grip the side table next to me in order to stop my knees from buckling. On Evander's other side, Viviane didn't have anything to brace herself on and she dropped to a knee with a gasp. My mind was screaming at me to kneel too, but I sucked in a desperate breath while trying to fight off what my instincts were telling me.

"I can speak to you however I like if this is how you treat me," Anron said. Fury and power flashed in his sharp blue eyes as he locked them on Volkan. "I came here as an ally, and this is how you repay my friendship?"

Prince Volkan looked like he was trying very hard to focus as he blinked before slashing a hand through the air. "You talk of friendship and yet you tried to have me poisoned when I visited your camp?"

The invisible power around Anron increased. I clutched the table hard as my knees started shaking, but on the inside, I was cackling. This had been so worth it.

As soon as I had heard that High Commander Anron was coming to have dinner with Prince Volkan, I had gone to Hilver. That night when I had gotten him and his friends off Idra's training duty, they had said that they owed me one. And tonight, I had collected that favor. Volkan had checked the dining room right before Anron arrived. But what he didn't know was that Hilver and his boys had snuck inside in the few minutes when the Prince of Fire had gone to meet his guest. Between the five of them, it appeared to have been an easy task to remove one chair and put a pillow in its place. And the result was... better than expected.

"I did not try to poison you," Anron sniped back. "Why would I? Out of all the people around that table, why would I try to poison *you*? We have an understanding. I help you now, and then you help me later. Trying to kill you makes no sense."

Volkan looked flustered but he shook his head and stabbed a hand towards the pillow on the floor. "Exactly. The same reasoning applies to this situation. If you are helping me become the next King of Elves, why would I make such a pathetic attempt to insult you?"

"Because you thought I had tried to poison you."

"Which you had already assured me that you hadn't."

Anron narrowed his eyes but the power crackling around him decreased. "Then it appears to be a misunderstanding. On both occasions."

"Yes."

The urge to kneel lessened to its usual intensity as the High Commander blew out a breath and nodded, but I swore I could still see a kernel of suspicion in his eyes. Evander hid a slight smile as he looked at me while straightening.

"Viviane," Volkan barked. "Go get another chair brought in."

The dark-haired female swallowed as she struggled back to her feet. "Yes, sir."

While she staggered out the door, Prince Volkan turned his annoyed gaze on Evander. "And you, while we wait, what is the most important event coming up in the Court of Trees at this time of year?"

"Oh, uhm." Evander licked his lips as he considered.

I could almost see the struggle behind his dark green eyes. If he told Volkan the truth, then the Prince of Fire would be in a position to sabotage the other princes even further. But if he lied, and Volkan caught him...

As if he could read the struggle as well, Volkan cocked his

head while fire flickered to life around his fingers. Panic shot across Evander's face.

"There is a party next week," he blurted out. "The nobles in the Court of Trees always arrange it to honor Prince Iwdael. To show their appreciation for him."

The fire disappeared as Volkan drew his hand along his jaw instead. "Ah, yes. I seem to remember being invited to that as well."

"What are you thinking?" Anron asked.

He turned to face the High Elf again. "Iwdael's power comes from his ability to make people feel good about themselves. So, what if we could get him to insult all of his nobles in one fell swoop?"

"Interesting."

"Yes." Volkan shifted his attention back to Evander. "Is there a way to stop him from attending the party?"

"Well…" Evander licked his lips and swallowed again. "He forgets things very easily. So if you wipe it from his calendar, and also make a note in his attendants' calendars that he has decided not to go, then he won't get there. Princess Syrene always kept track of all those things for him, but with her gone…"

"He's far too disorganized to remember all his commitments," Prince Volkan filled in.

"Yes."

"Where are all these calendars kept?"

"In the main study."

A vicious grin spread across Volkan's face as he snapped his attention to me. "You. Get on it."

I nodded. "Yes, sir."

His yellow eyes grew harder. "And Kenna, if Iwdael

somehow makes it to the party, I will hold you personally responsible. Understood?"

"Yes, sir."

"Good." He slid his eyes back to Evander. "How long would it take to sneak in and change those calendars?"

"Oh, uhm." Evander scratched the back of his head. "The main study is deep inside the castle and there are often a lot of people there, so it would take at least four hours to get in, wait for everyone to clear out, change it, and get back out again."

It took all of my self-control not to turn and stare at him in surprise. I knew which study he was talking about, and while it was indeed rather deep in the castle, it wasn't a very crowded area. It should take no more than an hour, maximum, to complete the mission.

"Alright, then you have four hours, Kenna," Volkan said. "Make a plan for how to get it done and tell Idra once you're ready."

"Yes, sir."

Noise came from the door as Viviane returned with two muscular elves who were carrying a chair. I took the opportunity to glance at Evander. A smile tugged at the edge of his lips as he winked at me.

Warmth spread through my chest.

He had deliberately lied about the complexity of the mission in order to buy me a few hours of unsupervised time. And I knew exactly who I wanted to spend that precious time with.

CHAPTER 20

Night had fallen over the castle and left its twisting corridors empty and silent. The feeling of passing through a curtain of silk sheets enveloped me as I phased through the wall of the main study and returned to the deserted hall outside. Just as I had predicted, sneaking into the room and changing all of the calendars had taken less than an hour, which meant that I had roughly three hours to spare. Staying in the shadows, I made my way towards my exit point.

It was at times like these that I truly realized how clueless people were about magic such as mine. They had wards against worldwalking, and gates and soldiers that guarded all the entries and exits, but no one seem to understand just how ineffective most of those security measures were against someone who could literally just walk *through* the walls. Now, if only I had the ability to worldwalk as well, then I would be truly unstoppable.

Voices sounded from the corridor up ahead. I paused. My

heart pattered in my chest while I waited to see if the voices were moving. A thump sounded. It was followed by the faint clink of glass against wood, but the sounds seemed stationary. Staying close to the wall, I snuck forward until I could peek around the corner.

"What's wrong, my prince?"

Prince Iwdael Vineweaver was sitting on the floor halfway down the corridor. His legs were sprawled before him and his back and head were slumped against the wall behind him. A half-empty bottle of liquor rested against his thigh.

"I'm tired," the prince said.

"So come to bed."

The second voice belonged to a gorgeous male elf with long golden hair. Both of them were dressed in shimmering outfits that made them look like they had just left an extravagant party. Gold glitter was splashed across their skin, and gilded branches and leaves decorated their hair.

"Not like that, Augustien." Prince Iwdael traced his fingers over the male's cheek before letting his hand fall back to the floor. "I'm tired in my soul. I don't want people to be sad. I want them to feel good about themselves and about life. But I'm also so tired of pretending to be happy and carefree all the time. I used to be like that. But I'm not. Not anymore."

The golden-haired elf, Augustien, kneeled next to his prince and took his hand. "Talk to me."

"I miss her."

His words were more of a sigh than anything else, but I could still hear him clearly. I knew that this was a private moment. Not meant for anyone else's eyes and ears. But for some reason, I couldn't tear my gaze from the elven prince slumped against the wall. I had never seen him like that before, and perhaps that was why I stayed even though I knew I shouldn't have.

"She planned to kill you, my prince," Augustien said gently.

"I know." Iwdael blew out a sigh and stared up into the ceiling. "But that still doesn't just erase all the years I spent loving her."

"No, of course not."

"We always had an open marriage. Even from the start. Because she was always a little distant and I have always believed that love is too wonderful a force to limit to only one person, but I really did love her. *Do* love her."

Augustien squeezed his hand again. "I know."

Iwdael tilted his head to the side and looked into his eyes. "So how do you stop loving someone?"

Pain swirled in Augustien's golden eyes. "I don't know, my prince."

"Yeah. Neither do I."

Tearing my gaze from the two of them, I retreated into the corridor again. The conversation was getting far too personal and I could no longer justify my presence there with simple curiosity. After a quick look over my shoulder, I left the Prince of Trees to his emotions and disappeared through another wall.

Silent corridors made of dark wood watched me as I made my way back outside, but I still couldn't quite get Prince Iwdael out of my head. I knew that Iwdael had taken a number of lovers during the course of his marriage to Syrene, which she had known about. And since I had talked to Princess Syrene after she was imprisoned, I also knew firsthand that she had only married Iwdael for power and that she had indeed planned to kill him along with all the other princes after she had assassinated the king. But he still missed her. Still loved her. I guessed that was the thing about love. It didn't need to make sense.

Cold winds rattled the branches above me as I phased through the high defensive walls around the castle and started into the dark woods. Prince Volkan had only set my range to the palace and a short distance outside the walls, so I couldn't travel anywhere. But that didn't mean I couldn't bring people to me instead.

After checking to make sure that no one was following me, I snuck up to a dark cottage at the edge of the tree line and walked right through the sturdy wall.

Steel hissed into the darkness. I jerked back as five gleaming blades were pointed straight at me from the middle of the room.

Moonlight fell across the four startled faces before me. A smile slid home across my lips.

"Seriously, Kenna?" Eilan arched an eyebrow at me. "You could have simply used the door."

With that wicked grin still on my face, I winked at him. "What would be the fun in that?"

He huffed out a laugh and shook his head. Steel glinted in the moonlight as he spun his twin knives in his hands before returning them to their holsters. Next to him, Mordren was sheathing his knives as well, while Hadeon rammed his sword back into the scabbard across his back. Ellyda remained motionless by the kitchen counter, staring straight at me. I smiled at the four of them. It was the first time that I had been able to talk to all of them privately since before I traded myself to Volkan and left for the Court of Fire.

"I didn't think you..." I began but then trailed off when Eilan closed the distance between us in two long strides.

A small noise of surprise escaped my lips as the gorgeous

elf drew me into a hug. I stiffened in shock for a moment, but then I returned it.

"Thank you." Eilan withdrew and took my hand instead. Holding my gaze, he gave my palm a quick squeeze before stepping back to the half-circle that had formed before me. "Thank you for what you did for me."

"Oh, uhm, sure." I gave him a self-conscious smile. "Anytime."

"No, not *anytime*. I don't think you quite realize what you did."

Light flickered to life in the small kitchen as Ellyda lit the candle on the wooden counter. I swept my gaze between the four of them, trying to understand why they all looked so serious. Yes, I had traded myself into slavery partly to save Eilan, which was a nice thing to do, I supposed. But it didn't quite warrant… this.

"Volkan had me, and it was only a matter of time before he figured it out," Eilan said. "And once he knew that it was me in that slave collar…"

"He would have held Eilan's life over my head," Mordren finished, his eyes far too serious for my liking. It was the first time he had spoken since I arrived and even the sound of his voice was grave. "He would have made me do anything he wanted, in exchange for Eilan's safety." He lifted his shoulders in an unapologetic shrug. "And I would have let him."

"And between my ability to shapeshift," Eilan continued, "and the entire Court of Shadows as his puppet, he would've had everything he needed to get rid of the other princes without taking any of the heat himself."

Hadeon nodded. "But you stopped that. Before Volkan had even realized what he actually had."

Looking from face to face, I wasn't sure how to respond to that. Of course I had done it in part to save Eilan, but I did have a plan too, so it wasn't fully as selfless as they were making it sound. "I–"

"Are you okay?" Ellyda interrupted before I could say anything else. Her sharp violet eyes had not left mine for one second since I had stepped through the wall.

"Yeah, I'm fine."

"It has been almost three weeks now."

"I know."

"She's right," Hadeon added. "Three weeks is a long time to withstand Volkan's attempts to break someone. We can stop this at any time, you know. Get you out."

A small smile drifted over my lips at their concern, but I shook my head. "No. I told you, I have a plan and I'm going to see it through. And besides, if it weren't for me, there would be no strain between Anron and Volkan."

Hadeon let out a long sigh, but then he nodded. As did Eilan. From her place by the kitchen counter, Ellyda only continued staring at me with those sharp eyes of hers, but I got the feeling that she understood as well.

"We have to go," Eilan said in a gentle voice. "We can only fool the chaperone for so long."

Disappointment tumbled into my stomach. "Already?"

"Well..." He winked at me. "Mordren is staying for a while."

"Oh." I glanced at Mordren. "Good."

"Whatever you need, just write it in the traveling book and we'll get it done." Hadeon held my gaze until I nodded in acknowledgement. Then he threw an arm around his sister's shoulders. "Come on, El. Let's give them some privacy."

Eilan tipped his head in their direction. "What he said. Anything at all, just let us know. I'll see you soon, Kenna."

And with that, the three of them disappeared out the door.

Leaving me alone with the Prince of Shadows.

CHAPTER 21

For some reason, I suddenly felt awkward. The small cabin was cramped with furniture but it still somehow felt too large. Too empty.

I hooked a loose red curl behind my ear, not meeting Mordren's gaze. "How long can you stay?"

"As long as you want me to."

"Okay."

The word sounded silly even to my own ears. It was as if I suddenly didn't know how to behave. The mood surrounding me and Mordren had been many things over the months we had known each other, but awkward had not been one of them.

Last time I had been able to talk to him like this, back in the Court of Water, I had told him what I wanted him to do. How I wanted him to treat me. But I had still felt that something was off with him. That something had changed between us the moment I traded myself for Eilan. I hadn't been able to put my finger on exactly what it was before, but now after he and the others had given me this great speech about the enormity of what I had done for them, I was beginning to realize what it was. And now, I couldn't shake the feeling that Mordren was just doing whatever I wanted out of some misplaced debt of gratitude.

I cleared my throat and looked up at him. "So, I had to wipe Prince Iwdael's calendar so he won't be coming to the party. But I'm going to need you to come. All of you. So that you can talk to his nobles and help mitigate the damage."

"Of course. Whatever you need."

There it was again. His uncharacteristically submissive choice of words that made uncertainty flicker in the back of my mind, wondering if he agreed to what I asked because he wanted to or because he felt indebted to me. I hated it. I hated doubting my relationship with someone. Second-guessing every move they made. Every word they spoke.

"Stop it!" I snapped.

Mordren blinked at me in shock. "Stop what?"

"Stop looking at me like that. Stop doing whatever I say. Stop walking on eggshells around me!"

"I'm not."

Anger roared inside me. Trying to sabotage Prince Volkan from inside his own court, while also trying to keep him from breaking me with his mind games, was all I could take. I was barely holding it together as it was, and I couldn't start doubting one of the few genuine relationships I had as well.

"Yes, you are! And it's driving me nuts. I told you to treat me the same way you always have, but here you are acting like... this. Every time I say anything, you answer something along the lines of 'if you want me to' or 'of course, whatever you want'. Like some kind of submissive servant."

"I'm not."

"Stop saying that!"

Since this was a stealth mission, I had been allowed to wear a pair of black pants, boots, and a shirt, but I still didn't have any weapons. So instead, I snatched up a pan from the kitchen counter next to me and hurled it at Mordren.

He jerked back and stared at me while his shadows shot out and stopped the flying projectile mid-air. I threw another pot at him. It came to an abrupt halt in a mass of twisting black tendrils, but I just sent another plate flying towards him.

"Kenna, what are you doing?"

There was barely enough time for him to set the kitchenware down on the table beside him before I hurled another piece at him. Grabbing whatever I could get my hands on, I continued throwing stuff while stalking towards him.

"I'm proving my point." Stopping two steps in front of him, I raised my chin and spread my arms wide. "Go ahead. Fight back. Make me stop throwing stuff at you."

Hesitation flickered in his silver eyes.

A snarl ripped from my throat. Snatching up a kitchen knife, I shot forward and gave his chest a shove. He tried to step back but tripped over the stool I had deliberately backed him towards.

Dull thuds echoed into the deserted cabin as Mordren crashed down back first on the ground. I flashed down after him. With one knee on either side of his chest, I leaned forward and placed the knife at his throat. He didn't even try to stop me, which pissed me off even more.

"*This* is what I'm talking about," I snapped and motioned with my free hand towards his impassive form. "At no other point, since the day I met you, would you have *ever* let me do something like this unchallenged."

"I'm not letting–"

"Yes, you are! Because you suddenly feel indebted to me."

"I don't–"

"Yes, you do. I made you snap out of your guilt last time but you still don't know how to act around me because you feel indebted to me."

His eyes flicked to the side for a moment before he met my gaze again. "It's not…"

"Not what?"

"Well…"

Barking out a cold laugh, I shook my head and sat up straighter, removing the knife from his throat. "Oh, the feared Prince of Shadows. Doesn't even dare to answer a question honestly anymore."

Fury flashed like lightning in his eyes. I let out a yelp as cool black tendrils wrapped around me and yanked my whole body to the side, flipping me over on my back. The impact was hard enough to make me suck in a gasp, but before I could do anything else, Mordren was straddling my chest while his shadows kept my arms pinned to the floor above my head. He had ripped the knife from my grip and flipped it in his hand before pressing it to my throat instead.

"Of course I feel indebted to you!" he snapped back. "You traded yourself into slavery to save my brother. And in doing so, you not only saved Eilan from eternal servitude to the person who murdered our parents, you also saved *me* from a fate worse than death."

"What?" I frowned up at him. "What fate worse than death?"

"You saved me from becoming Volkan's *bitch*." Leaning down over the knife, he growled that final word in my face. "Don't you get it? Volkan would have made me his bitch. Because if he'd held Eilan's life over my head, I would have done whatever he wanted. Obeyed his every command. I would have gotten down on my knees and surrendered my whole court to him if it meant he let Eilan live. I would have begged and groveled and licked his fucking boots if he ordered me to. *That* is what you saved me from. So of course I feel indebted to you. I could spend my entire life doing everything you asked, and it would still not be enough!"

His shadows snapped back inside him as he pushed to his feet, leaving me lying on the floor. A sharp thud sounded as Mordren threw the knife at the counter. It vibrated where it sank into the dark wood. Raking his fingers through his long black hair, Mordren shook his head while pacing back and forth across the floor.

Blowing out a long breath, I climbed to my feet as well. "So there we have it."

"Yeah."

"Good."

Turning slowly, he frowned at me.

"Now that we've gotten to the heart of the problem, we can do something about it." Crossing my arms, I locked eyes with Mordren from across the now messy kitchen. "You owe me a favor."

The confusion on his face deepened. "What?"

"You feel indebted to me, so to square that debt, you will owe me a favor."

"A favor? That is not even close to being adequate payment for not having to lick Volkan's boots for the rest of my life."

"Fine, let's add a bit to it then. The favor is completely open-ended, and when I call it in, you can't say no. So I can ask you for anything, and no matter what it is, you can't refuse." I flashed him a quick grin. "Meaning that if I called it in and told you to get down on your knees and lick Volkan's boots, you would have to do it."

A surprised huff of laughter escaped his lips. "Handing you that kind of power would indeed balance the scales again." He was silent for a while, considering, before finally giving me a firm nod. "A favor, then."

"A favor." I held his gaze. "When I want to call in that favor, I will tell you. Then, and only then, will you have to do as I say. So that means that at all other times, this will have no impact on our relationship. You could fight me or make me grovel at your feet... Hell, you could even try to kill me if you want. Because you don't owe me anything except that one favor." I arched my eyebrows at him. "Deal?"

He looked at me in silence for a few seconds. Then a small but grateful smile spread across his lips and he nodded. "Deal."

"Good. Now that that's settled, I can see in your eyes that there are things you've been wanting to do to me since the moment I walked into this cabin." Uncrossing my arms, I waved a hand in the air. "What is it?"

Power and authority settled around his body again like a sharp suit. I raised my eyebrows at him, daring him to say it out loud. Mordren took a step forward.

"I want to yell at you for coming up with this ridiculously dangerous plot of yours." He took another step forward. "I want to make you beg my forgiveness for going rogue and deciding to put yourself in danger without talking to me first." Another step. "I want you to understand how stunning you are when you scheme like a ruthless traitor." Eyes locked on me, he stabbed a hand towards the wall on my right. "And I want to push you up against that wall and make you forget your own name."

He had stopped only a breath away. Craning my neck, I looked up at him. Hunger and awe and unwavering power swirled in his silver eyes as he stared me down.

A challenging grin spread across my lips. "Then do it."

I sucked in a gasp as his hand shot towards the back of my neck, but he stole the breath from my lips when his mouth crashed into mine. His fingers threaded through my hair at the nape of my neck before tightening and forcing my head back. I grabbed the front of his shirt and yanked his body closer to mine while he backed me across the floor.

Something hard hit the back of my thighs. I barely had time to register that it was the edge of the kitchen table before Mordren's other arm snaked around me and lifted me up onto the tabletop. With a decisive thrust of his hips, he sent me sliding more firmly onto the smooth surface. I laughed against his mouth.

His hand released my hair and trailed around my neck before wrapping around my throat. Tearing his lips from mine, he positioned his thumb under my chin and forced my head back while locking eyes with me. "This plan of yours is ridiculously dangerous."

I grinned up at him. "I know."

Reaching up, I dragged my hands through his dark silken hair before pulling his lips back to mine. He relaxed his grip and drew his fingers up along my jaw instead while his lips ravaged mine. I drew my hand down from his neck, across his muscled chest, and down over the firm ridges of his abs. A shudder went through his body as I traced the top of his pants. Hooking two fingers over the black fabric, I yanked his hips closer to me.

A dark moan escaped his lips.

I wrapped my legs around him while crushing my mouth harder against his. A pleasant shiver coursed through me as he trailed his fingers down my body. And then another gasp ripped from my lips as he lifted me off the table and carried me towards the wall.

Smooth planks met my back as he pushed me up against it while his strong arms still held me up. I unwrapped my legs from around his waist. While still kissing me senseless, he gently lowered me to the floor.

As soon as my feet touched the ground, I tried to get back the upper hand but Mordren wouldn't allow it. Pushing me harder against the smooth wood, he rested his knee against the wall between my legs and then planted his hands on either side of my head. I drew my fingers up his stomach and chest until I reached the top button of his shirt.

He dragged his lips from mine and kissed a trail over my jaw and down my throat while I began unbuttoning his shirt. My fingers fumbled as my body shuddered with pleasure. Sucking in a desperate breath, I tried to force my mind to continue working while his fingers found the edge of my shirt and started pushing it upwards. His hands were warm against my already heated skin as he edged the dark fabric up my stomach.

At last, the final button of his shirt slid out of its hole. Victory sparkled inside me as I finally moved to run my hands over his naked skin. My fingertips had just barely brushed the ridges of his abs when something cool and silken wrapped around my wrists.

Blinking, I tried desperately to get my eyes back into focus.

Mordren smirked at me as his shadows forced my hands away from his body and pinned them against the wall above my head.

I narrowed my eyes at him. "Really?"

The wicked smile on his face widened. "Tell me how sorry you are for going rogue."

When I said nothing, he drew his fingers along my ribs and leaned down to kiss my throat. My toes curled as he reached that sensitive spot below my ear. Yanking against the restraints, I tried unsuccessfully to get my hands back to his hard body without having to give in to his power play.

His fingers brushed the skin just above my pants.

"Fine," I gasped. "I'm sorry for going rogue."

A dark laugh danced over my skin. While his fingers continued their teasing movements, the shadows around my wrists disappeared. I wrapped my hand around the back of his neck and forced his lips to mine before finally dragging my fingers down the lethal muscles of his chest and stomach. His skin was hot against mine.

Tracing the contours of his muscles, I moved my hands upwards and then pushed the crisp black fabric off his shoulders. He took his hands from my body for a second to shrug out of the shirt. I used the second of clarity to grab the hem of my own shirt and pull it up over my head. It fluttered through the air before joining his on the floor.

Mordren's eyes were dark with desire as he raked his gaze up and down my body. I started to take a step forward, but his hand shot out before I could get far.

With one hand against my collarbones, he pushed me back against the wall and held me trapped there while his intense gaze seared into mine. "You are stunning when you scheme, you ruthless little traitor spy."

A villainous smile spread across my lips as I let out a dark laugh. "Good." Tracing my fingers along his jaw, I winked at him. "Now, how about the part where you make me forget my own name?"

He smirked back at me while moving his hand down to my shoulder. "Oh you just wait."

His other hand gripped my hip. With that devilish smile still on his lips, he steered me away from the wall and backed me towards the couch in the living room.

Something firm appeared against the back of my legs. Mordren placed a hand against my chest and then pushed. I sucked in a gasp as I tipped backwards but Mordren used his shadows to maneuver me into position against the soft pillows while he climbed onto the couch as well.

The wide piece of furniture creaked slightly as his knees landed on either side of me. Leaning forward, Mordren placed a trail of kisses across my stomach, over my ribs, and up between my breasts. I bucked my hips as his teeth grazed my skin.

Lowering himself further, he pressed his hard body against mine while his lips continued up over my throat. Breathless, I raked my fingers through his hair. Mordren stole a few ravenous kisses from my lips while his hands made their way up my body.

He traced his fingers over my arms before taking my wrists in a firm grip. After guiding my hands back down he pinned them against the couch on either side of my face.

His eyes glinted as he leaned closer and breathed against my mouth, "*Now*, we are getting to that part."

Trapped by his strong grip and those glittering silver eyes,

I smirked up at him and traced my lips over his. "Do your worst, *my prince.*"

Mordren's dark laugh was like an intoxicating midnight wind against my heated skin. I drank in every sight and every touch as we lost ourselves in each other and pretended, for just a few hours, that the dangerous game that awaited us outside didn't exist.

CHAPTER 22

The rustle of clothes and clinking of jewelry filled the throne room as the remaining courtiers were ushered towards the exit. Golden light from the setting sun streamed in through the open doors at the far end of the hall and added gilded hues to the red stone. I watched the light sparkle off a glittering bracelet as a redheaded elf in a shimmering green dress made her way across the floor. The Prince of Fire had already left his throne room but several of his slaves helped escort his nobles towards the doors.

Since my mission in the Court of Trees last night had gone according to plan, Volkan had allowed me to simply stand in the throne room without having to do anything while he handled the courtiers who had come to see him. Little did he know that I had also spent three hours with Mordren. And all thanks to Evander's quick thinking. I glanced at him where he was showing a couple of blond humans towards the doors. After making a note to actually say thank you at some point, I turned back to the rest of the room.

My eyes swept over the redheaded elf in the green dress

again. I started. Flicking my gaze back to her a third time, I stared at her left wrist. The bracelet was gone. Why would she have taken that off? A blue-gray shadow glided unnoticed across the floor before disappearing into the corridor to my right. I cast a quick look over my shoulder to make sure that Prince Volkan had truly left before I followed.

It was probably nothing, but my gut was telling me otherwise and I had learned to listen to it long ago.

Torches burned brightly along the walls as I snuck down the corridor as well. Moving on silent feet, I hurried to catch up to my prey.

A skirt the color of a stormy sea fluttered around the final corner. I drew myself up against the wall and then peeked into the corridor that housed all our rooms.

Viviane was standing a few doors down. After pushing down the handle, she disappeared into her room. I furrowed my brows.

Apart from the times when Volkan called the three of us into a meeting about how to strike at the other princes, I hadn't really talked to Viviane, but she seemed far too cautious to risk stealing a bracelet right off someone's wrist. Stealing something from a bag or even a pocket was one thing, but taking something that rested against someone's skin without them feeling it took a lot of skill.

I drew back. No. That noble lady back in the throne room must have simply taken the bracelet off. Though, there was something about the way Viviane had moved that was… familiar. That reminded me of…

A door clicked shut on the other side of the corner.

Edging forward, I risked another glance into the corridor. Viviane had just closed the door to her room and was heading towards our shared bathrooms. A large towel was draped over her arm.

Indecision flitted through me. It was none of my business what she may or may not be doing, but I had spent most of my life finding out other people's secrets and the urge to figure out what she was up to was difficult to ignore.

Once I had heard the door to the bathroom close farther down, I slunk around the corner and approached her room. There was no lock on the door but I still chose to walk through it rather than open it, just in case she turned out to be the paranoid type.

Silk brushed against my skin and then I was standing inside a room that was identical to my own. One small bed, a nightstand, and a trunk were all it contained. For a moment, I remained motionless just inside the threshold.

Viviane had left the candle burning on the nightstand, which meant that she wasn't planning on being away for very long. If I was going to do this, it would have to be now.

A pang of guilt flashed through me. I shoved it aside. If I was right, this would give me some leverage, and I would need all the leverage I could get if I was to survive the dangerous scheme I was engaged in.

With quick and precise movements, I searched through all the obvious locations in Viviane's room. They only contained things we were allowed to have, but if she was as good as I suspected, then that wasn't exactly a surprise. I swept scrutinizing eyes through the room again. My gaze snagged on the wall next to the trunk.

Years of unearthing secrets and blackmail material had left me with a very good sense of when things were out of place. I dropped to a knee and ran my fingers over the red stones. One of them looked less... neat. The color around the sides was slightly off and the edges looked smoother. I poked and tugged at it from different angles.

It moved. A villainous grin spread across my lips as I dug my fingers into the small gap and pulled out the loose stone from the wall.

Light from the burning candle fell across a small but glittering pile. I stuck my hand into the opening and pulled out the sparkling bracelet that the redheaded elf had been wearing earlier. The smooth jewels glinted in the candlelight. With an impressed nod, I returned the bracelet to the pile of stolen necklaces, rings, earrings, and other jewelry before straightening again. Leaving the hiding place open, I took up position by the other wall.

Coolness from the stones seeped into my bare shoulder as I leaned against the wall and crossed my arms. And then I waited. But I didn't have to wait for too long.

Barely a few minutes later, the handle was pushed down and an elf with eyes the color of a storm-swept sea crossed the threshold. The door had just closed behind her when she froze.

"Kenna?"

Still draped against the wall, I gave her a nod. "Viviane."

Her dark hair was damp and dripped water down her shoulders while the towel hung from one of her hands. For a moment, she just stared at me, her mouth slightly open in surprise. Then her eyes darted towards the loose stone by the wall. All color drained from her face.

"You're a thief," I said.

It was more of an observation than an accusation, but panic flashed in Viviane's eyes. "No."

"And judging by the contents of your stash," I continued as if she hadn't spoken, "you're a very skilled one too."

"I have no idea what you're talking about." She threw the wet towel towards the incriminating evidence as if that would make it any less real. The heavy fabric flapped through the air before landing right on top of the loose stone I had pulled out. Lifting one shoulder in a shrug, she stepped farther into the room. "That must have been left by the person who used this room before me."

"Hmm, yeah. Must've." I nodded slowly before pushing myself off the wall. "Well, we'd better go and tell Prince Volkan about it then so that you won't get in trouble for something you haven't done."

I made it all the way to the door before I felt movement behind me. With her arms spread wide, Viviane threw herself between the door and me to block my path.

Desperation bounced around in her eyes. "Don't."

I had to suppress the wicked smile that threatened to slide home on my lips. So much of blackmailing was just about calling the other person's bluff. And it almost always worked. Keeping the smug expression off my face, I instead raised my eyebrows in a show of surprise.

"Please, don't," she said, her voice soft.

With my eyebrows raised, I just continued looking at her in silence. Another core part of blackmail: never bid against yourself.

She lowered her arms but didn't move out of the way. Her eyes flicked to the wet towel that was currently hiding half of her stolen loot and I could almost read the thoughts flying through her head. If Prince Volkan found out that she had been stealing from his nobles, then she would once more be on the receiving end of his cruel visions. And based on her reactions in that meeting room the other week, that was something she desperately wanted to avoid.

Viviane was a slave. Same as me. And I would never have actually ratted her out to the Prince of Fire. But she, of course, didn't know that.

"What do you want?" She swallowed, but she couldn't quite get the pleading note out of her voice. "Name it and it's yours."

"I would actually love some help."

"What kind of help?"

"Something that you and your skills are uniquely suited for."

She furrowed her brows. "Which is what?"

"I don't know yet." I shrugged. "So, how about you just owe me a favor?"

The confusion on her face deepened. "That's it? That's all you want? A favor?"

"Yeah."

Light danced across her features as she searched my face. I said nothing as I looked back at her. After a few more seconds, she seemed satisfied with whatever it was that she had been looking for in my eyes because she stepped aside. I took that as my cue to leave and started for the door once more, but I had only managed to place my hand on the handle when she spoke up again.

"Kenna?"

I turned back to face her. "Yeah?"

"One favor is an incredibly disproportionate price for keeping this kind of dangerous secret from the Prince of Fire. It's not nearly as steep as it should have been." She bit her bottom lip while considering me. "You could have demanded anything, *everything*, and I would still have agreed to it."

"I know."

"So why didn't you?"

Holding her gaze, I lifted my shoulders in a light shrug. "I need your help, but I would much rather have you as an ally than an enemy. Like I said, based on the contents of that stash, you're exceptionally skilled at this." A small smile drifted over my lips. "I'm actually friends with a couple of thieves on the outside. They'd be seriously impressed by you."

An answering smile tugged at her lips as well. "I hope I get to meet them one day then."

"How does..." I trailed off before starting again. "You don't have to answer this, but how does it work? How can you steal things right off someone's body like this without them feeling it?"

She took a step closer to me. Mischief danced in those storm-swept eyes of hers as she raised a hand towards my arm. "Like this."

I waited for her fingers to trail across my skin but nothing happened. Blinking in surprise, I stared down at my arm. Confusion swirled inside me.

"You're touching me," I said, frowning down at the hand she was dragging down my arm. "But I can't feel it."

"That's the beauty of it. And the curse." A wry smile slid across her lips. "Being born with magic like this, it's as if I was destined to steal stuff."

After studying her hand for another moment, I looked up and met her gaze. "Is that how you ended up here?"

"Yeah." Taking her fingers from my arm, she dragged them through her damp, blue-black hair. "I used to work for Prince Rayan. In his castle. And I stole some stuff from time to time because... well, because I can. One day, they realized that things were going missing. I panicked and ran. I thought they were closing in on me so when Prince Volkan offered me a deal, I took it. In hindsight, I'm not even sure that they ever actually figured out that it was me, but now it's too late." She shrugged, making her hair brush the top of her shoulders. "Eternal servitude to the Prince of Fire because of one panic-filled moment. Talk about making life-altering decisions for the wrong reasons."

"I'm sorry."

She waved a hand in front of her face as if to say that it didn't matter, and then nodded towards her pile of stolen jewelry. "Well, as you can see, I still haven't kicked the habit so I guess I haven't learned that much after all."

"Or maybe you've just been keeping your unique skills up to date."

A soft laugh escaped her lips. "That too, I suppose." Her face took on a serious expression again as she held my gaze. "Whenever you need help, just say the word."

"Thanks."

After giving her a sincere nod, I slipped out the door and closed it behind me.

That had gone better than expected. I had followed a hunch and now I was owed a favor by a master thief living right under Prince Volkan's nose.

Now, I just had to figure out how to use that to my advantage.

CHAPTER 23

Noise and color assaulted me as I walked through the open doors and into the ballroom. The night of the party had finally arrived and all of the nobles from the Court of Trees turned towards the doorway with hope shining in their eyes. It was promptly strangled and drowned in a frozen black lake when they realized that it was Volkan Flameshield who strode inside and not their own prince.

Guilt wormed its way through my chest. Because of my actions, all of Iwdael's attendants in the castle believed that he had cancelled, and the Prince of Trees himself didn't remember that he had been invited to a party in his honor.

Irritation started mixing with the disappointment that blew across the crowd.

"Has anyone seen Prince Iwdael?" A male elf in a bright blue shirt spread his hands and looked from face to face. "Anyone?"

"I'm sure he has better things to do," Volkan answered loudly as he stalked across the floor.

I suppressed the urge to cringe. This certainly wasn't

helping Prince Iwdael's image. I would have to find a way to mitigate the damage. But without Volkan noticing.

"What makes you say that?"

A malicious glint crept into Volkan's eyes as he turned with deliberate slowness towards the source of the voice.

The colorful crowd of elves and humans parted as a black-clad male prowled towards us. In the corner, the musicians halted their playing. Watchful eyes flicked between the two colliding forces.

"Ah, little Mordren," Prince Volkan said.

Idra took a step forward but was waved back by the Prince of Fire before she could get into position. Since Mordren was approaching alone, Volkan apparently didn't want it to look as if he was afraid or needed the protection from anyone.

"What makes you say that he had better things to do?" Mordren repeated, his voice cutting through the tense silence like a knife. Coming to a halt two steps in front of Volkan, he arched a dark eyebrow. "Iwdael loves to party, sometimes more than is decent. Barring some kind of catastrophic event, he would never miss a party of this scale."

Murmurs of agreement spread through the gathered nobles as they met each other's gaze and nodded. Some of the dissatisfaction evaporated as Mordren's words helped chase away their insecurities. They might feel self-conscious because Prince Iwdael hadn't shown up, but in their hearts, they must know that he loved to party and that it was unlikely that he would decide not to go when an event like this was arranged in his honor.

Annoyance rippled off Volkan as he glared back at the Prince of Shadows, but he just lifted his arms and motioned at the ballroom around them. "Then why isn't he here?"

Mordren held his gaze. "You tell me."

"Are you implying something, little prince?"

"Is there something to imply?"

"What happened to the music?" A light voice suddenly called into the crackling tension that was building. "My wife and I would like to dance."

Flicking my gaze to the side, I found Prince Rayan gliding through the crowd with a smile on his face. The Prince of Stone was of course nowhere to be seen since he detested parties, but thankfully the smooth and diplomatic Prince of Water had decided to make an appearance.

The lethal conflict staggered to a halt as Rayan and Lilane swept onto the dancefloor while the musicians in the corner started up a merry tune. Light shimmered across her dress as the Princess of Water spun in her husband's arms and then let out a rippling laugh. That broke the spell.

Elves and humans shook themselves out of their stupor and some joined the dancing couple while others drifted towards the tables filled with sparkling wine and mouthwatering pastries. The brightly colored ribbons that hung across the ceiling of the whole wooden hall swung gently as someone sent a fluttering of fresh leaves whirling through the air around them.

Volkan clicked his tongue before a smile dripping with malice slid across his mouth. "Yes, perhaps some dancing is in order." Holding Mordren's gaze, he snapped his fingers in front of my face. "Kenna."

I shot Mordren a sharp look to remind him not to take the bait, and then stepped up to place a hand on Volkan's arm. Mordren curled his fingers into a fist but then simply scoffed and strode away.

"Oh, your lover pretends not to care but I can hear his teeth cracking from clenching his jaws too tightly," Prince

Volkan said as he led me onto the dancefloor. "Now, let's give him something to really fume about."

An exasperated sigh slipped my lips.

Volkan snapped his gaze to me. "What was that?"

"Nothing, sir," I amended quickly.

"Answer."

I hesitated for another second before doing as he ordered. "It's just... we've done this exact same thing quite a few times now. Every time Mordren has been in the room, you've used me to try and make him jealous or pissed off. It's getting pretty repetitive. I mean, aren't you getting bored of doing the same thing over and over again?"

"Bored of messing with Mordren? Never. Besides, I'd say it's working perfectly every time."

Following his gaze, I found Mordren tracking our movements as we made our way onto the dancefloor. Cold murder burned in his eyes.

"And as for you," Volkan continued as we came to a halt just as another song was about to start. "You'd better get used to these *repetitive* events, because it's now your sole purpose in life. The only reason for your continued existence is to do these same things over and over again. To make Mordren jealous and pissed off. Am I making myself clear?"

Glancing up, I met yellow eyes that burned with power. If it was meant as a reminder of what he'd do to me if I stopped following orders, it served its purpose perfectly.

I swallowed the answer I had been about to give him and instead dipped my chin. Well, it had been worth a shot.

"Yes, sir," I replied instead.

The song that filled the high-ceilinged hall was fast-paced and powerful. Pushing aside the flash of nerves that shot through me, I placed one hand in Volkan's and moved the other to his shoulder. He rested his other one on my waist in turn. And then we danced.

Say what you will about the Prince of Fire, but he was a very good dancer. Holding me tightly to him, he moved us expertly through the steps and it was all I could do to keep up with his rhythm.

"Is he watching?" Volkan asked.

I flicked my gaze to Mordren, who stared at the two of us with lightning flashing in his silver eyes. "Yes."

"Good."

Volkan threw me out in a twirl before pulling me back towards him again. As soon as my body connected with his muscular form, he slid his hand from my waist and planted it on the small of my back. Keeping me pressed against him, he steered us through the sea of colorful dancers while making sure that we were always in view from where Mordren was standing.

I cast another glance at the Prince of Shadows. Mordren had picked up a glass of wine and was gripping the delicate stem so hard that I feared it might break. The red liquid inside rippled as he flexed his fingers before tightening his grip again.

My frustrated sigh was thankfully drowned out by a series of gasps around us. While still continuing the dance, both Volkan and I turned towards the cause of it.

High Commander Anron strode into the ballroom with the watchful Captain Vendir next to him. Both of them were dressed in gleaming bronze armor decorated with artful leaves. I stole a glance at Volkan's face.

He hid it well behind a pair of raised eyebrows, but this close, I could read the satisfied gleam in his eyes. The two of them must have planned this.

"I was looking for Prince Iwdael," the High Commander said. "But I can't seem to find him. Is he not here?"

Several of the nobles flushed in embarrassment at having the leader of the High Elves show up at their party only to discover that the prince they had arranged it for hadn't even bothered to show up.

When an elf in a shimmering purple suit explained that Prince Iwdael was not in attendance, Anron gave them all an understanding nod. "I see. Well, I suppose princes have a lot of important matters to handle and that business must take precedence over pleasure."

The mood shifted slightly and a ripple of discontent spread through the crowd again. I fought the urge to groan.

"But you are of course welcome to stay, High Commander," the elf in purple said and then looked at Captain Vendir as well. "Both of you."

"Are you sure?" Anron answered. "We would not want to intrude."

"Of course, we would be honored to have you here."

Prince Volkan threw me out in a twirl again while the two High Elves nodded and made their way into the party. A firm hand appeared against my lower back as I slammed back into Volkan. He steered us closer to where Mordren was still standing but I kept my eyes on the two threats who had just walked through the door.

A cluster of elves from the Court of Trees approached Anron and Vendir as they came to a halt by a table overflowing with glasses. Vendir simply watched in silence but his High Commander raised his eyebrows in a show of surprise as the group of elves actually kneeled down to bow before them.

I narrowed my eyes at them. Everyone in the kneeling group wore a black bracelet around their wrist. Murmuring spread through the ballroom at the display of deference, but no one said anything. Sweeping my gaze through the room, I located my allies.

Hadeon was standing next to a pair of guards from the Court of Trees while Ellyda was seated with a group of people by the couches on the other side. Halfway between them was Eilan. A large group of well-dressed nobles from this court had gathered around him. Just as I had instructed, they were all busy speaking to different members of the Court of Trees so that they could drop subtle hints that would help salvage Prince Iwdael's reputation. But now, all three of them were studying the High Elves and their bowing fanatics. As was everyone else.

Intense silver eyes met me.

Well, everyone *except* Mordren, apparently. I shot him a pointed look, but he simply continued staring at me and Volkan as we moved across the polished wooden floor. Tearing my gaze from the furious Darkbringer prince, I fixed my attention on Volkan instead.

"They're setting themselves up as gods," I said while Anron motioned for the kneeling elves to rise.

Volkan's eyes snapped to me. "Excuse me?"

"The High Elves." I nodded towards Anron and Vendir as another group approached. They weren't wearing black bracelets, but there was awe on their faces. "People have started acting as if they are gods."

"I already know that some people have started worshipping them, but why would that concern me?"

"I'm just worried about you, sir." I let a mask of sincerity settle on my face as I looked up at him. "If the High Elves are setting themselves up as gods of this continent and all its people, why would they need you?"

Anger flashed in his eyes and he tightened his grip on both my hand and my back. "You dare speak to me in such a way? You are a slave. Your sole purpose is to be a weapon against Mordren. So shut your mouth and do as you are told."

"Yes, sir." I dropped my gaze, both as a show of submission but also to make sure that he couldn't see the wicked satisfaction gleaming in my eyes. "Sorry, sir."

He might have dismissed my comment and hid it behind his anger, but I could see the idea taking root behind his eyes. It wasn't enough to set him against the High Elves, but it was a start. A seed planted that would hopefully grow with the careful nurturing that my future sabotages would bring.

The song was reaching its crescendo. Powerful tunes swelled and echoed across the room as we sped up to match it. The low-cut golden dress I was wearing fluttered around my legs as Volkan moved us closer and closer to Mordren.

Just as the final notes crashed over the ballroom, Volkan slammed us to a halt and dipped me backwards in a swift motion.

My long red curls brushed the polished floor. With my back arched across Volkan's arm, I could see Mordren upside down where he was standing only a short distance away. Lightning storms flashed in his eyes.

Volkan's other hand had released mine and instead moved to my leg. As the song died out, he drew his hand up my bare leg while keeping my hips pressed against his.

Glass shattered.

The delicate crystal goblet in Mordren's hand had been crushed into sharp pieces. Red wine ran like blood over his hand while shards of glass rained down and clinked against the hard floor.

Prince Volkan leaned down and breathed against my ear. "Good job. Now, keep this up."

While he pulled me back up, I let out a sigh that could have been interpreted as simply a long breath after a challenging dance.

Yes, I might have planted a seed of doubt in Volkan's mind. But all my planning and scheming would mean nothing if we couldn't somehow get through this night without the Prince of Shadows committing violent murder.

CHAPTER 24

Violent murder was looming closer with every passing hour. After the dance and the shattered glass, Mordren had managed to pull himself together enough to make a few rounds through the ballroom to help salvage Prince Iwdael's reputation. But the Prince of Fire was no fool and he knew exactly how to push Mordren's buttons.

Surrounded by his courtiers, Volkan was lounging on one of the soft brown couches by the windows. With me sitting on his lap. He was talking to a pair of well-dressed elves from his own court while he casually rested a hand on my leg, his fingers brushing the inside of my thigh. Idra was standing a few steps behind the backrest, her body alert but her face an impassive mask. I matched the expression on her face as I swept my gaze through the ballroom.

Mordren was standing halfway across the room and, based on the way shadows flickered around the cuffs of his suit jacket, he looked about ready to rip Volkan's heart from his chest. But thankfully, he remained where he was. I continued my scan of the room until I found the person I was looking for. Eilan.

Elves and humans in various stages of intoxication had gathered around Eilan and were batting their lashes at him. Seemingly oblivious to the attention, the gorgeous elf was laughing and entertaining the group around him.

As if he could feel my gaze, he discreetly shifted his stance. Light green eyes met mine. I flashed him a subtle hand gesture before glancing away again.

A moment later, Eilan excused himself and made his way towards the bathrooms.

I dragged my attention back to the scene around me just as Prince Volkan snapped his fingers above his shoulder.

"Evander." The Prince of Fire nodded towards a pair of humans who were eating strawberries by the tables to our right. "Those two?"

Leaning down over the backrest, Evander spoke softly. "Lord and Lady Blackbriar?"

"Yes. I thought you said they would be among those most offended by Iwdael not showing up."

"Yes, sir."

Volkan narrowed his eyes. "They don't look very offended."

Worry flickered across his face as his eyes darted between the smiling humans and the dissatisfied prince. "No, I suppose not."

"You suppose not? Go check." Volkan cocked his head while fire burned in his yellow eyes. "And if they're not, make sure they are by the time you leave."

"Yes, sir.'"

Prince Volkan didn't usually bring Evander to events and meetings, but since this one was in the Court of Trees and

Prince Iwdael wasn't attending, Evander's presence had been requested. His mission was to supply Volkan with information about the nobles from the Court of Trees, and with no Prince of Trees there to recognize him as Syrene's former spy, he could do so more or less unhindered.

While he made his way across the polished wooden floor, I watched the way the light played across the white dress shirt he had been allowed to wear. After all, showing up half-naked to a formal party would not have drawn the right kind of attention.

A female elf with long blond hair and sparkling blue eyes passed him in a swishing of hips while he drew closer to his target. As he reached them, I shifted my gaze to the beautiful female instead and tracked her movements across the floor. She was approaching one of Volkan's scribes.

Seated alone by a table, the scribe was busy writing in a small journal. He was an unassuming male elf with short sandy hair and a jerky way of moving that made him look a bit like a startled bird. The only reason he had been allowed to come was because Volkan wanted a report on which nobles from the Court of Trees had been most affected by Prince Iwdael's decision not to attend.

The blond female picked up a glass of sparkling wine and dropped down in a chair across the table from him with a contented sigh, as if tired from a full night of dancing. Jerking his head up, the scribe blinked at her as he realized that she had said something. She flashed him a smile that made him blush furiously. After casting a quick look in Volkan's direction to make sure the prince's attention was focused elsewhere, he closed his journal and answered something that I was too far away to hear.

Suppressing a smile, I slid my gaze back to Evander and the two humans.

By the time he finally left them, they looked much more irritated. It was rather frustrating. I had some people drifting through the party trying to mitigate the damage, while Volkan kept sending out people to make it worse. Every time we managed to calm someone down, another enraged person popped up.

Volkan tightened his grip on my thigh. I glanced down in surprise before turning to meet his gaze. With his eyes tracking Mordren, who had finally donned a mask of indifference, he spoke quietly in my ear.

"Lean against me," he ordered.

I blew out a sigh but leaned my body against Volkan's shoulder. Evander, who had reclaimed his position behind the couch by now, met my gaze. His dark green eyes were filled with sympathy. After giving him a small smile, I glanced around the room again.

Mordren was thankfully still not looking in our direction, and the other couple I had been searching for was looking far too drunk to notice anything else that was happening around them.

My eyes found a pair of red ones across the sea of glittering dancers. Hadeon held my gaze for a few seconds before looking away. Then he stalked towards us.

Ellyda fell in beside him and they cut through the laughing partygoers while their eyes were locked on the Prince of Fire. Sensing that something was about to happen, Volkan shifted his gaze to the approaching siblings. His hand stayed firmly on my thigh.

From behind me, I could hear Idra moving. The leather of her armor groaned faintly as she positioned herself in front of the couch instead. Hadeon was wearing his ceremonial leather armor as well, and he cut a striking figure as he came to a halt in front of the Prince of Fire and crossed his arms.

"The hell is your problem?" Hadeon demanded as he stared down at Volkan.

"Excuse me?"

Hadeon waved a hand to indicate me sitting on Volkan's lap. "You think this is appropriate for a formal event?"

The courtiers around us sucked in a surprised gasp at the way he was addressing their prince, but Volkan only seemed amused. Cocking his head, he let a cold smile stretch his lips.

"You think you're the right person to lecture someone on proper etiquette?" Volkan let out a derisive laugh. "You're nothing more than a simple brute. I'm surprised you're even allowed into these types of events. Shouldn't you be out playing with swords in the mud or something?"

Ellyda's eyes snapped into focus. Ever since they had stopped in front of the couch, she had been looking at a spot on the wall somewhere above Volkan's head but now her eyes bored into his.

"If you ever speak to my brother like that again–" she began but Volkan cut her off before she could finish.

"Ah, lady Steelsinger. Finally rejoined reality, have you?" He raised his eyebrows at her. "How was the latest trip to crazy town?"

Hadeon moved like a viper. One second, he was standing with his arms crossed. The other, he lunged towards Volkan with his arm out as if to strangle him.

White hair fluttered in the air as Idra flashed forward as well and blocked his way before he could reach the Prince of Fire. Her hand shot out towards Hadeon's chest and he redirected his attack to match hers.

The courtiers on the couches shrank back while staring at the two warriors.

Idra had her palm firmly planted on Hadeon's muscled chest while his strong hand was wrapped around her throat.

"I suggest you withdraw that hand," Idra said.

Her voice was calm and the expression on her face was as blank as always. It was the disinterested look of someone who had long since stopped fearing death. Not for the first time, I wondered who she had been before she had become Volkan's slave.

"Or what?" Hadeon growled in her face. Tightening his grip on her throat, he forced her chin up. "Am I supposed to be scared of you?"

"Yes."

He scoffed. "Well, sorry to break it to you, but I'm not. So either follow through on your threat or stand the fuck down."

Surprise flickered in her black eyes for a moment. It was there and gone again so fast that I wasn't even sure if I had really seen it. She opened her mouth to reply, but before she could, Volkan spoke up.

"So aggressive. You really are proving my point, aren't you? But given your parentage, it's not surprising. By the way, how is the family?" A wide grin slid across Volkan's lips as he shifted his gaze between Hadeon and Ellyda. "Oh, right, I forgot…"

Fury flashed in Hadeon's red eyes and his muscles twitched as he got ready to throw Idra out of the way by her throat. But before that could happen, a sharp voice cut through the violence.

"How is the rest of your inner circle? Oh, right, I forgot…" Ellyda's cold violet eyes slid briefly to Idra in a pointed look before returning to Volkan. "She's the only one left."

Volkan shot to his feet. I stumbled as he shoved me aside to accomplish it. Tripping over a pair of legs, I slammed into a nervous-looking elf and knocked her glass right out of her grip. Wine splashed over me and ran down my legs.

"Let's go, brother," Ellyda said, her sharp smile directed at Volkan.

Hadeon took his hand from Idra's throat and gave her a short shove backwards before falling in next to his sister. It took great effort to hide the wicked grin on my lips as I watched them stride back across the dancefloor.

Anger burned in Volkan's eyes as he stared after them. With a snarl, he whipped back towards me. Whatever he had been about to say died on his tongue when he noticed the wine running down my legs.

"Go clean yourself up," he snapped and jerked his chin in the direction of the bathroom.

"Yes, sir."

Evander gave me a puzzled look as I passed him. I only shot him a satisfied smile in return and then began weaving my way through the crowd.

Most people stepped out of the way when they noticed the sticky mess that was attached to me but one person stayed his course as he strode towards me from the same direction that I was heading. Mischief glinted in Eilan's light green eyes as he winked at me. I grinned back at him as we passed each other and continued in opposite directions.

Pushing open the door to the bathrooms, I took in the wide space before me. A row of gleaming white sinks had been placed underneath a gigantic mirror that covered the whole wall. But that was not what I was really after.

In the corner, sitting on the floor with his knees drawn up and his forehead resting on top of them, was the scribe with sandy hair from the Court of Fire. His head jerked up when he heard the door close behind me.

"Oh," I said, my voice the epitome of surprise. After staring at him for a few seconds, I made a show of narrowing my eyes in recognition. "It's Tristan, isn't it?"

"Kenna," the scribe, Tristan, moaned pitifully. "Please, don't tell anyone."

"Tell anyone what?"

His cheeks were flushed red and his eyes were having difficulty focusing. He looked ridiculously drunk. I suppressed an evil smile. Just like he was supposed to be.

"I'm drunk," he confirmed. "Really, really drunk. I'm supposed to be keeping track of the nobles but I can't even count them anymore. Let alone make out where their heads are at."

Drifting closer, I crouched down in front of him and placed a hand on his knee. "Don't worry. Just come by my room tomorrow morning and I'll help you fill in the blanks. I'm standing next to Volkan all evening anyway, so making notes of the nobles will be no trouble. I'll cover for you."

"Really?" Hope sparkled in his eyes. "Would you really do that?"

"Of course." I gave him one of my kindest smiles. "But I'll need a favor too."

"Anything."

"I'm going to need you to make some documents."

He nodded enthusiastically. The movement apparently made his stomach turn because he slapped a hand in front of his mouth as if to stop himself from vomiting. After patting him on the knee, I drew back and walked over to one of the sinks.

"Oh, I shouldn't have," Tristan mumbled from by the wall. "But she was so beautiful. So, so beautiful."

Turning on the water, I began cleaning off the wine that still covered my legs. While I bent down to wipe my shins, I finally let the evil grin I had been holding in spread across my lips.

Yes, that blond female had been very beautiful. And with her flirting and smiling it would have been impossible for someone like Tristan to refuse when she kept offering him drinks, which had led him to his current predicament. But see, that's what happens when you're targeted by a shapeshifter.

And then, all we needed was to stage a confrontation with Volkan that just so happened to end with me getting wine all over my legs so that I would have to visit the bathrooms at that particular point of the evening too.

One flirting shapeshifter and two scheming siblings later, and I was suddenly owed a rather huge favor by one of Volkan's scribes. Oh, it truly was a wonderful feeling when wicked plans came together.

CHAPTER 25

The most important thing when planting a document is to put it somewhere people will find it, but without making it too obvious. Putting something in the middle of the table is out of the question because it instantly makes people suspicious. What you want to do is place it a little to the side, so that you notice it without making it the center of attention.

Paper rustled faintly as I positioned the document in the right spot while keeping one eye on the door.

The handle was pushed down.

My heart leaped into my throat, but the paper was already in place so I just threw myself backwards and melted into the shadows at the back of the room.

"You timed your entrance perfectly the other night," Prince Volkan said as he strode across the floor and dropped into the armchair in front of the fire. Leaning back, he swung his feet up and rested them on the low table. "Mordren was almost starting to get through to people, but your arrival helped distract them."

THE FIRE SOUL

High Commander Anron lowered himself into the armchair opposite the Prince of Fire. "Yes, he seems quite... persistent. Is he going to be a problem?"

"No, he's nothing more than a spoiled brat. I can handle him."

"Are you sure?"

"Of course I'm sure." There was a hint of annoyance in Volkan's voice but he shook it off as he leaned further back against the soft cushions. "I was fighting my way to power before he was even born. I know exactly how to break him."

"Good." A smirk pulled at Anron's lips as he glanced sideways at Volkan. "And I hear that the nobles in the Court of Trees have become even more dissatisfied with their prince. Apparently, his attendants all swear that he cancelled while the prince himself says that he just didn't know about it."

Volkan answered with a wicked smile of his own. "Yes, what an unfortunate situation for him."

Fire crackled in the hearth by the wall, but the heat wasn't as oppressive this time. Perhaps Volkan had decided that he didn't need to keep up with his power plays against the High Elf Commander. From my place in the shadows of two stone bookcases, I watched them grin at each other.

"So, we've hit Rayan, Edric, and Iwdael," Anron began. "That leaves Mordren."

"Oh, I have something special planned for him."

My chest constricted at his words but I forced myself to keep breathing softly. Golden light from the setting sun fell in through the window and set Volkan's yellow eyes ablaze as he leaned forward in his seat and rested his elbows on his knees.

"And then, we will start all over again," he said. "Rayan

needs to be hit extra hard next time since he managed to escape our last trick more or less unscathed."

"Do you think it was Kenna's doing?"

"I can't be sure, but let's just say that I suspect she wasn't trying her hardest that time."

"And now?"

"Now she knows the consequences of failure. I've been able to work on her in the breaking room almost every night, and I'm getting closer." Dragging a hand through his long blond hair, he leaned back again. "She's barely holding on. I just need to find that one thing that will shatter her spirit. Everyone has something. I just need to figure out what it is."

Dread swirled in my chest. He wasn't lying. The sessions in the breaking room were getting more and more intense and it was taking everything I had to put myself back together after the visions he showed me.

"I'm sure you..." Anron trailed off as his eyes snagged on a paper at the edge of the table. "What's this?"

Narrowing his eyes, he sat forward and pulled out the document from the stack of notebooks, papers, and ledgers that covered the tabletop. Ice seeped into his sharp blue eyes as he scanned the contents of the page.

"What's what?" Volkan asked with a lazy wave of his hand.

"You're planning an attack."

"The hell are you talking about?"

Anron shot to his feet and shook the document in front of Volkan's face. "This is a report detailing how your court would go about attacking my camp."

Snatching it out of the air, Volkan straightened as well and then frowned down at the paper. "This is nonsense. I haven't had a report like this made."

"Then what is it doing here?"

"I don't know."

"You don't know?"

Hidden deep in the shadows between the bookcases, I let a victorious grin spread across my lips. Oh, how terribly inconvenient it must be having a traitor spy living under one's roof. Especially one who can walk through walls and plant forged documents on one's desk right before a meeting with one's ally.

"No. And I don't appreciate your tone."

High Commander Anron drew himself up to his full height, which was a good head above Volkan. "You don't appreciate my tone? Well, I do not appreciate backstabbing liars."

Fire roared in the hearth as Volkan took a step forward. "You're calling me a liar?"

The air crackled around Anron as he stared him down. "You do not want to play this game with me."

"Likewise."

The flames in the fireplace flared up, almost singeing the ceiling, while fire sprung to life on Volkan's skin. Orange light danced across his face as flames whooshed down over his arms. Something snapped in Anron's cold blue eyes.

I staggered into the bookshelf behind me. If it hadn't been for its sheer mass holding me up, I would've dropped to my knees right then and there.

Power the likes of which I had never felt before pulsed through the room. Every cell in my body was screaming at me to get down on my knees and beg the High Elf's forgiveness, even though I wasn't the one who had offended him. There was nothing visible around him. No magic. But something inside me was still screaming that I was about to be in mortal danger any second.

Volkan seemed to feel it too because he stumbled back a step and the fire in the hearth died down to its original form. Then anger flashed across his face.

"Don't you threaten me," he growled. "I'm the one who should be suspicious of *you*. You're the one who's setting himself up as a god. This is my continent. And I will not have you stealing it from me."

Wicked satisfaction bloomed in my chest. My words from the party the other night really had taken root in Volkan's insecurities.

Anron stared at him while the sense of danger grew more and more intense. "I have no desire to stay on this little island of yours."

"Then why are you making people worship you as gods?"

"I am not the one making anyone do anything. The people worshipping us are simply recognizing what their ancestors did and they are the ones who have decided to bow to us again. You are the one who is scheming behind my back."

"I am the one who is on your side."

"My side? Then why are you planning an attack?"

"I'm not plotting an attack!" In a gesture of frustration, Volkan let the fire along his arms die out as he slashed a hand through the air. "If I was planning something like that, do you really think I would be stupid enough to write it down and then leave it lying around?"

Anron narrowed his eyes. For a moment, only the faint popping of the fire broke the silence as the two of them continued staring each other down. I held my breath. This was it. I might be able to break Anron and Volkan's alliance right here, right now.

"You're right," Anron said at last. The terrible sense of danger disappeared as he relaxed his stance and gave Volkan a nod. "That would indeed be the work of an amateur, and based on everything I have observed about you, you are many things, but you are not an amateur. My apologies for overreacting."

It was so small that I almost missed it, but Volkan blew out a soft sigh of relief before waving a hand in front of his face. "Don't worry about it. I apologize for my accusations as well. They were unfounded."

Disappointment ran like cold poison through my veins. It had almost worked.

"Water under the bridge," Anron assured him before his eyes turned suspicious again. "So, who could have planted it?"

"Several servants have access." Volkan ran a hand over his chin while considering. "And then, of course, there's Kenna..."

My heart leaped into my throat. Not hesitating a second, I threw myself through the wall and reappeared in the hallway I had used to gain access. With my pulse smattering in my ears, I sprinted back towards the throne room.

If Prince Volkan decided to go back and realized that I wasn't there, I didn't even want to think about what would happen.

Golden fabric fluttered behind me as I skidded around another corner before darting down the next hallway.

A shadow fell across the floor from the opposite direction.

I leaped through the wall. Buckets and mops rattled in surprise as I slammed into them but my hands shot out and grabbed them before they could topple. While the cleaning supplies glared at me in sullen silence, I waited for the person in the corridor to walk past.

When I estimated, based on the average person's walking pace, that they were long gone, I let go of the disgruntled mop handles and phased back into the hallway.

It was empty.

Blood pounded in my ears as I ran the final distance to my entry and exit spot, and then stepped through the red stone wall.

A grand throne room appeared before me.

Evander started slightly as I suddenly appeared out of nowhere, but he recovered quickly. With casual movements, he discreetly moved the large fan he had been using to hide the fact that I had disappeared for a while. Picking up the jug of water, I straightened as the rest of the room came into full view.

"Did it work?" Evander breathed while keeping his eyes on the opposite wall.

I flexed my fingers on the handle of the jug. "Partly."

As soon as the word was out of my mouth, Volkan and Anron came striding back into the throne room. I made sure that my face wore a slightly bored expression, as if I had been standing there doing nothing for a long time, while my eyes stared blankly towards the other side of the room.

Even though I wasn't looking at him, I could feel Volkan's gaze burning holes in my body. I resisted the urge to hold my breath.

Agonizingly slow seconds passed. Then the two lethal elves disappeared into the corridor and presumably went back to the meeting room. I dared a small sigh of relief. That had been far too close. And my plan had only partly worked.

Conflict was always good because once you had gotten that first fight out of the way, it was easier to get another started. Between the attempted poisoning, the missing chair, and now the document detailing an attack, Volkan and Anron had started to fight more regularly.

I cast a glance at the space they had been standing in earlier.

Now, all I had to do was keep putting a strain on their relationship so that they wouldn't be able to make their move before I made mine.

CHAPTER 26

Steel clanged between the red stone walls as Volkan slammed his sword into mine. I deflected it and twisted around to jab my blade into his side. It was knocked aside as Volkan rammed his fist down on my arm. Leaping back, I narrowly avoided his retaliatory strike.

"You wouldn't happen to have anything to do with that planted document this afternoon, would you?" he demanded.

"What document?" I asked.

Fire flared to life in his hand. I barely managed to throw myself aside as Volkan hurled a fireball at me with terrifying speed.

"Don't lie to me."

Rolling to my feet, I raised my sword again. "I'm not."

Volkan drew back his arm again. Panic screamed inside me as a spear of flame shot right towards me. I dove to the side.

Another fireball exploded a mere breath from my body. Orange embers sailed into the air around me as I desperately scrambled to my feet to avoid the next flaming projectile.

"I'm not lying," I called while jumping out of the way of another fire spear. "Please. I don't know what document you're talking about."

Volkan had been furious all evening after his showdown with Anron earlier, and he had apparently decided to take it all out on me. The fact that I was indeed responsible for it was of course entirely beside the point.

Fire flared to life along the floor until I was surrounded by an entire barrier of it. With panic still screaming inside my mind, I backed towards the wall while the ring of flames rushed towards me.

I knew I could leap through the wall to safety, but if I did, there would be hell to pay. So when the cold stones appeared at my back, all I did was twist my body to the side and cover my face with my arm.

Crackling fire sped towards me. My heart was thumping in my chest. Flames exploded against the wall and I crouched down to shield myself from the burning wave. But none of it touched me. Before I could even frown in surprise, something else happened that made my heart stop.

"What is the meaning of this, Volkan?"

I snapped my head up and whipped it towards the sound of the voice. Utter shock filled my chest as Mordren Darkbringer sauntered across the threshold.

"Ah, glad you could make it, little prince," Volkan replied.

Mordren's silver eyes found mine for a second and they were full of concern. Then it disappeared as he tore his gaze from me and slid it back to the Prince of Fire.

"I had much more riveting things planned for tonight than spending it with you," Mordren said and raised his eyebrows. "So, get to the point. Why am I here?"

A smug smile spread across Volkan's lips. "I have a deal to offer you."

"So you said. What kind of deal?"

"By now, I'm sure you're aware of my... interest in the lady Steelsinger." When Mordren only continued staring back at him in silence, Volkan pressed on. "What if I were to tell you that I could be persuaded to never go after dear Ellyda again."

Mordren scoffed. "As if I would ever take your word for anything again."

"I've drawn up a contract." He started towards a table by the wall while jerking his chin towards Mordren. "Come take a look."

While Volkan's back was turned, Mordren flicked another glance at me. I shrugged in response to his silent question.

After another moment of consideration, Mordren followed the Prince of Fire to the table. Paper rustled into the silence as Volkan picked up an official-looking document and handed it to him. A scowl appeared on Mordren's brow as he read through it.

"You think I would seriously agree to this?" he demanded and shook the paper in front of Volkan's face. Scoffing, he threw the document down on the table again and stalked towards the door. "Goodbye, Volkan."

"You would really throw away this one chance to keep what remains of your family safe?" Volkan called after him. "I have no interest in your annoying brother or that brute of a warrior. But Ellyda... You know that I will stop at nothing to get her."

Mordren trailed to a halt. For a moment, he remained motionless on the floor with his back still to Volkan. I had pushed to my feet and was watching the exchange with furrowed brows.

"You would throw away the chance to protect someone you have known your entire life, for someone who you have only known for a few months?"

With a start, I realized that I was somehow a part of this deal.

Turning with calculated slowness, Mordren faced him again. "You murdered my parents."

"And I will keep coming after Ellyda until she is bound in slavery to me." Malice gleamed in his yellow eyes. "And if I cannot have her, then I would rather put her in the ground before I let you keep her."

Shadows shot out around Mordren. Sauntering closer to him, Volkan flicked a hand and let out a short laugh.

"Oh, don't even try it. You're alone in *my* court now." The Prince of Fire came to a halt a few steps away. "But this is a one-time offer and you have to decide now. So, what's it going to be?"

Indecision flashed over Mordren's features. Twisting his head, he met my gaze. Guilt swirled in his eyes as he looked at me.

"How severe would we be talking?" he asked reluctantly.

"Just enough to cripple. Let's say, cut one hamstring and damage the muscles of one arm."

Dread exploded in my chest as I suddenly realized what this was. *This* was the special thing Volkan had planned in order to break Mordren. To make him choose between me and his family.

"And then you will leave her alone after that?" Mordren said, his eyes still on me. Pain and intense guilt were burning in his face. "Kenna, I mean. If I do this, you won't try to hurt her anymore either."

"Agreed."

I swallowed. "Mordren, what are you…?"

All the hesitation and guilt disappeared from Mordren's face and a cold mask took its place. "Deal."

A wide grin stretched Volkan's lips. While Mordren pulled back his shadows, Volkan stepped in front of him and held out his hand. I couldn't see Mordren's face since Volkan was blocking the view, but their shoulders moved as they shook hands.

Worry seeped into my bones as I moved closer and tried to catch Mordren's eyes. He must have a plan for how to get out of this.

Steel sang into the silence. I froze in my tracks as the Prince of Shadows drew his twin knives and advanced on me.

"I'm sorry, Kenna," he said. "I know that this is way more than you signed up for, but there is nothing I wouldn't do to keep my family safe."

Volkan's laugh echoed between the red walls as he stood watching from a short distance away. "Apparently, including crippling his former lover."

Fear mingled with the dread as Mordren advanced on me, but I forced it aside as I locked eyes with him and whispered, "So what's the plan?"

"This is the plan."

He swung his knives at me. I leaped back.

"I'm sorry, Kenna," he said, his voice flat. "But keeping Volkan from getting Ellyda is more important right now."

Sudden clarity hit me like a lightning bolt. Coming to a complete stop, I lowered my sword and let out a disbelieving laugh. I couldn't believe that I had almost fallen for it.

"This isn't real," I said, and looked at Volkan. "This is just a vision. Mordren would never actually do something like this."

Pity swirled in Volkan's eyes as he shook his head at me.

"Oh, you clearly don't know Mordren as well as you think. Lovers he can get in droves. But his family…"

"Right," I scoffed before turning back to Mordren. Raising my chin, I spread my arms wide. "Then go ahead. Cut me."

Something I had figured out during all these sessions with Volkan was that his magic couldn't create physical things. All it could affect were my sight and my hearing. Which meant that his apparition of Mordren wouldn't be able to actually hurt me.

Pain shot up my arm. I sucked in a gasp and whipped my head back down. Staring at my forearm, I found a cut across my skin. Blood welled up and ran down my arm.

For a moment, my mind refused to process what I was seeing. The cut. The blood. Mordren standing in front of me with his bloody knife raised.

Then I snapped out of it and leaped backwards. Panic pulsed through me. This was real. Mordren had really chosen to take Volkan's deal.

Backing away across the floor, I tried to mount some kind of defense but I was suddenly having trouble breathing. After everything I had done for him, he had agreed to cripple me in order to save Ellyda.

"Volkan can just have someone heal you afterwards," Mordren said as if he could read my mind.

"That's not the point!" I snapped as I threw my short sword up to block his next attack. "Don't do this."

He flicked his wrist, sending my sword sliding off his knife while ramming his other blade towards me. "I have to."

Metal vibrated into the air as I slammed my sword down on top of his to stop it but Mordren was picking up speed now. Darting across the floor, he attacked with single-minded fury. With my small, low-quality sword, it was difficult to evade his strikes. But that wasn't the biggest problem. It was that the stunned shock still ringing inside me was clouding my brain and slowing my movements.

I backed towards the wall. If he was really planning to go through with this, I might as well escape through the wall.

Fire flared up around us until a ring of flames cut off my escape. From the other side of the burning barrier, Volkan was grinning at me.

The second of inattention cost me. With my focus elsewhere, and my limbs slow with shock, I didn't see the blow coming until it had already landed. Mordren's elbow cracked into my jaw and sent me crashing down on the floor. My sword scraped against the stone but I managed to keep a hold of it.

Twisting onto my back, I stared up at the dark-haired prince looming over me. His eyes were cold and his face impassive. At that moment, true terror flashed through me. He was really going to go through with it, which meant that I would have to hurt him in order to stop him.

"Don't," I breathed. "Please, don't."

"I'm sorry," he said in a flat voice.

He took a step closer. I struggled to my feet and backed across the floor while shaking my head. Heat seared into my back as the ring of fire came up behind me.

My heart slammed so hard against my ribs that it threatened to break free of my body.

Mordren wouldn't actually consider it. He wasn't actually going to cripple me. He couldn't. Not after everything I had done. After everything he had done. But still, I raised the sword and held it in the air between us. The blade shook slightly.

A small voice had been screaming desperately in my mind

for the past few minutes but I had been suppressing it. As I stared into those uncaring silver eyes, the voice finally broke free.

Fire billowed like wings behind me as I straightened my spine and raised my chin.

"No," I said. "I don't know how you're doing it, but this isn't real. Mordren isn't even here."

"You're really prepared to get crippled to prove it?" Volkan's voice came from outside the circle of fire. "Or to kill your lover to prove it?"

"Yes."

I swung.

Steel whooshed through the air as my sword sped straight towards Mordren's neck. Surprise registered in his silver eyes, and for a moment, I feared that I had made a terrible mistake. Then he yanked up his own blade and blocked mine before it could land. Metallic ringing filled the air as Mordren and I stared at each other from across our weapons.

His features flickered. And then Mordren's dark-clad body disappeared to reveal Volkan Flameshield. As the vision blew away, the version of Volkan who had been standing outside the flames vanished as well.

I sucked in a small gasp. So that was how he had done it. At first, Volkan had been real and Mordren had been the vision, but at some point he must have switched. Probably when they were shaking hands. Volkan had grafted a vision of Mordren onto his own features, in order to be able to carry out the fight, while the new Volkan was only an incorporeal figure.

My moment of relief and understanding cost me precious seconds. While I was still wrapping my mind around how Volkan had accomplished this rather complex and convincing vision, he shoved my short sword away and, as I twisted in reaction to it, positioned himself behind my now unprotected back. With the sharp edge of his blade across my throat, he forced me to take a step back and press myself against his chest.

"Ah, I was so close." Prince Volkan reached over my shoulder and stroked his other hand along my jaw, tipping my head backwards. "So close to breaking you. But now we're getting warmer. Soon I will have found the one thing you won't be able to stand. And then you will surrender completely."

Dread surged through me again. He was right.

He *was* getting closer. And the problem was that I wasn't entirely in charge of the timeline for my scheme. There were things that were out of my control that still needed to happen before I could get the endgame started.

Adrenaline from the fight mixed with the sudden onslaught of dread and panic and sheer terror, and it took all my self-control to stay on my feet.

At that moment I knew that if Volkan continued in this way, he would break me before I could strike the final blow. And then, it would all be over.

CHAPTER 27

I stumbled. Throwing out a hand, I braced myself against the cold stone wall to stop myself from falling. The adrenaline from the fight had drained from my body and left me a fragile shell. Trying to muster the strength to keep going, I staggered blindly down the hall and towards what I hoped was the slave wing.

My knees buckled.

The impact jarred my bones, but I had no strength left to break the fall so I simply crashed down on the floor. Another burst of pain pulsed through my numb body as my shoulder slammed into the wall, but at least it stopped me from toppling over. I drew in a ragged breath but I couldn't make my muscles obey me.

Something wet ran down my cheeks. Reaching up, I wiped a hand over my face and realized with muted surprise that I was crying. A lot. Tears streamed down my face and I couldn't seem to get them to stop.

My hands shook.

As I glanced down at myself, I realized that my whole body

was shaking. I was vaguely aware of something moving in the corner of my eye, but I couldn't tear my gaze from my trembling limbs.

"Kenna?"

The word cut through the fog in my mind. Moving slowly, I turned my head towards the sound. Apparently, I had collapsed next to a door because an elf with white hair was staring at me from a doorway only a stride away. It took another few seconds before my brain could process who it was. Idra Souldrinker.

"I'm sorry," I pressed out between ragged breaths as I realized that the noise I'd made as I collapsed must have been what made her open the door to investigate. "I didn't know this was yours." I waved a hand vaguely towards the wall behind me before placing both palms against the floor in an attempt to get to my feet. "I'll leave."

My arms shook violently but I managed to get myself off the floor. Emotions I couldn't decipher flickered in Idra's eyes for a moment as she watched me take a swaying step forward. Then she blew out a sigh and stepped out to push the door open wider.

"Get in," she said and jerked her chin.

I blinked at her in surprise. When she only jerked her chin again, I staggered the final two steps to her door and did as she said. The door clicked shut behind me a second later and then Idra was walking past me towards her bed. I swept my gaze through the space as I followed her.

Her room was bigger than those of all the other slaves. A double bed with white covers waited at the back of the room and there was both a full-sized closet and a desk along the wall. Idra was wearing the tight-fitting black pants and top that left her arms and stomach bare, as if she had been getting ready to head to the training room, and in her dark attire she stood out in stark contrast against the white furniture.

I had aimed for the chair by her desk, but didn't quite make it so I simply slumped down on the floor and leaned my back against her closet instead. It rattled faintly when I connected with it, which made Idra look back in surprise.

She had been heading for the foot of her bed, but now she paused on the floor a few strides away and looked down at me. "Volkan's breaking sessions?"

"Yes," I breathed.

"What happened?"

Tipping my head back, I rested it against the cold closet door and drew in a ragged breath. I wasn't actively crying but tears were somehow still running down my cheeks. "I can't tell what's real anymore."

Silence fell across the room. Since Idra was standing to my left, I couldn't see the look on her face or make out why she wasn't replying, but I didn't have enough strength to care so I just continued staring at the opposite wall.

Clothes whispered against stone.

I turned my head slightly and stared in surprise as Idra sat down on the floor next to me. Letting out a long breath, she leaned back against the closet as well. For a long while, we just sat there next to each other.

At some point, the tears must have stopped because when I reached up to wipe them off my cheeks, no new ones took their place. I sucked in a deep breath. When I spoke up again, I had to clear my throat and try again three times before I could get a full sentence out.

"I don't know how long I can keep going."

"Twenty-six."

I frowned at her. "What?"

"That's how long you've been here. Twenty-six days." Idra turned to look at me. "Most people don't make it nearly that long."

"I can see why," I replied, the words more a sigh than anything else. "I'm tired. I'm just so, so tired." Raking my fingers through my hair, I drew in another shaky breath. "Sometimes, I think that life would be easier if I just… let go. If I just stopped fighting."

"It is easier." Her face showed no emotion whatsoever. "It is easier to stop fighting and to just let go. And sometimes it's necessary. Sometimes you have to let go before the strain becomes too great and it snaps your mind completely and turns you insane."

Tilting my head, I met her impassive black eyes. Once more, I wondered who Idra really was, or would have been, outside of all this. "How long did you hold out? Before he found the thing that broke you?"

"He didn't."

"What do you mean?"

"He didn't need to."

She held my gaze but didn't offer any more explanation than that. I wasn't sure if it was because I was simply too mentally exhausted to worry about consequences, but I found myself blurting out a question I had already asked once, before I could stop myself.

"Who were you before all this?" As soon as the words were out of my mouth, I regretted them. Last time I had asked her that, she had kicked me out. When I saw those same emotions flicker in her eyes this time too, I pressed on before she could say anything. "I'm sorry. I shouldn't have asked that."

Idra was silent for a few seconds. I watched the way the

candlelight danced over her shining white hair while she considered me.

"Why did you get involved with Prince Mordren?" she suddenly asked.

"Oh." I blinked at her in surprise but then drew my legs up underneath me and turned so that I sat facing her instead. While hooking a stray curl behind my ear, I met her gaze again. "I guess it was because I... didn't have anything else." A short chuckle escaped my lips. "How pathetic that sounds when I say it out loud. But yeah, I guess I got involved with him because I didn't know what to do with my life and I wanted to try and figure it out."

"And did you?"

"Yes. And no."

She cocked her head, making her hair brush her scarred shoulder. "How so?"

"I just arrived at the same conclusion as before I joined up with him." When she raised her eyebrows in silent question, I gave her a casual shrug. "I want to rule."

To my surprise, she didn't laugh. She just studied me with those bottomless eyes for a few seconds and then nodded.

"That's a dangerous thing to say in the Court of Fire," she said at last. A calculating glint crept into her eyes. "How do you know that I won't go straight to Prince Volkan and tell him everything you told me tonight? That he is close to breaking you. And that what you really want is power. He would know exactly how to use that against you."

"Yeah, I know. But I don't think you will."

"And why is that?"

"Because if you were the kind of person who rats others out, you would've already told Prince Volkan how good I *really am* at fighting by now."

Idra let out an amused breath and raised her eyebrows, but didn't dispute it. I flashed her a victorious grin, which made her huff out another silent laugh and shake her head. When she didn't say anything else, I took that as my cue to leave. "I'll let you get back to... whatever it was that you were doing when I banged into your wall."

Uncrossing my legs, I pushed to my feet again. Idra did the same. Only the soft rustle of clothing broke the silence that fell while I brushed off my rather rumpled golden dress. When I looked back up, I found Idra watching me intently. I gave her a nod and then began to turn around, but before I could, her hand shot forward and grabbed my arm.

"Hey."

I turned back fully and met her gaze again. "Yeah?"

She didn't reply. Confusion and surprise swirled in her eyes as she looked from her hand on my arm and back to my face several times, as if she was trying to figure out what had just happened. Then she snatched her hand back.

Raising my eyebrows, I looked back at her. "What's wrong?"

"You didn't flinch." Her brows were thoroughly furrowed as she stared at me. "You didn't flinch when I touched you."

"You've touched me before, when we've sparred."

"Yes, but that was under the rules of the fight. This wasn't."

"So?"

She cocked her head while her normally so impassive eyes flickered with emotions I couldn't read. "You do know that I can kill anyone with a single touch, right?"

"Yeah, I know."

"So why didn't you shy away?"

"Did you mean to kill me with that touch just now?" I chuckled and spread my hands in a confused gesture.

"Because if you did, then I read this situation completely wrong."

"No, I didn't."

"And that's why I didn't flinch."

"Huh." Idra was still staring at me, her mouth slightly open. "You're a very strange person."

I tipped my head from side to side. "I've been called worse."

She shook her head. "Most people just assume I'll kill them if I touch them."

"What an odd way of looking at the world."

Another confused look passed over her face.

I shrugged. "Just because I own a sword doesn't mean I plan to run you through with it. I would assume the same logic applies to magical powers."

And then something so unexpected happened that I really did jerk back. Idra laughed. It was such a shocking sound that for a moment, I could only stare. In all the weeks I had known her, I had barely seen her smile, and the amused huffs from a few minutes ago didn't even count as real laughs. But now she was laughing. Really laughing. It was actually a very pleasant sound.

Light from the candles glittered in her dark eyes as she drew her fingers through her hair and at last inhaled deeply, shaking off the last of the laughter. "That is indeed a very logical assumption."

"Well, not to brag, but I have been known to say the occasional smart thing or two."

Idra opened her mouth, and for a moment, it looked like she was about to say something else, but then she just closed it again and shook her head. While I desperately wanted to know what she had been about to tell me, I also didn't want to push her. So, I kept my questions to myself and instead just reached out and gave her arm a quick squeeze.

"Thanks." I motioned vaguely at the room with my other hand. "For, you know…"

Odd emotions drifted across her face again but then she crossed her arms and cleared her throat while giving me a single nod. "Yeah."

After a nod back, I turned and walked back towards the door. A torchlit hall of red stone met me outside as I closed the door to Idra's room behind me. There was always something… removed about her. Something distant. As if she was watching life and everyone else from a distance. But tonight, I had seen a shadow of emotions in her eyes. I still didn't understand what they meant or what had made her like this in the first place.

But maybe someday, I would.

CHAPTER 28

Footsteps echoed between the red stone walls. Before I could get out of sight, a lean elf with light brown hair rounded the corner from where the scribes worked. He moved carefully, like someone who spent more time sitting and reading than engaging in any physical activity, and in his hands, he held a mountain of papers. Since they were upside down, I couldn't read what they said but I wouldn't have had time to either.

The brown-haired elf looked up from his pile when he saw me but he didn't stop. Standing conspicuously by an empty wall, I watched him in silence. He held my gaze for another few seconds before turning his attention back to the corridor ahead. Paper flapped faintly in the draft he created as he left me behind and disappeared towards the main exit.

Remaining motionless, I listened for any other sounds of approaching people. When there were none, I blew out a soft sigh and continued sneaking towards the study that Prince Volkan had retreated to earlier.

Orange light from the low-hanging afternoon sun fell in

through the windows as I reached my destination. It had been two days since my little breakdown in Idra's room and I had finally recovered. More or less, anyway.

I was exhausted but couldn't allow myself to feel it. After all, there were favors to collect and schemes to plot.

After phasing through the wall of the opposite room, I moved back to the door and unlocked it from the inside. With careful movements, I cracked the door open a little and peeked out through it right as a shadow fell across the stone floor. A second later, a bunch of footsteps sounded from the other side of the corridor.

Staying perfectly still, I watched the scene outside.

An elf with long red hair came striding up the hall from the direction of the throne room and the main entrance. He looked as if he knew where he was going, but there was a nervousness to him. When he saw the group of people heading towards him from the other direction, he paused for a second. But then his eyes fell on the gold collars around their throats and he started back up again.

Twisting his body slightly, he weaved through the cluster of slaves while keeping his eyes on the door set into the left wall.

Firelight cast shimmering highlights in dark hair before the silent elves had cleared the hall and disappeared towards the throne room. The nervous-looking one stopped in front of the door he had been approaching. After running a hand through his long red hair and readjusting his satchel, he rolled his shoulders and then raised a hand to knock.

"Enter!" came the command from inside.

The redhead drew in a breath and then pushed the handle down and slipped inside.

I shifted my weight but remained where I was, watching the now empty corridor from the small crack in the door.

For a minute or so, nothing happened.

Then, soft footsteps sounded again. I watched as a dark-haired female hurried past from the same direction the redhead had come.

Keeping my eyes on the door to Prince Volkan's study, I shook out my muscles to prevent stiffness. Another few minutes dragged by.

At last, the door to the study was shoved open. I barely dared breathe as Volkan and the redheaded male crossed the threshold.

"Be back same time next week," the Prince of Fire said.

"Yes, sir," the other elf replied.

A soft click sounded as Volkan closed the door and locked it. His guest shifted on his feet and glanced up and down the corridor as if he wasn't sure whether he had been dismissed or not. Since he apparently wasn't sure, he remained hovering by the door while Volkan straightened again. The Prince of Fire looked him up and down before striding away. The redhead bowed, but Volkan only made it two steps before he turned back around.

"Oh, and Erik?" Volkan leveled a stare dripping with threats on him. "Last week, you missed that the guy was incredibly skilled at using throwing knives. If you have missed anything in that report," he nodded towards the now closed door to the study, "then I might start to wonder if you were trying to sabotage me on purpose."

Erik's face drained completely of color. "Y-yes, sir. It won't happen again, sir."

Realization dawned on me. So that was how he had known that Eilan's shapeshifter persona *Julian Bladesinger* had been an impostor. He had Erik, the elf in charge of organizing the tournament, do background research on anyone who entered. Or more specifically, he had Erik research the challenger's fighting technique so that he could give Volkan a report the day before. When there had been nothing to find on the fake Julian Bladesinger, it had raised a whole bunch of red flags. I stifled an impressed huff.

Though I might thoroughly despise Volkan Flameshield, I had to admit that he was an intelligent one. Not only did this little precaution ferret out potential impostors, it also allowed the Prince of Fire to learn each challenger's strengths, which meant that he could decide on an effective fighting style to counter that beforehand. Clever, indeed.

Erik bowed low again while Prince Volkan spun on his heel and stalked deeper into the castle.

Another elf appeared from around the corner he was just about to round. The slim female leaped out of the way and bowed low as well. She kept her head down while walking backwards until the Prince of Fire was gone. Once he had disappeared from sight, the female whirled around.

A sharp thud rang out as she slammed right into Erik, who had been straightening from his bow as well. He stumbled backwards and his satchel slipped from his shoulder and hit the floor, scattering the contents on the red stone.

"Oh by the spirits, I'm so sorry!" she said.

"It's fine." Erik quickly dropped to his knees and began gathering up his things. When the female elf crouched down to help, he waved a hand at her. "It's fine. I've got it."

She straightened and lingered awkwardly for another second before giving him a nod that he couldn't see. "Oh, okay. I'm sorry again."

"Don't worry about it."

"Sorry."

Backing away a step, she continued looking at him for another few seconds before turning around. As she started towards the throne room, she glanced in my direction.

Eyes the color of a storm-swept sea met mine and a brief smile flickered over her lips. Brushing her hands down her body, she straightened her dress and the golden slave collar around her neck before she broke eye contact and hurried away.

Torchlight shimmered in hair that was so black it was almost blue.

And then she was gone.

On the other side of the corridor, Erik had straightened once more but he hadn't started walking. Instead, he was standing rooted in place while his eyes stared in disbelief at the paper in his hands. When he finally moved, it was to jerk his head up and cast a panicked look at the now locked door to the study before staring down at the paper again.

I closed the door and locked it from the inside again before walking straight through it. Making sure to keep my footfalls silent, so that he wouldn't realize that I hadn't come from all the way down the corridor, I approached Erik.

"Is something wrong?" I asked once I was only two steps behind him.

He practically jumped out of his skin and whipped around. Panic darted in his eyes as he met my gaze. I donned a mask of innocence and open curiosity as I looked back at him. It appeared to work because his posture changed from 'cornered animal about to attack' to 'terrified squirrel about to drop his nuts' and he raked his free hand through his hair.

"I just…" He cast another desperate glance at the locked

door and then cleared his throat. "I just realized that I missed a paper that I was supposed to have put in a folder in there."

"Oh." I followed his gaze as if I hadn't been staring at that same door for the past ten minutes. "Do you want me to put it in for you?"

His gaze snapped back to mine. Confusion blew across his face as his eyes dipped to the golden slave collar around my neck before he looked back up again. "You have a key?"

"Well, no. But I don't need one."

The surprised frown stayed on his face.

I held out my hand. "Which folder is it?"

Looking down at my open palm, Erik hesitated for a moment. I could almost see him playing out the possibilities in his head. Clearly, I wasn't supposed to read whatever was written on this document, which was something that could get him in trouble. But on the other hand, not getting the paper into the folder would be even worse. The Prince of Fire was not someone who tolerated repeated mistakes.

Erik swallowed. And then he slowly placed the document in my waiting hand. "It's the red one. On the desk. At the top of the pile on the right."

Taking the paper, I nodded and then moved past him towards the door.

"Could you..." He cleared his throat. "Could you make sure that this is the third document in the folder?"

"Sure."

I glanced back at him and nodded again before taking a decisive step right through the stone door. There was a small gasp of surprise behind me, but it was cut off as I left the hallway behind and reappeared in the study.

Red light from the setting sun fell across the room and deepened the color of the walls and the floor. I swept my gaze over neatly organized bookcases before heading straight for the desk.

There was indeed a red folder at the top of the pile on the right. I skimmed the pages inside before placing the document under the first two, just as I had been instructed. They contained information about the male elf that Prince Volkan would be fighting in the sixth tournament match tomorrow. Since it was of little interest to me, I left my snooping at that and instead made my way back into the corridor.

Wide eyes met me when I stepped back into the torchlit hallway.

"You can...?" Erik trailed off.

I gave him a smile. "Yeah."

"And you put it in the folder? As number three?"

"Yes."

Relief washed over him like an ocean wave. Slumping back against the wall, he pressed a hand to his forehead and heaved a deep sigh. Then he met my gaze again. "Thank you. You saved my life. Literally."

"Don't worry about it."

He straightened and took a step closer to me, his eyes darting down to the slave collar around my neck again for a second. "If there is ever anything, anything at all, that I can help you with, just say the word."

"Thank you. I will."

Reaching out, he pressed my hand before dipping his chin and then turning around to hurry back out of the Court of Fire. I watched him leave.

Still standing there in the now empty hallway, I finally let a villainous grin spread across my lips. How easy it was to screw someone over when you were owed a favor by a magically gifted thief.

Hilver and his friends had been happy to help cover Viviane as she stole the document right out of Erik's satchel when he first arrived and squeezed past that, oh so inconveniently timed, group of elves. And then Viviane just hurried back through the corridor so that she could approach from the same direction again, thus making it seem even more like it was someone else entirely that second time.

After Volkan had left Erik, all Viviane had to do was accidentally bump into him and sneak the document back among his things. The fact that he had also dropped the satchel had been a complete coincidence. Or so I thought, at least.

Just when the poor tournament organizer was imagining all the horrible methods that Prince Volkan would use to kill him, someone who just happened to be able to walk through walls showed up and solved his problem. If Viviane hadn't been as skilled a thief as she was, and if Erik had been a bit less worried about being turned into charcoal, he might have been suspicious.

It truly is marvelous what the fear of violent death can do to a person's decision-making process. And it really was immensely helpful to have several people owe you favors.

Particularly when you were trying to screw over a prince.

CHAPTER 29

Fire roared across the throne room. I flinched as the heat rolled over me, and several of the other slaves outright ducked to avoid the wave of flames that shot out from Prince Volkan. Since he wasn't actually aiming it at anyone, everyone managed to escape unscathed, but that didn't stop the air of fear that descended on the castle like thick mist. While everyone desperately wanted to run in the other direction, with the Prince of Fire this angry, no one dared to leave their posts either. So we all remained standing along the walls of the throne room as Volkan Flameshield bellowed in frustration.

"I give them all spectacular fights!" he screamed. "And this is how they thank me?"

The loud whoosh of fire magic echoed through the high-ceilinged hall as Volkan slashed his arms through the air and threw more flames at the walls. They exploded against the red stone and rained down to the floor like a glowing orange waterfall.

"By not even showing up to watch!" Volkan continued.

Whirling around, he stabbed a hand towards the person behind him. "How many?"

Idra, the only person in the room who appeared completely unaffected by Volkan's flame-throwing, looked back at him with impassive black eyes. "About a quarter, sir."

"A quarter?" Fire rushed up and down Volkan's arms before finally disappearing. Reaching up, he raked his hands through his long blond hair. "Never, in the history of this tournament, have so few people attended a match. Never."

From a couple of strides away, Idra said nothing. The rest of the room held its breath. I studied the thin cuts with dried blood along Volkan's arms while I tried very hard to keep a neutral expression on my face. His sleeveless tunic of dark red was rumpled, and sand clung to his boots. By the looks of him, his latest tournament match had been a fantastic display of fighting skills. Too bad almost no one had been there to see it.

Volkan snapped his gaze to the slaves along the walls, as if noticing for the first time that we were still there. The ones he stared straight at flinched back a step. Anger still burned in his yellow eyes but he flicked a hand.

"Get out," he ordered. "All of you."

Feet smattered against stone as people vanished almost before he had even finished speaking. I met Evander's gaze from a short distance away. He nodded.

Turning around, I started towards one of the side corridors. From behind me, Volkan's voice rang out once more.

"Idra!"

"Yes, sir."

"Make sure everyone knows how displeased their prince

is. If the arena isn't packed beyond capacity for the final fight next week, make sure they know exactly…"

His voice quieted as I moved out of earshot and disappeared down a narrow hallway. Slipping through a few walls, I picked up a surprise before I finally ended up outside the door to the greenhouse. After phasing through that one as well, I unlocked it from the inside and then moved to a secluded spot farther in.

The air was warm and moist, and I could almost feel the condensation around me like thin mist. Running a hand over a cluster of green plants, I turned down another pathway and then dropped down on the floor. With a smile playing over my lips, I rested my back against the stone wall of a plant bed while I waited. The smell of damp earth and herbs surrounded me. I drew in a deep breath.

A few minutes later, soft footsteps came from the door to the greenhouse.

"Can you believe it?" Evander said as he rounded the final corner to where I was sitting. "Only a quarter of the usual audience was there to watch the fight today."

"Yes," I replied. "It's almost as if someone had informed people that the match had been pushed back a few hours."

Matching grins spread across our faces as we looked at each other. And then I burst out laughing.

Evander lowered himself to the floor opposite me, leaning back against the wall of another plant bed. "That was pretty amazing."

"Well…" I flashed him a satisfied smile. "I called in some favors."

Glass clinked faintly against stone as I took out the bottle I had stolen on my way here, and showed it to Evander. He raised his eyebrows. Continuing to grin at him, I uncorked it before raising it in the air.

"Here's to screwing with Prince Volkan's source of power while he tries to do the same to everyone else!" I drank deeply from the wine bottle before handing it to Evander.

He lifted it in the air as well. "Here's to you." After taking a large gulp, he lowered it and shook his head while a disbelieving smile drifted over his lips. "I don't understand how you do it."

"Well, you help too."

"Yeah, not really."

"Yes, you do." I took the bottle from him and drank from it again. "I wouldn't be able to do half the things I'm doing if you weren't covering for me."

His fingers brushed mine as he reclaimed the wine and took another swig. An embarrassed look drifted across his face while he raised his other hand and scratched the back of his head. "I don't know about that."

"I'm serious." Leaning forward, I placed a hand on his arm. "I know we have a… complicated past. But I really appreciate everything you do to help me now. Covering for me while I sneak around, helping me make poison, lying to Prince Volkan so that I could get a few hours alone. All of it."

"I'm glad to hear that." Glancing up, he met my gaze. In the golden sunlight falling in through the glass ceiling, his dark green eyes glittered like emeralds. "And I'm glad we could… get past, well, everything that's happened."

While things could never go back to the way they were before he betrayed me, I found that I was rather satisfied with this development too. After all, it was always better to have more allies than enemies.

"Me too," I said.

Only the muted sound of water dripping slowly onto leaves pierced the silence that settled for a while. Taking the bottle from Evander, I drank some more wine. With the blow I had dealt Prince Volkan today, I was on track with my scheme. Soon, this would all be over. Or so I hoped.

"By the way, what did you do with those three extra hours I bought you when you were breaking into Prince Iwdael's castle?" Evander suddenly asked.

"I spent them with Mordren, mostly."

"Oh." Emotions blew across his face, but they were gone before I could decipher them. He shifted his weight on the red stones, which made a bead of sweat run down the muscles of his bare chest. "Doing what?"

Fighting, flirting, and fucking. Though, I didn't really want to tell him that, so instead I said, "Scheming. There are always some things that I can't do from in here, that I need him and his court to do from the outside."

Evander seemed to relax slightly. "I see. What kind of things?"

"It's safer for you if you don't know. If Prince Volkan were to find out that you're somehow involved in what Mordren is doing, he would…" I shook my head. "I can take that risk because Volkan already knows of my connection to Mordren, but I don't want you getting hurt because of my actions."

Blowing out a sigh, he drew his fingers through his short brown hair. "I just wish I could do more."

"You're already doing enough."

Slightly awkward silence fell across the greenhouse. We were back to the question about trust. Evander knew that the plan was to take down Volkan and that we would be free afterwards, but beyond that, I always kept him strictly on a need-to-know basis.

A cloud of fragrant air, smelling of basil and rosemary, drifted past us. I drew a deep breath and then drank some more wine.

"This will work, right?" Evander's suddenly worried eyes searched my face while he motioned towards the gold collar around his neck. "Your plan? You will get these off us and we'll be free. Right?"

The image of me breaking down and bawling my eyes out on Idra's floor flashed across my vision. If Evander knew just how close Prince Volkan was to breaking me, he might get cold feet. So I shoved the memory out of my mind and instead summoned all the confidence I could muster.

"Yeah, of course." I gave him a firm nod. "We're almost there now. Just a little while longer."

He studied my face as if checking to see whether I was lying. Seemingly satisfied, he nodded back. "Good." Reaching out, he took my hand in his while holding my gaze. "I'm here. For whatever you need."

I squeezed his hand. "Thanks."

Guilt wormed its way into my chest. We were supposed to be rebuilding our friendship, but here I was, lying to him again. Or maybe not lying, but at least withholding information. But there was no point in telling him just how close to the breaking point I really was or just how dangerous my scheme really was.

After Prince Volkan's fiasco of a match today, he would need someone to take out all his anger and frustration on. And I had a distinct feeling that I was that someone.

It was all I could do to keep myself together, so if Evander started doubting me now, I was sure to lose it.

So I did what I always do.

I lied.

CHAPTER 30

"Your presence is requested in the Great Hall."

I drew up short. Blinking in surprise, I stared at the guard wearing the red and gold armor of the Court of Fire as he stopped right in front of me. He wasn't angry, but he looked on edge, and he was blocking the way down the corridor that I had been following.

"Okay?" I answered carefully. "When?"

"Right now."

Suspicion flared up inside me but I only nodded. "Alright."

Without another word, the guard turned on his heel and motioned for me to follow him. I did.

We walked in silence as we made our way through the red stone castle and towards the grand dining room that was known as the Great Hall. My heart pattered in my chest. Whatever this was, I was certain that it was nothing good.

The murmur of people chatting in soft voices drifted towards us from the open doorway at the end of the hall. This was one of the narrow servants' corridors that was used by the people who waited the tables when Prince Volkan arranged dinners in this room. Firelight flickered from beyond.

My pulse sped up.

I hadn't seen Volkan all day, so he must have been preparing something spectacular.

When we reached the end of the corridor, I had to remind myself to keep breathing normally. However, before we could step across the final threshold the guard held out an arm, blocking my way.

Coming to an abrupt halt, I turned and looked up at the guard in silent question. He only continued staring straight ahead into the dining room, but he kept his arm like a barrier in front of my chest so I stayed put. Since I was apparently supposed to wait here for now, I instead shifted my gaze to the Great Hall in order to try to figure out exactly what I was doing here.

Thousands of candles covered the room. Golden candleholders were positioned down the entire length of the long table in the middle, and sparkling gold candelabras lined the walls. Everything with a wick had been lit. The firelight combined with the gold decorations cast the whole room in that same glittering hue. And the room wasn't deserted.

About fifty people in splendid outfits were standing in various groups around the room. There was a mix of both humans and elves, but based on their attire, they were all nobles. I narrowed my eyes as I realized something else.

They weren't exclusively from this court. In fact, nobles from every court were here, and there even seemed to be a fairly balanced number from each. The suspicion inside me grew. What was Volkan up to?

Sweeping my gaze across the nobles shimmering in the golden candlelight, I located the Prince of Fire. He was standing roughly halfway between the bedecked table and the large open doors on the other side, and there was a grin on his lips. It looked like he was waiting for someone. I flicked my gaze to the open doorway just as a shadow fell across the floor.

My stomach dropped.

Mordren Darkbringer sauntered across the threshold with lazy grace before coming to a halt a few strides from Volkan. His chaperone, the blond elf called Remus, followed him inside but took up position by the wall instead.

"What's with the sudden dinner invitation?" Mordren said. A slight smirk played at the corner of his lips as he cocked his head to study Volkan. "Perhaps it has something to do with the fact that no one came to watch you fight yesterday. Is that it? You needed a bit of attention?"

A malicious smile spread across Volkan's mouth. "Not at all. I simply figured it was high time we talked."

"Is that right?"

"Yes."

The rest of the dining room had gone dead quiet. Fear flickered around the groups of nobles as their eyes darted between Volkan and the Prince of Shadows. Prince Volkan was not someone that they wanted to cross, and they were even more scared of Mordren, so between the two of them, they cast an almost tangible air of lethal danger over the room.

"Well," Volkan began and motioned towards the table, "shall we?"

Mordren's answering smile was a slash of white, but he moved towards the chair at the edge of the table. After a few nervous glances towards their host, the nobles scrambled towards their seats as well. With Volkan and Mordren taking up the ornate chairs on each end, the other guests filled the long sides of the table between them.

After sitting down, Mordren adjusted his sharp black suit. Light that reflected off the gold plates and cups along the table painted gilded highlights in his night-black hair. Arching a dark eyebrow, Mordren met Volkan's gaze from across the table.

"If you wanted to talk," Mordren began and flicked a lazy hand to indicate the sea of nobles between them, "then why are all these people here?"

"They are high-ranking nobles from every court."

"I can see that." The Prince of Shadows nodded towards the middle left of the table. "Those over there are even from my court."

"Yes." A calculating glint crept into Volkan's eyes. "And they are all here to bear witness."

Alarm bells suddenly went off inside my skull. Whatever Volkan's plan was for taking out Mordren's power source, it was going down right now. I glanced up at the guard next to me again. Still keeping his arm raised in front of my chest, he only continued watching the dining room before us.

"Ah," Mordren said with a smug smile. "Are you scared that I will try something?"

Volkan scoffed and then gave him a wicked smile of his own. "Oh, you wish."

Lifting a hand, the Prince of Fire snapped his fingers. At last, the guard beside me turned to face me.

"Prince Volkan has declared that you will serve him and Prince Mordren tonight," he said in a low voice. "Only the two of them. Got it?"

Dread welled up inside me but I managed to reply, "Got it."

The guard nodded and then lowered his arm. From all the

other hidden servants' corridors, other slaves had already appeared and had started serving drinks to the nobles at the table. Swallowing, I steeled myself and then stepped into the Great Hall as well.

Volkan turned and looked straight at me, which made Mordren follow his gaze too. His handsome face betrayed nothing, but he gripped the arms of his chair hard. Tearing my gaze from his, I picked up one of the decanters on the side table by the wall and moved towards Prince Volkan.

The Prince of Fire had turned back to Mordren and was grinning at him. Thankfully, he had recovered enough to only look back with a mask of mild disinterest, but I knew that he was furious.

"You wanted to talk," Mordren said and leaned back casually in his chair. "So, talk."

"I see you still haven't learned any manners, little prince."

"And you have still not learned how to get to the point."

I reached the table and lifted my decanter. With a steady hand, I poured red wine into Prince Volkan's cup. Just as I was finishing, I felt a hand on my hip. Volkan traced his fingers up towards my waist while keeping his gaze locked on the Prince of Shadows.

Lightning flashed in Mordren's eyes and he tightened his grip on the chair before forcing his hands to relax again.

"Problem?" Volkan shot him a satisfied smirk. "Oh, you were probably just waiting for your wine." Drawing his fingers from my waist and around the small of my back, he continued grinning at Mordren before he lifted his hand and gave me a smack on the ass. "Go serve him some wine."

"Yes, sir," I said while keeping a carefully neutral mask on my face.

The silent nobles tracked my movements as I walked

towards the other side of the long table. Mordren's eyes were locked on Volkan's the whole time.

When I finally reached him, I positioned myself so that only he could see my face. Raising the decanter once more, I began pouring the wine while speaking in a soft whisper.

"This is it. Whatever he is doing to damage your reputation, he's going to do it now." I leveled a hard stare at Mordren that I knew he could feel even though he was pretending not to pay any attention to me. "So no matter what Volkan does, don't go along with it."

The gold goblet before Mordren was full, so I drew back and started retreating towards the wall. However, before I could make it two steps, Volkan spoke up again.

"Kenna." He twitched his fingers at me. "Over here."

"So, now that we have both gotten our wine," Mordren said in a dismissive voice while spinning a hand in the air. "Why don't you get to the point already?"

"Ah, yes," Volkan replied. "This situation with the High Elves… I was wondering what your opinion is on it all."

Since my back was now to Mordren, I couldn't see his face but the slight pause made me think that he was frowning.

"What about it?" he asked.

"What do you think about the High Elves?"

Candlelight danced across the nobles' faces and set their expensive jewelry glittering. As I made my way back down the table, I realized something that made the blood in my veins run cold. Every single noble inside this room was wearing a black bracelet. Was Volkan trying to somehow set them all against Mordren by making him say that he didn't like the High Elves? But that didn't make any sense. How would that damage his reputation?

"I do not discuss my court's stance on political topics with the rabble," Mordren replied contemptuously.

Since I had finally arrived next to him, Volkan wrapped his arm around my back and rested his hand on my hip again. With calculated movements, he traced his fingers in lazy circles up my side. I suppressed an eye roll.

"Political topics, you say?" Volkan continued. His hand moved back down to my hip and then continued towards my thigh. "Wouldn't you say that this is more of a religious matter?"

Mordren's eyes had gone dark. "Take your hands off her."

"Pardon me?"

"You only get this one warning, Volkan," he said, his voice cold and dangerous. "Get that hand off her."

The nervous nobles flicked their gaze back and forth across the table, darting from one prince to the other, and I could almost swear that none of them were breathing. I shot Mordren a pointed glance, but he wasn't looking at me. His murderous gaze was locked on the Prince of Fire.

"She is my slave." Volkan's eyes gleamed with malice. "And I can do whatever I want with my slaves."

"You–"

Volkan shot to his feet. I barely had time to gasp before his strong hand wrapped around the back of my neck and he slammed me chest first down onto the table. On instinct, I had thrown my hands out to brace myself on the tabletop, but Volkan's superior strength had my chest and cheek pressed against the cold stone anyway. My breath was knocked out of me but I didn't even have time to register it before pain shot up my forearm as the Prince of Fire rammed his dinner knife through my hand.

A scream ripped from my throat.

The whole thing had taken less than a second, and now that the others around the table had finally realized what was going on, cries of alarm rose from the gathered nobles as well.

Right as the screaming started, black shadows shot towards me and wrapped around the hand that kept the knife pressed through my palm. Fire roared to life in response to it.

"Sit down," Volkan bellowed across the room of hysterical nobles.

At the same time as they all froze in their tracks, another voice cut through the room.

"Stop!" The surprisingly commanding voice came from Mordren's chaperone. Remus had closed the distance to the table and positioned himself between the two princes. Holding his arms outstretched, he faced the Prince of Shadows. "Prince Mordren. You have to stop this."

"He–" Mordren began before Remus cut him off again.

"I know what he is doing, but the cold hard truth is that no matter how much you wish it were otherwise, that woman over there is Prince Volkan's slave. And what he does with his slaves is his business. I will forgive this first outburst because of the sheer *barbarity*," Remus shot a sharp look at the Prince of Fire, "of Prince Volkan's act. But if you continue to attack him now, I will have no other choice than to report you to King Aldrich. Because whether you like it or not, Prince Volkan *is* free to do whatever he wants with his slaves."

From my position, I couldn't make out the expression on Volkan's face, but I could see Mordren clearly. His silver eyes slid back to me where I was bent across the table, my chest and cheek pressed into the smooth stone by Volkan's grip on my neck, and my hands splayed against the tabletop with a knife still pinning my right palm to the table. Utter fury mixed with terrible desperation in Mordren's eyes.

If he attacked Volkan right now, the king would strip him of his title and his court. But if he didn't, the Prince of Fire could continue to hurt me unchallenged. I could see the impossible choice roaring inside him. Holding his gaze, I gave him an almost imperceptible shake of my head.

Mordren continued staring at me. I glared back, urging him to remember my earlier warning that this was Volkan's big play and that he shouldn't go along with it. There was only one choice, and we both knew it. Losing his court was not an option, especially not over this.

Ever so slowly, the black tendrils around Volkan's wrists withdrew. The gathered nobles heaved a sigh of relief as it became clear that they were not about to become trapped in a battle between two lethal elven princes. Remus gave Mordren a brief nod and retreated towards the wall.

For a few seconds, the grand dining room was dead quiet.

Then Volkan ripped the knife from my hand before ramming it back down again.

Another scream forced its way past my lips. Gritting my teeth, I tried to stop a sob from escaping my throat and curled my other hand into a fist in an effort to prevent my knees from buckling. Pain pulsed from my hand and all the way up my arm.

From halfway down the table, Mordren stood frozen on the floor. He was grinding his teeth together so hard I could see the muscles of his jaw flicker and he kept clenching and unclenching his hands, but thankfully, he didn't attack again.

"Do you want me to stop?" Volkan said from somewhere above me. There was a dangerous note to his voice. "Then beg."

The nobles sucked in a collective gasp. No one told the Prince of Shadows to beg. Ever. Surprise and confusion rippled across the room and chased the terror away. What was happening here was something unprecedented.

Volkan twisted the knife in my palm. I managed to stifle the scream but not the whimper that spilled from my lips.

Shadows flickered around Mordren's body. Locking eyes with him, I silently begged him to just return to his seat and not attack.

"Drop to your knees and beg me to stop," Prince Volkan repeated.

Mordren took a step forward. Panic cut through the pain as I realized that he wasn't going to let this slide. He was going to attack. Several half-formed plans flashed through my mind as I tried to figure out how we could win this fight while also making sure that King Aldrich didn't strip Mordren of his title afterwards.

No adequate solution presented itself.

I was running out of time. Mordren had closed the distance between them and stopped two strides away from Volkan. Tearing his gaze from me, he locked eyes with the Prince of Fire. Black tendrils were still whipping furiously around Mordren's body. What could I do to tip the scales of this fight?

There had to be something.

Anything.

My mind went blank.

Every single thought was wiped straight from my head.

The whole room stared in utter disbelief as the Prince of Shadows slowly lowered himself to his knees.

I swore I could hear the sound echo through the entire room as his first knee hit the red stone with a thud. Keeping his eyes locked on Prince Volkan, Mordren placed his other knee on the floor as well.

"Beg," Volkan Flameshield commanded.

"Please."

"Please what?"

"Please stop hurting her."

A shocked buzz went through the nobles around us as they stared at the impossible scene playing out.

Volkan yanked out the knife. I sucked in a sharp breath between my teeth and braced myself for the next strike, but he only released my neck and stepped back.

Using my uninjured hand, I pushed myself off the table and straightened. My legs wobbled and blood leaked from the hole in my palm, running down my arm and dripping from my elbow towards the floor as I raised it to inspect the wound. I tried to bend my fingers but they didn't move.

Terror flashed through me. This was my sword hand. If I couldn't move my fingers, I wouldn't be able to use my sword. Mordren seemed to be thinking the same thing because the dread welling up inside me was mirror in his eyes as well.

"Do you want me to have her hand healed?" Volkan said as he came to a halt a single stride in front of Mordren. "Then grovel."

Still kneeling on the floor, Mordren snapped his gaze back to the Prince of Fire. Now that I was standing, I could finally see the expression on Volkan's face. His eyes burned with delight and a mocking smile stretched his lips.

He shifted his hand and pointed at the floor. "Bow before my feet."

Fury and panic and desperation flashed past in Mordren's eyes. Only the faint rustling of clothing and hiss of fire broke the silence as Volkan dared him to humiliate himself even further in front of an entire room full of nobles from every court. The tension was so thick I could have cut it with a knife.

"This isn't it. I'm not calling it in now," I said into the oppressive silence, reminding Mordren that he didn't owe me anything until I called in that favor. And I sure as hell wasn't calling it in now. "So don't you dare."

Giving me a tired smile, Mordren sat back on his heels. "I know."

Shocked gasps bounced across the room as the feared Prince of Shadows placed his palms on the red stone and pressed his forehead to the floor in front of Volkan's feet.

My heart broke.

Pain that had nothing to do with the bleeding wound in my hand shot through me as everything inside me shattered like broken glass. Mordren had sworn that he would burn his own court to the ground before he ever bowed to the Prince of Fire. And yet, here he was, kneeling on the ground and groveling before Volkan's feet. For me.

Not because he was repaying a debt. But because…

I drew in a shaky breath.

If I had ever doubted Mordren's feelings for me, there was no mistaking them now. Mordren Darkbringer kneeled for nothing and no one. Except his brother. His family. And me, apparently.

"What a sight this is," Prince Volkan said and spread his arms. "The Prince of Shadows, the Darkbringer prince that everyone is terrified of, is on his knees before me. Groveling." A wide smile decorated his lips as he swept his gaze over the gathered nobles. "What a story you will have to tell once you get back to your courts."

A cold sinking feeling spread through my stomach.

Prince Volkan slid his gaze back to the bowing elf before him. "Little Mordren, finally right where you belong."

Wildfire rage burned through me and smothered everything else in its roaring path. Mordren was *mine*. And no one treated my people in this way.

With blood still running down my arm and dripping to the red floor, I turned to stare at the Prince of Fire. A malicious smirk curved his lips as he watched his enemy bowing before him.

I was going to kill him for this.

CHAPTER 31

*L*oud crashes echoed into the night. Rage burned inside me as I picked up another training dummy and hurled it into the wall.

Prince Volkan had stayed true to his word. Once Mordren and the others had left, he'd had a healer fix my ruined hand. And I was currently using both of my now undamaged hands to tear through the training room in a storm of fury.

"What are you doing?"

I whipped around to find Idra Souldrinker leaning against the doorjamb with her arms crossed. Her impassive eyes glided across the mess I'd made before finally settling on my face. She raised her eyebrows, waiting for an answer.

"I am going to kill him," I announced.

"Who?"

"Volkan." Twisting around, I kicked at another training dummy with all my might. It shot backwards across the floor before crashing into the wall behind with a loud bang. "I am going to kill the fucking Prince of Fire."

"No, you're not."

"Watch me," I spat back and stalked towards the wall next to her.

Idra moved forward and blocked my way. I changed direction and started towards the now empty doorway instead, but she followed.

"Get out of my way," I growled.

Before I had even finished speaking, she flashed across the floor. I threw myself backwards to escape her attack, but the anger roaring inside me was clouding my mind. Curling my hand into a fist, I swung at her in an attempt to make her draw back again. But instead of retreating, she simply grabbed my wrist mid-air and used my momentum against me. While throwing my body down on the floor, she twisted my arm up behind my back.

I slammed into the training mat hard enough that my breath was driven from my lungs. Idra used that second of inattention to lock me down. With one hand forcing my arm up against my back, she crouched down and pressed her knee between my shoulder blades. Her other hand appeared at the back of my neck, holding me against the floor.

Struggling against her grip, I banged my fist against the ground in frustration. Idra didn't let up. I spat out a few curses and tried again, but in the position she had me trapped in, there wasn't a lot I could do. At last, I stilled.

When she still didn't release me, I swallowed my anger and humiliation and tapped my hand against the floor in submission.

For a moment, nothing happened.

Then, she leaned down and spoke close to my ear. "When I allow you to get back up, we are going to sit down and have a conversation like civilized people. Understood?"

"Understood," I pressed out.

The pressure on my wrist, neck, and back finally disappeared. I pushed to my feet and turned to face Idra. Her eyes searched my face as she looked back at me, but for a few seconds, she said nothing.

"Come sit down," she said at last.

Without waiting to see if I would follow, she strode towards the nearest bench and dropped down on it. I briefly entertained the idea of just stalking out, but then did the same. The torches along the walls hissed faintly and cast dancing shadows over the red walls. I glared at them in sullen silence.

"This is about what he did to Mordren," Idra finally said.

It was more of a statement than a question, but I answered anyway. "Yeah."

"Everything would be much easier if you just stopped caring."

"Is that what you did?" I spat back. "Give up and just let him do whatever he wanted?"

"Yes. And no."

"What's that supposed to mean?"

Clothes whispered against stone as Idra shifted her position on the bench so that she faced me instead. This close, I could see that she also had faint scars all over her face. Her dark eyes took on an intensity that I had never seen before as she cocked her head and stared back at me.

"Do you really want to know?" she said. "Who I was before I came here?"

The question took me completely by surprise. Startled out of my anger, I jerked back and blinked at her before finally managing a nod.

"I was a slave." Reaching up, she hooked two fingers under her silver collar and lifted it slightly before letting it drop back against her collarbones again. "I have worn this exact collar almost my entire life."

The last flames of my fury sputtered out and died as I stared back at her in shock.

"Yeah." She shrugged, her shining white hair brushing the top of her shoulders with the movement. "I was born in a tiny village in the mountains. A long, long time ago. When my magic manifested, and people realized that I could kill them with a single touch... Well, let's just say that they didn't like it. They feared me. Even my own family. They thought I was possessed by a demon from hell. So in order to get it out of me, they did what all rational people would do. They tried to torture it out of me."

"What?" I breathed.

"I escaped and sought refuge with the elven... ruler who lived up there by the mountain. In exchange for a position that would make me untouchable, I offered him my services as a soldier. With my magical abilities, I knew that he would accept. And he did. I worked for him for a while." She let out a humorless laugh. "But I was young and inexperienced back then, so when he told me that I should wear this silver collar as a mark of my station, I didn't think twice. He put the collar around my throat, poured his magic into it, and then I was trapped."

"It works in the same way as these ones?" I asked and motioned towards the golden one around my own neck.

"Yes, and no. Volkan tried to replicate this one, which is what led to the creation of the ones you all are wearing, but this is one of a kind. As with yours, it allows the master to set a range that the slave is allowed to move in and it prevents them from killing their master. But yours can be taken off at any time if the master pours his magic into the collar. Mine cannot. My collar can only be taken off after the master is dead."

"By all the gods and spirits." I shook my head. Watching her, I realized that she didn't even look sad. Only tired. "But so, the elven ruler was Volkan?"

"No. I was bound in slavery for many, many years before I met Volkan. Though, I wasn't so much a slave as I was a… research experiment."

"What?"

"Once the elf who became my master found out that I could kill people with a single touch, he hatched a plan. The first step was to create this collar from some kind of lost High Elf lore. And once it was on, he started his experiments. He thought that if he could only figure out how my power worked, he could share it with all his other soldiers and then he could take over the entire continent." She shrugged again. "So he strapped me to a table and cut me up to see what was inside."

I jerked back as if someone had slapped me. "He did *what?*"

"He had me healed after the experiments every day to make sure I didn't die but…" Lifting her arms, she turned them over and glanced down at them. The scars crisscrossing her entire body shone in the firelight. "After a few years, it started becoming more and more difficult so the scars became permanent."

I wasn't sure I was breathing at that point. "Did you…?"

"Feel everything he did to me?" she finished, her eyes still impassive like pools of black water. "Yes."

Terrible realization dawned like a red sun. Suddenly, I understood why Mordren's pain magic didn't work on her. It wasn't because she was magically gifted at shielding, which I should have known since worldwalking was the only secondary power a person could be born with. Idra wasn't an impossible exception who could somehow use shielding in addition to her death magic and her worldwalking. Her pain threshold was simply off the charts.

"I lost track of the years after a while, but eventually, Volkan found out about what he was doing. He had become the Prince of Fire by then and he wasn't interested in being challenged, so he took his army of soldiers there and wiped him out." Idra drew her fingers through her hair in a casual gesture. "After it was over, Volkan found me in the basement. Since my master was dead, the collar could finally be taken off but the problem is that I can't be the one to remove it. Not to mention that I was still strapped to that stone table, broken and bleeding."

It felt as though the blood had frozen inside my veins. I could only stare back at her in mute horror.

"Volkan knew what I could do, so he gave me a choice." She blew out a humorless laugh. "Death or eternal servitude. If I was alive, there was still a chance that I would one day be free. But if I was dead, I would never have that chance. And he also promised that he would never experiment on me. So I agreed. Volkan poured his own magic into my collar and snapped it shut again." She spread her hands. "And here we are."

"By all the gods and spirits," I breathed.

Suddenly, my own life didn't feel all that difficult anymore. Compared to everything that Idra had been through, my life might as well have been a sunny walk in the park.

"I'm so sorry," I said.

"Yeah." Leaning back, she stretched out her legs before her. "So when I tell you that it's easier to let go, I'm speaking from experience." Black flames suddenly flared in her eyes. "Don't get me wrong, I would love to kill him. I know everything there is to know about anatomy after all the years my old master spent picking me apart, so I know every single way that I could kill Volkan. But I can't."

The dark flames in her eyes lit the ones in mine as well. This talk with Idra was supposed to have calmed me down. To have smothered my anger. But all it had done was to make it burn even hotter. After everything that Idra had been forced to endure, she'd finally had freedom within her grasp. And then Volkan had snapped that collar shut around her throat and made her a slave again. Everywhere he went, he brought misery and death.

"And neither can you," Idra finished while motioning between our slave collars. "Not as long as we have these on."

I turned and stared towards where Volkan's bedroom was located behind rows upon rows of walls. A cold smile spread across my lips as I slid my gaze back to Idra.

"Oh, I will make him take mine off." The promise dripped from my lips like poison. "And then I will kill him."

CHAPTER 32

The guard at the end of the hall snapped to attention as he heard my footsteps echo between the red stone walls. Since I wasn't even trying to mask my approach, I simply strode straight towards him.

"Prince Volkan asked me to come and see him," I said and offered him a shrug. "Something about Prince Mordren."

Surprise flitted over the guard's face. "Oh. He hasn't said anything to me about it."

In situations like these, it's always best to say as little as possible. If you argue too much, the other person becomes suspicious. But if you just stand there in silence until the other person becomes awkward, chances are they're going to start doubting themselves and do what you want.

So that was exactly what I did. Coming to a halt a single step before the confused guard, I simply looked up at him and waited for him to open the door.

He cleared his throat. "Right. I'll check with him to confirm." After rapping his knuckles on the door, he pushed down the handle and then twisted to speak into the gap he had opened. "Prince Volkan, I have–"

I moved like a viper.

In one fluid motion, I yanked the sword from his belt and darted through the door. As soon as I was inside, I kicked hard, slamming the door shut right in the guard's face, and then moved so that I wouldn't have it directly behind my back.

It crashed open a second later as the guard darted inside as well.

"Stay out of this," came a commanding voice.

Prince Volkan was standing halfway between his bed and the door. He was still wearing his sleeveless red tunic and dark pants, but he had taken his boots off and looked like he had been about to head into his private bathroom. Now he held up a hand towards the guard to further enforce his command. There was a dangerous gleam in his yellow eyes and they never left mine.

"I want another try," I declared. "And if I win, you take this collar off me right here, right now."

"Kenna," Volkan said, his voice deceptively pleasant.

The guard was still hovering awkwardly in the doorway, and when I had kicked the door shut, he must have called in reinforcements because the noise of trampling boots echoed from the corridor behind him.

"What's wrong?" I challenged. Spinning the stolen sword in my hand, I raised it and leveled it at his chest from across the room. "Are you suddenly scared of fighting me?"

If he knew how good I really was at swordplay, he would be. But he didn't. So my taunt accomplished exactly the thing I wanted it to do. It made rage flicker in his eyes.

The running guards had reached the door by now, but

they stopped as Volkan turned his commanding stare on them and flicked his hand. They withdrew, closing the door behind them.

"You have some nerve." Volkan walked over to where his sword hung on the wall and drew it slowly, as if savoring the sound of steel singing into the silent room. "Forcing your way into my private chambers and demanding things from me."

Holding my sword at the ready, I advanced on him. "You do not get to talk about forcing people to do things."

Firelight from the shallow flame pools along the walls painted his face with streaks of red and deep orange as he prowled towards me. The middle of his room was a relatively open space and the floor was covered by a large carpet made of rich red and gold thread.

My dress brushed against my bare legs as I took the first step onto the carpet. On the other side, Volkan did the same. There was a cold smile on his face.

"Tell me," he began, raising his curved sword, "does this by any chance have something to do with what I made Mordren do earlier today?"

"You used me to make him get down on his knees and bow before your feet." Fire burned inside my soul. "In front of nobles from every court."

"Yes. And now they will tell everyone… that Mordren is my bitch."

I attacked.

Leaping forward, I twisted and swung with all my might. Volkan read my movements and threw up his own sword to block mine while aiming a punch towards my other side. I rammed my closed fist down on his wrist. The force knocked his arm off course and allowed me to disengage our blades and jump backwards again.

"What even is your problem with Mordren?" I snapped as I lunged at him again. "What could he possibly have done to make you hate him this much?"

Volkan dodged my strike and swiped at my ribs. "He was born. That's reason enough."

"No, it's not."

"He's a spoiled brat who's never known what it is to fight. To struggle. To always have to watch his back for threats. He was born into a royal family where succession is hereditary. He was just handed his crown and his court without having to fight for it."

I slammed my sword into his. "You killed his parents!"

Grabbing my wrist, he yanked me closer. "Of course I did!" he snarled in my face. "They were growing too powerful. And with little Mordren manifesting his powers, they were becoming a threat. So I did what anyone would've done. I eliminated the threat."

Since he held my arm in an iron grip, I couldn't pull away. Changing tactics, I twisted my hips and kicked hard at the side of his knee. He hissed.

The fire in the flame pools surged upwards. I rolled out of the way as they shot towards me, but before they could hit and set the carpet on fire, they vanished. Unless Volkan was prepared to burn his own room down, he would have to get through this fight without his fire magic. I jumped to my feet again.

"Eliminate a threat?" Whirling around, I darted towards him again. "You took his parents and their friends and made them kill each other!"

Metallic ringing filled the air as our swords clashed. I shoved his aside and swiped downwards, but my attack fell short when he drove his fist down on my arm. Pain pulsed through my forearm. Recovering quickly, I ducked under his oncoming blade and jabbed at his side instead. He leaped aside. When he landed and was still trying to stabilize himself, I seized the moment and kicked at his hip. Stumbling a step back due to the surprise hit, Volkan swung his sword wide.

"So?" he spat back at me, picking up the thread of conversation while advancing again. "And Mordren has never killed anyone, is that what you're saying?"

"It's not the same thing!"

I rammed my sword towards his heart. He sidestepped and swung at my back while I was still trying to recover from the failed lunge. Since I was too far out of position, I barely made it in time. Diving forward, I tried to escape the blade but the sharp edge grazed my skin. I could feel a few drops of blood trickle down my skin from the thin cut. My dress was tangled around my legs, but I shot to my feet anyway.

"Mordren kills people to make sure that no one betrays him like you did." I aimed another attack towards his heart. "It's not the same thing as just killing people for the hell of it."

Wildfire rage flashed across Prince Volkan's face.

Alarm bells blared in my head and I leaped backwards, crouching down and throwing an arm over my head right as a wave of flames cut through the room.

When the deadly flames disappeared and I looked back up, there was an army of Volkans standing in the room. All of them looked identical. And since I had been busy ducking the fire, I hadn't been able to mark the real one.

The one on the left attacked. I whirled towards him and yanked up my sword to block his, but it passed right through it. With the unexpected lack of resistance, I stumbled forward just as a hard kick hit the back of my knees.

Pain crackled through me as my knees hit the carpeted

floor with a bang. I tried to convert the crash into a roll, but a sword sped towards me from straight ahead. Diving to the side instead, I managed to get out of reach. But I quickly realized that it had been another fake Volkan because another leg smacked into my ribs from the other side.

I sucked in a gasp as I was thrown off my knees and tumbled across the floor. Another wave of pain shot through me as I slammed to a halt against the stone frame of Volkan's bed.

Legs and arms and swords descended on me from every direction. Choosing a side at random, I swung my sword wide to stop a few of them. The blade passed straight through everything.

Right as my arm reached the other side, something solid hit my wrist. I cried out as my elbow bent too far back and I lost the grip on my blade as another real foot kicked it out of my hand.

The army of Volkans disappeared and only one remained. Standing over me where I was slumped against the foot of his bed, he pushed the tip of his sword against the base of my throat. Fury burned in his eyes.

"You think Mordren and I are so different in that regard, but we are the same!" He pushed the sword harder into my skin. "You defend him and you hate me, but he and I are exactly the same. You think I don't know anything about broken trust?"

Paralyzing fear washed over me as I wondered if he was actually going to kill me right here. End my life and find some other way to rattle Mordren. I had always banked on the fact that no matter what I did, Volkan wouldn't kill me because he still needed me as a weapon against Mordren. But as red flames danced across his furious face, I wasn't so sure.

"This." Volkan's hand shot towards me and grabbed my collar. With a savage tug, he used it to yank me to my feet until I was standing before him with my back pressed against his bedpost. Leaning closer to my face, he pulled hard on the golden collar again. "*This* is the only way to make sure that people won't betray you."

My eyes widened in fear as he raised his sword, but he only threw it on the bed behind me. The brief moment of relief was short-lived when he moments later drew back his fist.

Air exploded from my lungs as he drove it into my stomach. I sucked in a desperate gasp as I doubled over, but the strong fingers curled around my collar kept me upright. My eyes watered but Volkan only pulled me further up by the collar until I was forced to stand on my toes.

"I trusted people before too," he said, his voice a deadly whisper. "And I have also been betrayed."

I drew in another shaky breath while trying to block out the dull pain spreading through my body.

Volkan traced his fingers down my cheek in an almost loving gesture. "She was just like you. Beautiful. Devoted." A coldness seeped into his eyes. "Or so I thought. Right up until the moment when I woke up to her plunging a dagger into my chest. Turns out all she wanted was my throne. And she was willing to lie and fuck her way to it until she could kill me."

From the fog of agony and terror, I managed to blink at him in surprise. A cruel smile spread across his lips. Grabbing the top of his tunic, he pulled it down to reveal a jagged scar right next to his heart. I had seen it before but never thought much about it.

"I still keep the scar. As a reminder that no one can be trusted. A reminder that fear, and *this*," he tightened his grip on my collar again and gave it a firm tug, "is the only way to make sure that no one can betray you."

Without warning, he released me and I collapsed to the floor when there was suddenly nothing holding me up anymore. On my knees on the floor, I stared up at the Prince of Fire who still loomed above me. And at that moment, I realized something terrible.

At the heart of it, we were all the same.

Me. Mordren. Volkan.

We had all been betrayed by people, hurt by people, used by people. And what we wanted was enough power to make sure that we were in control of the situation, so that no one could ever do it to us again.

I still hated him. I hated Volkan with every fiber of my being. Hated him for what he had done to Idra. To Hadeon and Ellyda's parents. To Eilan and Mordren's parents. For everything he continued doing to Mordren. For everything that he was doing to me. But now I understood why he was doing it, because at the heart of it, he and I were driven by the same motivation. And that terrified me.

The need for power and control so that no one could use me again, so that I could make sure that no one hurt me or my friends again, burned inside me. And that same fire burned in Volkan's soul too. I would stop at nothing to get what I wanted, which meant that neither would he. Our motivations might be the same, but I couldn't help the awful feeling of dread that surged up as I seriously considered that, against someone like Volkan Flameshield, I might be thoroughly outclassed.

Volkan reached down and grabbed my arm. After hauling me to my feet, he dragged me across the floor and towards the door. "You will be punished for this insolence. Coming to my bedroom like this and making demands."

Yanking open the door, he practically threw me at the cluster of guards waiting there. They started in surprise, but the dark-haired one I had been hurled into caught me before I fell.

"Get her to her room and make sure she stays there until tomorrow morning," Prince Volkan ordered.

"Yes, sir."

The door banged shut behind me.

While the guard escorted me back to my room, I tried to keep the runaway panic inside me from turning into a full-blown stampede. It only partly worked. But at least I managed to keep my face a blank mask as we walked through the red halls.

When the door to my room at last closed behind me, I let it slip. And then the tears came. Drawing ragged breaths, I managed to keep myself together enough to write a quick note to Mordren in the traveling book. Then I collapsed on my bed and pulled the covers up to my chin in order to stop my body from shaking.

I didn't want to admit it, but behind all my anger and all my scheming, I was terrified.

There was a reason why Volkan was the Prince of Fire, and had been for so long. And there was a reason why he never lost any of the fights in the tournament. He was powerful, intelligent, and utterly without morals or compassion.

In the face of all that, who was I to think that I could take him down? Me. A bastard-born half-elf with control issues and delusions of grandeur. What chance did I really stand against the power of Volkan Flameshield?

CHAPTER 33

A black castle rose before me. I watched the morning sunlight reflect off the glass-like material while the first winds of spring ruffled my hair. Seeing Mordren's castle again filled me with both longing and dread. Mostly because the Prince of Fire was next to me as we strode towards it.

"This is your punishment," Volkan said as we were escorted towards the main entrance by one of Mordren's guards. "You hated seeing Mordren bow to me. Well, let's see if we can't get him to do it again."

I had recovered from my moment of fear and doubt last night. Or at least partly, anyway. So even though Volkan was trying to get under my skin, I managed to keep my expression neutral as we entered the Court of Shadows.

Since I hadn't known that we would be coming here until it was already too late, I hadn't been able to warn Mordren about this. I could only hope that he would be able to deal with whatever Volkan was going to do. I glanced at Idra. She kept her eyes straight ahead, not acknowledging me, as if our moment of bonding in the training hall had never happened.

Looking away, I slid my gaze back to the corridor in front of us as well.

Only the sound of our footsteps broke the silence as we made our way deeper into the black castle.

When we at last saw the light flickering from inside the doorway up ahead, my heart was thumping in my chest. There was a throne room in this palace, but since Mordren didn't allow courtiers inside anymore, it was rarely used. Instead, the guard was taking us to the cozy dining room I had spent so much time in when I was living here.

"My prince," the guard said as he stopped in the doorway, blocking our way forward. "Prince Volkan is here to see you."

There was a beat of silence. Then Mordren's voice cut through the stillness.

"Send him in."

The guard had barely taken a step to the side before Volkan was stalking past him and into the dining room. Idra and I followed him.

"Volkan, what a terribly dreary surprise to find you in my home this early in the morning," Mordren said.

He scoffed. "Little Mordren, how unsurprising to find you–"

"Kenna," a stunned voice cut him off.

An affronted look flashed across Prince Volkan's face at being so rudely interrupted, but I barely caught his expression before my eyes found the source of the voice and I blinked in surprise.

The Court of Shadows had been in the middle of having breakfast when we had barged in, and the polished table was filled with plates and cups, as well as a variety of pots and pans. Mouthwatering scents of toast and fried eggs and grilled sausages hung over the whole room. Between the mountains of food and the glittering candles were six people.

Mordren, his face the epitome of haughty indifference, was sitting next to Eilan. The shapeshifter was absentmindedly spinning a knife in his left hand but his pale green eyes were taking in every detail of the scene. Across from the two of them were Hadeon and Ellyda. As usual, Ellyda was lost in a book and appeared not to have even noticed our arrival. Hadeon, on the other hand, tracked Idra's every move with sharp eyes. But none of them were the reason for my surprise.

The source of the interruption was a skinny human with loose brown curls and perceptive brown eyes. Valerie. I flicked my gaze to the blond man sitting across from her. Theo.

"Oh," was all I managed in reply.

"Who are you to interrupt an elven prince when he is speaking?" Volkan Flameshield demanded, his voice dripping with threats.

With an unbothered expression on her face, the brown-haired thief turned to Volkan and lifted her narrow shoulders in a shrug. "I'm Valerie." She flapped her hand in her friend's direction. "And this is Theo."

Theo lifted a hand and gave the Prince of Fire a little wave.

I almost laughed. In fact, it took all my self-control not to burst out laughing. Prince Volkan had probably expected a worried reply, a stammered apology, or maybe even terrified silence. Whatever he had been expecting, that had at least not been it, because he was staring at the two thieves as if they had suddenly grown three heads.

"What do you want, Volkan?" Mordren prompted. Shining black hair slid over his shoulder as he cocked his head. "I would like to finish my breakfast without your breath poisoning the air."

A malicious smile slid home on Volkan's lips. "So cocky for someone who bowed before my feet just yesterday."

Silverware rattled as Hadeon banged his fist onto the table and shot to his feet. Idra took a step forward in response to it, which made Valerie and Theo scramble out of their seats as well.

"Always hiding behind your general." Hadeon flicked his eyes to Idra before fixing Volkan with a scornful look. "Are you that scared of us?"

"Scared? Of you?" Volkan cut a dismissive hand through the air. "You can't even move without your little chaperone tattling to the king."

Mordren and Eilan exchanged a look. With terrifyingly synchronized moves, they slowly rose from the table and prowled towards the Prince of Fire. Hadeon rounded the table and joined them on the right while the two human thieves completed the half-circle on their left.

Volkan swept his gaze around the room. "Speaking of, where is little Remus?"

A wicked glint crept into Mordren's eyes as he flashed him a lethal smile. "Not here."

Idra stood her ground, her face impassive as always, but there was a tiny spark of alarm in Volkan's eyes as he searched for the chaperone he had no doubt counted on to be here.

Shadows swirled around the dark fabric of Mordren's suit as he took another step closer. Beside him, Eilan, Hadeon, Valerie, and Theo moved with him.

Volkan's gaze darted from face to face, as if he was only just now realizing that he was outnumbered six to two. And there was no chaperone to protect him.

A wide grin spread across my lips.

"I think you should leave," a voice cut through the tension like a sharpened blade.

Both Volkan and I turned to look at its source. Still seated at the table with an open book before her, Ellyda had finally looked up from its pages and was staring straight at the Prince of Fire. Her violet eyes were cold enough to cause frostbite.

While continuing to casually twirl a knife in his left hand, Eilan locked eyes with Volkan and jerked his head in Ellyda's direction. "What the lady said."

"Don't test me, Mordren," Prince Volkan growled. "You don't want to find out what happens if you start something right now."

Dark tendrils slithered across the floor as Mordren grinned. "Is that so?"

I let out a yelp. Grabbing me by the arm, Volkan yanked me sideways until I was standing in front of him. Fire whooshed to life in his other hand.

"Back off," he warned. Raising his arm, he held his flame-covered hand next to the side of my head. "Because I promise you, you won't like how this ends."

All five of them froze in their tracks. To my right, Valerie and Theo stared at me with panic and worry darting in their eyes. Hadeon and Eilan, on the other hand, only looked angry. It was strange, because it was the same emotion, but it manifested very differently on their faces. For Hadeon, it was hot rage that roared like red flames in his eyes, while Eilan stared at Volkan with cold fury. Cold, like the space between the stars.

Wood scraped against the floor. Ellyda had pushed her chair back and stood up, watching the scene before her with sharp eyes.

Volkan looked from face to face and a slight frown blew across his brow. Then he tightened his grip on my arm and jutted out his chin. "What's it going to be?"

"Leave." Mordren's whole body radiated power as he took a single step forward and pointed towards the door behind us. "While I still let you."

For a moment, it looked like Volkan was going to do something else, but he only snarled and jerked his chin at Idra. "Let's go."

Still keeping a firm grip on my arm, he pulled me with him as he stalked towards the doorway. After another few seconds, Idra followed. I cast a quick look over my shoulder and managed to catch Valerie's eye. She still looked worried but gave me a nod. I flashed her a satisfied grin.

Then the view was cut off as we disappeared back into the black corridor.

About halfway to the front door, Volkan finally let go of my arm. I rubbed the spot where his fingers had dug into my skin but said nothing. However, when we finally strode out into the mild spring morning, I could no longer keep the wicked smirk from my lips.

The scent of new grass and melted snow filled my lungs as I drew a deep breath and grinned at the pale sun rising over the city below. For the first time since the training room, Idra turned to look at me. Slight confusion swirled in her dark eyes, but she remained silent as we stopped just outside the high defensive walls.

With that smirk still on my lips, I looked up at Volkan. "Wow, you really lost that one, didn't you?"

Anger sparked in his yellow eyes again, just as I had known it would, but I had decided to taunt him anyway so I only raised my eyebrows. He took a step forward, forcing me to crane my neck to meet his eyes. A dangerous, triumphant expression settled on his face. Even though I had deliberately provoked him, I couldn't stop the spike of terror that shot through me when he looked at me like that.

"Oh, not at all," he began.

Leaning down, he drew a hand along my jaw. I flinched back a step at the vicious look in his eyes, my heart suddenly thumping in my chest.

A smile that was pure evil spread across his mouth.

"Because now, I finally know how to break you."

CHAPTER 34

"You're afraid."

Pacing back and forth across the floor inside my room, I let out a shaky breath. "Wouldn't you be? I'm barely holding it together as it is."

Evander's face was full of concern as he looked up at me from where he was sitting on my bed. "You shouldn't have provoked him."

"Yes, I should."

"Because he made Prince Mordren grovel at his feet in front of nobles from every court?"

I slowed my pacing enough to glance at him, but I didn't reply.

Evander blew out an exasperated breath and raked his fingers through his short brown hair. "You really care about him, don't you?"

For another few seconds, I continued saying nothing. I didn't really want to talk to Evander about my relationship with Mordren because I knew that he would never understand it.

But in the end, I still let out a sigh and replied, "Yeah, I do."

"I don't understand why. He is as bad as Prince Volkan. If not worse. The only reason he's gotten anywhere in life is because he manipulates, threatens, and blackmails people into submission. Not to mention that he actually kills people too. How could you possibly like someone like that?"

Because I'm exactly the same.

"He–"

A sharp knock came from the door.

My heart leaped into my throat, but I forced myself to walk over and push down the handle. The door swung open to reveal one of Prince Volkan's guards.

"Follow me," he said.

A surge of panic coursed through me. It was time. I swallowed. After twisting back to give Evander a small wave goodbye, I followed the guard into the torchlit hallway.

I hadn't been able to concentrate on anything since Volkan's declaration this morning. Being a master at psychological warfare, he hadn't taken me to the breaking room straight away. Instead, he'd gone about his day as planned. All the while, the dread inside me had been building and building with every passing hour until I was almost driving myself crazy trying to figure out what he was going to do to me.

The door to the breaking room appeared at the end of the corridor and the guard motioned for me to enter. At that point, I had to force myself to keep breathing. With blood pounding in my ears, I steeled myself and walked across the threshold.

Prince Volkan was already waiting for me inside.

And so were seven other people.

Cold dread washed over me as I stopped just inside the door. It banged shut behind me.

"Kenna." A wide smile cut across Prince Volkan's face. "Welcome to your own personal hell."

"No," I breathed as my eyes darted around the room.

There were seven pyres spread out along the walls and one person was tied to a pole on top of each of them. Mordren. Eilan. Hadeon. Ellyda. Valerie. Theo. Even Eilan's shapeshifter alias, the blond warrior by the name of Julian Bladesinger, was standing atop a pile of wood. Fear flickered in their eyes.

"This isn't real," I said.

Volkan cocked his head, his long blond hair rippling with the motion. "Isn't it?"

Raising both arms, he spun in a circle. Blades of fire shot out around him and ignited the wood below the visions of my friends. I tried to smother the runaway terror. This wasn't real.

Metallic clanking filled the room and temporarily drowned out the crackling of the fire that was taking root on all the pyres. I looked down at the short sword Volkan had thrown before me.

From across the room, he drew his own sword. "Go ahead. Fight me." Holding out his blade, he turned in a slow circle and used it to motion at my friends. "But the only way *this* stops, is if you submit."

Steeling my mind once more, I bent down and picked up the sword.

The fires around the room flared up.

Valerie let out a whimper.

I closed my eyes for a second, forcing the sound out of my mind, and then advanced on Volkan. He grinned at me but didn't move to meet me. Instead, orange light flashed across the walls as the flames burned brighter.

The pyre directly behind Volkan held a bound Ellyda and she was struggling against her ropes as the fire crept forward, licking her boots. I forced myself to keep my eyes on the Prince of Fire.

Logs popped from the pyre on my right. Hadeon sucked in a sharp breath between his teeth in response to it.

I swung my sword at Volkan.

With that malicious grin still on his mouth, he sidestepped it.

That's when the screaming started.

It was a high-pitched, desperate sound and I whipped my head towards it instinctively.

Standing atop the pyre to my left, Valerie was screaming in terror as flames ate their way up her legs. Panic shot up my spine.

"It's not real," I whispered to myself. "It's not real."

Eilan's scream cut through the room. I flinched. Forcing myself not to look at him, I dragged my eyes back to Volkan instead. Wicked satisfaction burned in his eyes.

"During that little visit to the Court of Shadows, I finally figured it out," Volkan said. "I saw the way they all reacted when I threatened you. They all care about you. Which means that you care about them. And that's when I finally remembered why you traded yourself to me in the first place. It was to save little Julian Bladesinger, the person you love."

As if on cue, Eilan's shapeshifter alias screamed in pain.

"So the thing that you fear most," the Prince of Fire continued, "isn't that something or someone will hurt you. It's watching someone hurt your friends."

Pure terror washed over me. Volkan had finally done the

one thing I had been desperately hoping he wouldn't be able to do. He had found my deepest fear. The one thing that could break me.

I shook my head. "It's not real."

Volkan laughed. It was a cold mirthless sound. Locking eyes with me, he grinned and raised his arms. "Then this won't matter."

The fire clinging to every pyre roared upwards. Clothes caught fire. Hair caught fire. Earth-shattering screams, terrible enough to pierce the veil between the living and the dead, filled the room. Mordren was screaming like he was possessed as flames sped across his body. Next to him, Theo's body was spasming in a sea of fire.

My knees buckled.

Steel clattered against stone as I dropped the sword to press both hands over my ears. But it did nothing to block out the bloodcurdling screams.

A strong hand wrapped around my arm and turned me. Yanking my head up, Volkan Flameshield forced my eyes to the blond body writhing on the pyre before me. Tears rushed down my cheeks. I slapped a hand across my mouth to stop myself from throwing up as I watched the skin melt off his bones. Shattered screams of pure animalistic desperation pounded against my ears.

In all my life, I would never forget that sound. Or that sight.

Inside me, everything went black. It was like snuffing out a candle, leaving my heart and soul a dark empty void.

"Please, stop." My voice came out in a broken rasp. "Please."

"What was that?"

"Please, stop."

The vision disappeared in the blink of an eye. I sucked in a gasp as the suddenly deafening silence hit my ears like a physical blow. Without all my burning friends, the room was now empty except for me and Volkan. My whole body was shaking.

Wrapping his hand around my collar, Volkan pulled me to my feet and pressed the sword back into my hand. I stared up at him with wide eyes. After taking a step back, he twitched his fingers at me.

"Come on. You can still fight me."

Staring back at him, I threw the sword aside as if it had burned me. "No."

"Really?" He flashed me a mocking grin. "You were so confident this morning. Go ahead. Take your shot."

When I didn't immediately reply, the vision snapped back around me again. Fire. Screaming. Melting flesh.

"Stop." I dropped to my knees. Pressing my palms against the cold stone floor, I bowed my head in submission. "I'll do whatever you want. I'll follow every order without question, I'll never challenge you, I'll do... anything." I drew in a shaky breath. "Just please, no more. No more."

"You're surrendering?"

"Yes."

Volkan twitched his fingers in front of my face, silently telling me to look at him. "Then prove it."

Staying on my knees, I looked up at him.

Victory swirled in his eyes as he stared me down. "Who are you really?"

"I'm a spy," I blurted out. "I didn't trade places because I love Julian Bladesinger. I did it so that I could come here and spy on you for Mordren. So that I could mess with your relationship with High Commander Anron."

He raised his eyebrows. "Is that right?"

"Yes."

A wicked laugh bounced between the red stone walls. "Oh, I think you will be of great use to me."

With my heart and soul numb after the shutdown, I only looked back at him with impassive eyes.

Instead of me sabotaging Volkan's scheme, he would now use me to further his plans.

And I was going to let him.

CHAPTER 35

Salty sea air filled my lungs. The brisk winds blowing across the beach ripped through my hair, but I barely felt it. Idra was right, everything really was much easier if you just let go.

"Why did you bring her this time?" High Commander Anron said and jerked his chin in my direction.

"Because she has a lot of information," Volkan Flameshield said. "And she does whatever I tell her. Isn't that right, Kenna?"

A brief flash of burning pyres and earsplitting screams appeared around me before vanishing again. I flinched.

"Yes, sir," I replied. "Whatever you want."

"Huh." Anron stroked a hand over his chin as he watched me for another few seconds before turning his attention back to Volkan. "That is a very interesting power. I would love to hear more about how it works someday."

Volkan waved a hand in the air in a sort of noncommittal response before moving on. "We need a final push. Something to show King Aldrich that I am the one true candidate."

"Wouldn't it be better to keep hitting the other princes and undermining their power even more first?"

"True." Volkan crossed his arms over his chest. "But we also have to build up my reputation. Just making them look bad won't necessarily make King Aldrich like me better. We need to do something to make him notice me too."

"What about accusing them of colluding to kill the king? Then you could both tarnish them and make yourself look like a hero for uncovering the plot at the same time."

"It won't work."

"Why not?"

"He would never believe it." Volkan shrugged. "Not so soon after Princess Syrene tried to assassinate him."

Anron furrowed his brows. "Who is that?"

"Well…"

While the Prince of Fire recanted the whole story of how Syrene had almost managed to kill the King of Elves last year and take his throne, I stared at the horizon.

We were a safe distance away from the High Elves' camp and the spies that Prince Rayan had stationed there. Grasslands stretched out to my right before sloping upwards farther inland, and the beach we were standing on looked more gray than white in the light of the overcast sky. I stared at the dark smudge that marked the zealots' temporary camp.

Last time I'd been here, there had been a group of elves with black bracelets praying to the High Elves at the edge of their camp. That group had doubled in size now. But with my feelings this muted, I couldn't really bring myself to care about that.

"She sounds like an interesting one," Anron said once Volkan's story was finished.

"Yeah, well, she's currently sitting in the dungeons

underneath King Aldrich's mountain, awaiting execution, so perhaps not that interesting."

The High Commander smirked and waved a hand in the air. "Alright, so blaming them for a fake assassination attempt is out of the question. What else can we do?"

"Idra, any ideas?"

Her bottomless black eyes turned to Volkan. "No, sir."

"No, you never have, do you?" He sucked his teeth. "Killing really is your only skill, isn't it?"

For a brief moment, something flashed in her eyes. But then that impassive mask slid back on and she just went back to scanning the area for threats. Volkan blew out a dismissive huff and then turned to me.

"Kenna, what would you do?"

I considered in silence for a few seconds. "I would pretend to give him valuable information on a perceived enemy, sir."

He narrowed his eyes at me. "Explain."

"Right now, the biggest threat against King Aldrich is the High Elves. That means he would greatly reward someone who can help him with that problem." I shrugged. "So, you fabricate some supposedly valuable information about the High Elves, and then you present it to the king. That means he will both reward you for uncovering it, and it will also make him act on faulty information, which will put both you and High Commander Anron in an even better position to accomplish whatever it is you're planning to do."

Silence fell across the beach. I shifted my weight in the soft sand as another gust of wind whirled through the landscape and pulled at my hair.

"That's actually a very good plan, Kenna," Volkan said at last.

I didn't even bother feeling guilty. Instead, I just nodded in acknowledgement and then went back to staring at the horizon.

"I agree," Anron said.

"Hmm. So, what kind of information should we feed the king in order to do maximum damage?"

Waves crashed against the shore to my left. I watched the whitecaps move across the dark gray sea and tasted the rain in the air while the Prince of Fire and High Commander Anron plotted out a scheme that would screw over the King of Elves, and all based on advice that I had given them.

Yes, Idra had indeed been right.

It really was much easier if you just let go.

CHAPTER 36

Stunned silence spread across the room. For a moment, no one said anything as they stared between Prince Volkan and King Aldrich. Then, the king broke the stillness.

"That's... very well done, Volkan," he said with an approving nod.

A smug expression briefly flashed across Volkan's face before he inclined his head. "Thank you, my king."

Seated on the armrest of Volkan's expensive-looking armchair, I watched the expressions on the other princes' faces as they mulled over the fabricated information that they had just been given. Rayan was sitting on the couch to our left. With one leg crossed over the other and a slight frown on his face, he studied the Prince of Fire. Directly across was Prince Edric, and as opposed to Rayan's delicate frown, he was outright scowling. Mordren, who had taken up position to our right on the king's other side, looked like he was imagining the sound that Volkan would make if he plunged a dagger into his heart. The only one who appeared entirely unbothered was Prince Iwdael. Lounging on another sofa, he regarded the rest of the room with a bland expression.

"And how, exactly, did you come to be in possession of this particular piece of information?" Mordren challenged, his silver eyes fixed on Volkan's face.

"The same way everyone gets information." Prince Volkan rested a hand on my thigh and drew it upwards in a very deliberate gesture. "I used my *spies*."

Mordren's eyes flicked to me for a fraction of a second before he replied, "Is that right?"

"Yes. Isn't it great to have loyal people who can get past your enemy's defenses and right into their home?"

"It is indeed," King Aldrich agreed, completely ignorant of the underlying meaning to the words being spoken. "The only question now is, what do we do with this information?"

"My king," Rayan Floodbender began, "I think we should send additional spies to reconfirm whether this is in fact the truth, before we take any sudden action."

Even though I kept my gaze on the Prince of Water, I could feel Mordren's eyes on me as Rayan continued explaining his reasoning. Based on the smirk playing over Volkan's lips, I knew that he could see Mordren searching my face as if trying to figure out whether I had anything to do with the false information about the High Elves that Volkan had just presented to the king. I very much did since it had been my idea, but my face stayed an expressionless mask as I continued to stare at the red stone wall above Prince Rayan's shoulder.

"You're quite right." King Aldrich pushed to his feet.

Furniture scraped against the floor as the rest of the princes scrambled to do the same.

"We'll gather a bit more information before we act," the

king finished with a nod in Rayan's direction. Then he shifted his gaze to the Prince of Fire. "Well done, Volkan. This kind of initiative, hard work, and cunning is exactly the kind of qualities that a king needs. You all should aspire to be more like that too."

The scowl on Prince Edric's face deepened and a soft rumble went through the stones of Volkan's palace, but the Prince of Fire wasn't paying him any mind. Instead, he inclined his head in Aldrich's direction.

"Thank you, my king." A satisfied smile spread across his lips. "I am glad that my efforts are appreciated."

"Indeed." The king nodded back. "But now I really must go."

"Yes, there is actual work to be done," Edric grumbled and took a step towards the door to the meeting room.

"Of course," Prince Volkan said. "Oh, and I welcome you all to attend the final fight in my tournament in three days. It is bound to be spectacular."

Edric muttered something noncommittal while stalking out the door after King Aldrich, but Prince Iwdael gave Volkan a pleasant smile and a nod before he disappeared as well. Sensing the tension in the room, Rayan lingered by the roaring fire in the hearth as Mordren closed the distance between us.

"Is there a problem?" Prince Volkan challenged with raised eyebrows.

Hadeon fell in beside the Prince of Shadows as they crossed the floor. In response, Idra and half a dozen of Volkan's guards moved into the room to surround them from a distance. I watched them advance but did nothing else.

"Mordren," a clear voice suddenly cut through the room. There was a casual look on Prince Rayan's face, but he knew exactly what he was doing as he met Mordren's surprised gaze. "Would you mind joining me on the way back out? There is something I would like to discuss with you."

For a moment, it looked like he was about to refuse, but then he changed direction and started towards the door with Rayan instead. "Of course."

Without a second look back, the two princes and their companions disappeared into the torchlit hallway beyond. A flicker of annoyance blew across Volkan's face. Apparently, he wasn't at all satisfied that the confrontation had been averted because he stalked after them while snapping his fingers at Idra.

"Let's see them out," he said.

He didn't wait to see if she obeyed, but instead simply strode after the retreating princes. Idra did indeed follow, leaving me alone with a handful of guards and some of Volkan's other slaves. I stared at the empty doorway.

A log popped in the fireplace by the wall. Red and orange shadows danced across the stones as the flames around the meeting room flickered. For a few minutes, I just remained standing there. Then I finally drew a deep breath and started towards the door as well.

The idea I had given Volkan yesterday had made him look like a resourceful person fit to lead our lands, and it had started a scheme that would screw over the king and the rest of the princes. Sure, they were going to reconfirm it, but if I knew anything about Volkan then he would be able to fake whatever proof he needed to make it look real a second time. Mordren had known that it was me. As I wandered down the hall in the other direction, I couldn't help wondering if Edric and the other princes had figured it out as well.

"It's true, isn't it?"

I snapped my head up at the sound and came to a halt. Evander was standing in the middle of the corridor, blocking my way forward. His arms were crossed over his muscled chest and there was a disapproving frown on his face.

"Is what true?" I replied at last.

"That *you* are the one who helped Prince Volkan do this. That you're the one who came up with it."

Twisting slightly, I cast a glance over my shoulder. The corridor was empty except for us. "Yeah. So?"

Evander shook his head in disgust. "How could you?"

"You don't know what it's like."

Taking a step forward, I made to skirt past him but he moved sideways so that he continued blocking the way forward. I glared at him but he only looked back at me with raised eyebrows.

"Of course I do," he replied. "I've been through the exact same thing. But trust me, the fear wears off after a bit."

"Not with me. He keeps showing me these little glimpses to remind me of what he could do to me if I stopped obeying."

"He did the same thing with me. With all of us. But he will stop doing that after a while. Trust me, if you just hold out a little bit longer then you'll be fine."

"I don't care." Once again, I tried to move past him.

"Well, I do!" He threw out his arms, blocking my way again. His dark green eyes took on a pleading look as they met mine. "Come on, Kenna. We need to find some way to screw up Prince Volkan's final match. It might be the last really good opportunity we have."

An irritated expression flashed across my face. Raising my arms, I shoved him backwards. "When the hell did you become so invested in this scheme?"

"When did you decide not to be?" he snapped back. Closing the distance between us again, he grabbed me by the shoulders and gave me a small shake. "Pull yourself together, spiritsdamn it! We need to finish this."

I moved like a viper. Smacking away his hands, I took his wrist in a firm grip and threw him aside. He hit the red stone wall with a thud.

"No, we don't," I growled in his face while he was busy sucking air into his lungs. "Because I've had enough! I've had enough of sacrificing myself for other people. I sacrificed myself for my family, for Monette, for Valerie and Theo when I first met them, and all that got me was beaten up, robbed, belittled, and exhausted. And then I sacrificed myself for Mordren and his court, and now I'm a slave again." I threw my arms out in frustration. "I worked so hard to be free. Worked so hard to stop putting other people first, to start putting myself first, but now here I am making the same fucking mistake over and over again."

I had let go of his wrist but hadn't stepped back, so Evander was still standing pressed against the wall. Looking back at me, he spoke in a soft voice. "Caring about people is not a mistake."

"Yes, it is! Because I'm tired of caring. I'm tired of caring about other people. I've said it before but this time I'm serious. All it has ever done is hurt me."

"You don't–"

"Yes, I do." Raking my fingers through my hair, I shook my head at him. "You have no idea just how exhausted I really am. How tired I am of this life that I can never seem to escape, where I have to constantly walk on eggshells. I'm tired of having to analyze every single thing someone says to see if they're about to hurt me. Tired of always being on high alert. Of always having to carefully choose my words and then panic when someone might have interpreted them in a way that would make them mad. Caring and constantly worrying about every single thing I say and do is killing me! I can't take it anymore."

Evander blinked at me. He must have heard the raw truth that laced my words because genuine surprise suddenly blew across his face as he looked back at me, as if he was seeing a completely new side to me. Then his eyes darted to the right and he opened his mouth. But before he could say anything, I pressed on.

"So I don't give a fuck who runs this continent anymore," I snapped at him. "If it's Mordren or Volkan or the High Elves or the damn spirits of our ancestors. I don't care anymore. I just want people to stop hurting me."

"Really?" a voice dripping with threats said into the suddenly oppressive silence.

I flinched. Whipping around, I found Volkan Flameshield standing a few strides away. He cocked his head and looked from me to Evander. I took a step back while Evander remained frozen by the wall.

"You don't care if I rule or not?" Prince Volkan demanded.

"I..."

After an audible swallow, I flicked my gaze from side to side, but Evander kept silent. Volkan advanced on me. I flinched back another step, which made him shoot me a commanding stare. Swallowing again, I remained where I was but dipped my chin and lowered my gaze to the floor.

"Answer," Volkan ordered as he stopped right in front of me.

"I'm sorry, sir," I said, keeping my eyes downcast. "Of course I care if you rule."

He let out a cold laugh. "No, you don't." Before I could reply, he took my chin in a firm grip and forced my head up until he could lock eyes with me. "But you really want me to stop hurting you, don't you?"

"Yes."

"Hmm." He stroked his thumb over my jaw. "I could make your life here really comfortable. Like Idra's. You could have a nicer room, you could wear clothes of your own choosing, you'd never have to work hard again... And all you would have to do in return is obey my every command without question and do everything you can to rattle Mordren whenever he's in my presence."

"And you would never hurt me again? Or look for reasons to hurt me or invent reasons to hurt me just because you can?"

"Unless you outright betray me, I will never hurt you again."

Oh he was good, I had to give him that. The mistake that most people make when they try to make someone else obey them is to do it solely by force. But that only works to a point, which Evander was the proof of. However, figure out what it is that the other person really wants, or rather what they desperately *need*, and offer it to them... That is what makes someone submit completely.

"So, do we have a deal?" Volkan prompted.

Looking into his commanding stare, I hesitated for all of one second before answering, "Yes."

"Good." A satisfied smirk spread across Volkan's face as he released my jaw. "Then come with me."

Evander was still standing unmoving and quiet between

the burning torches, and I could feel his gaze on me. Ignoring him, I didn't even look back as I followed Volkan down the hall in the other direction.

A sense of relief spread through me as I walked. It was a calm and steady feeling and I recognized it well.

It was the feeling that washes over you when you know that you have made a good decision.

CHAPTER 37

Rippling anticipation hung over the whole city. It was the final day of Volkan's tournament and all the other princes would be there to watch. Even the king had decided to put in a rare appearance. Not to mention High Commander Anron and his Captain Vendir. Elves wearing black bracelets whispered excitedly as they moved closer to the great sandstone arena while a cluster of humans drank deeply from waterskins. The blistering sun shone down on them from the bright blue sky, heating their skin, as they waited in line to get inside. I kept my eyes on the towering walls ahead as I followed Prince Volkan towards the stairwell that would take us to the private balconies.

"Well, if it isn't the little Prince of Shadows," Volkan suddenly said.

Dragging my gaze from the hulking arena, I swept it over the dusty street before us until I found the reason for his remark. Mordren, Eilan, Ellyda, and Hadeon had rounded the building from the other direction and were heading towards the door to the stairs as well. They stopped when they noticed us.

On Volkan's other side, Idra kept walking with casual grace but her eyes were sharp as they flicked over the party now blocking the doorway. None of them wore any visible weapons, but the keyword in that sentence was of course 'visible', so Idra's dark eyes stayed alert as she assessed the threat level.

"Volkan," Mordren replied.

As we came to a halt two strides away, Volkan flashed him a taunting grin. "I wasn't sure you would come. Not after the humiliating experience you received at the opening of my tournament."

Ellyda was holding a cup of what looked like water in her hands. Up until that moment, she had only been staring unseeingly at the ripples that moved across its surface, but at the sound of Volkan's comment, her fingers tightened on the cup. Idra shifted her gaze to the blacksmith in response to it. A bead of sweat ran down her temple, presumably due to the heat rather than nerves. If it came down to a fight, Idra was the only one that I was certain would walk away alive.

"Of course we came," Mordren replied before any potential fight could break out. His cold smile was a slash of white. "We cannot wait to see you die in the final match."

"Always the same with you, little prince. A lot of talk but nothing to back it up."

Cocking his head, Mordren cast a pointed glance at me and the outfit I was wearing before sliding his gaze back to the Prince of Fire. "If you are so unconcerned about my actions, then why have you suddenly decided that you need a second bodyguard?"

Volkan lifted his hand and drew it over my shoulder and down my arm while satisfaction seemed to pulse from his whole being. "It's a reward." A malicious smile stretched his lips as he held Mordren's gaze. "For *loyalty*."

Mordren's eyes darted to me again.

After we'd made our deal three days ago, Volkan had indeed kept his word. He had moved me into a nicer room and I had been allowed to choose what to wear, which was why I was currently wearing a shirt and pants of dark leather that I had gotten from Idra. It was such a relief to be out of that skimpy golden dress. And in return for that small mercy, Volkan expected me to hold up my end of the bargain.

"Yes," I said before Mordren could reply. Locking eyes with the Prince of Shadows, I took a step closer to Volkan. "Thank you, sir."

Mordren's eyes flashed. And then I did the one thing I knew would make him lose all sense of composure and self-control. I rose up on my toes and kissed Volkan's cheek.

Black shadows exploded before us. Fire roared to life along Volkan's arms in response to it and Idra took a step forward, positioning herself between the Court of Shadows and her prince. No weapons had been drawn and no shadows had touched us, but the potential for violence hung like a crackling storm over our two groups. From a short distance away, Remus watched the exchange with sharp eyes.

"Mordren," Eilan said from behind his shoulder. There was a warning note in his voice.

"Yes, listen to your brother, little prince," Volkan taunted. "You really don't want to see how this plays out."

Dark tendrils whipped around Mordren's arms as he took a step forward. "Oh, but I think I do."

Hadeon moved with him. Taking a step forward as well, he twisted his body so that he would block Idra's path to Mordren. Leather creaked into the tense silence as Idra moved closer too.

"Then try it." The flames along Volkan's arms flared up as he too advanced another step. "I could do with a little warmup before my match."

Violence and death flickered from all sides. And then Ellyda did something that Volkan would not have expected in a million years. She threw her drink at him.

A loud splash echoed around us as the liquid hit Volkan over the chest, throat, and jaw. The fire covering his arms spluttered out. After looking down at the wet section of his tunic, he turned to stare at Ellyda in surprise. There was a look of stunned disbelief on his face. In this heat, the tunic would be dry by the time we reached Volkan's balcony, but that wasn't the point. No one threw drinks at the Prince of Fire. Except Ellyda, of course.

"Enough with the dick-measuring contests," she snapped. After cutting a sharp glare in Volkan's direction, she spun on her heel and stalked towards the doorway. "Mordren, let's go."

Hadeon let out a smug chuckle and then followed her. When Volkan's fire had died out, Mordren had pulled back his shadows as well, and now he was staring straight at me instead. I looked back at him with an impassive mask on my face. After a small nudge from Eilan, the two of them disappeared after the others as well.

Next to me, Volkan was still staring uncomprehendingly at the now empty place where Ellyda had been only moments ago. If it had been anyone else who had thrown that drink, the whole situation would have exploded into violence. But Ellyda was odd enough to get away with something like that.

And besides, it was no secret that Volkan still wanted to recruit her to his court.

"Sir," Idra said, her voice soft. "The time."

Volkan spat out a snarl but then stalked towards the entrance to the stairwell. "After this match, we're going to pay the Court of Shadows a little visit and I am going to make them all crawl before me." Twisting slightly, he cast me a glance over his shoulder. "Well done, Kenna. As long as you keep doing things like that, our deal is active."

"Yes, sir," I answered as I climbed the stairs behind him.

I could feel Idra's gaze on my back but I kept my eyes on the steps.

Excited murmuring met us as we crossed the final threshold and emerged onto Prince Volkan's private balcony. I stopped at the back and took up position by the wall while Idra followed him a bit closer to the railing. Volkan didn't stop until he was standing right in front of the stone balustrade, while Idra came to a halt a few steps behind him.

A warm wind blew across the balcony and ruffled my hair. I drew a deep breath. The air smelled of sand and warm stones. Standing in the shade, I watched from my position by the wall as Volkan threw his arms wide to silence the chattering crowd.

The stain from Ellyda's drink had already dried and the Prince of Fire only looked formidable as he stood there before his subjects. Light from the bright sun made the golden threads in his sleeveless tunic glimmer. The rich dark red fabric fell across his chest in a way that accentuated his muscled body, and his long blond hair rippled behind him as another warm wind blew across the arena. As a hushed silence spread over the crowd, I realized that everyone must be thinking the same thing that flashed through my mind at that moment. Challenging someone like Volkan Flameshield to a one-on-one battle was completely and utterly insane.

"My subjects," the Prince of Fire called in a voice that boomed across the arena. Turning to the right, he looked towards the other private balcony. "Fellow princes. High Commander." At last, he inclined his head to the white-haired elf seated in the ornate chair beside the four elven princes and their retinues. "My king." None of them answered his greetings, but Volkan hadn't been expecting them to either, so he just turned back to the crowd. "Many challengers were eager to measure themselves against the strength of their prince. Most of them dropped out after seeing the first two matches."

Nervous laughter echoed throughout the waiting audience.

"Now, we have arrived at challenger number seven," Volkan continued. "I think you all know how this is going to end by now."

Another bout of laughter that was as much fear and awe as it was actual amusement rippled across the humans and elves around us.

"Let's give Djimon Skybreaker a welcome worthy of someone who is about to die."

The crowd erupted in cheers as a muscular elf with long black hair strode onto the sands of the arena. There was a sheathed sword at his belt, but he made no move to draw it as he stopped in the middle of the circular space and raised his fists in the air to the roar of the audience. From atop the balcony, Volkan snickered at the confident gesture.

Blond hair billowed behind him as he leaped up onto the railing. "Let the match begin."

His red and gold tunic fluttered around him as he stepped

off the stone balustrade and plunged towards the floor of the arena. From this angle, I realized that the fall wasn't actually all that high. The move looked much more impressive from afar, which was of course the point.

A cloud of dust rose in the air as Volkan slammed down onto the pale sand. He dove forwards on impact and came up in a roll. Drawing his sword, he charged at Djimon Skybreaker.

Orange light flashed over the sands like a streak of lightning. The crowd sucked in a collective gasp. Prince Volkan had barely made it two strides when the odd lightning bolt hit him and he was engulfed in an explosion of red, orange, and yellow.

No one dared to breathe while they waited for it to die down. When the explosion ebbed out, another wall of fire became visible. Shooting up in a half-circle around Volkan was a shield of flames. Behind it, the Prince of Fire was grinning like a madman.

Djimon shoved his palm forward again. Once more, something that looked a lot like fireworks, *lethal* fireworks, shot out from his hand and sped across the sands towards Volkan. It hit his fire shield in a smattering explosion right at the same time as Volkan jabbed his other hand forward.

A series of fireballs shot forward. Djimon dove aside as the burning orbs hurtled straight for him, and threw another attack towards the prince at the same time. The fireballs exploded against the far side of the arena in a rain of fire and the crowd screamed in excitement. Deadly fireworks slammed into Volkan's shield.

He staggered a step back as one streak of orange lightning cut through the protective flames, but the fire covering his body absorbed the second hit. Drawing his right arm in a wide arc, he sent a wave of flames rolling across the sands. Djimon threw himself behind one of the pale stone walls that dotted the sand and provided cover. He barely managed to get behind it before crackling fire washed over it like a tidal wave.

Orange lightning streaked across the sand again.

Extending one hand out into the open, Djimon had sent another attack at Volkan while he had been busy looking at the side where his opponent had disappeared. While Volkan yanked his flame shield to the side in order to block it, Djimon jumped up from his cover and shoved his palms forward over and over again.

Volkan parried them with his shield while hurling another fireball towards him. The ball of fire struck one of Djimon's lightning attacks and exploded in a blinding eruption of flames. A boom shuddered through the arena.

Dodging fireballs and tidal waves of crackling flames, Djimon was shooting lightning bolt after lightning bolt at the Prince of Fire, preventing him from concentrating enough to use his powers to cast a vision over Djimon. Heat washed over the audience and burning embers blew through the air. It was by far the greatest show of battle pyrotechnics I had ever seen. Based on the roar of the crowd, they agreed.

The only one not watching the spectacular fire magic below was Mordren. He was staring at me. Even from this distance, I could feel the intensity in his silver eyes as he kept them locked on me. I turned to meet his gaze. For what felt like a very long time, the two of us only stared at each other from across the arena while crackling fire exploded below us.

Idra glanced at me from where she stood by the railing.

I slid my gaze back to the battle below.

Fire whooshed across the sands. Volkan was getting frustrated by now. It was clear that he had expected this fight to be much more one-sided than it had turned out to be. His fire magic was not limited to only one thing, as Djimon's was, and he could also plant visions across people's eyes, which meant that this should have been an easier win. But the problem was that Djimon was *fast*. His deadly fireworks streaked across the sand and hit the Prince of Fire in rapid succession, barely leaving him time to both block and counter.

The crowd sucked in a gasp as Volkan suddenly let his flame shield drop and threw out both arms. Djimon seized the opportunity to shoot more orange lightning at him, but while he attacked, so did Volkan. Slamming his hands forward, he raised a wall of fire so tall it reached halfway up the arena. At the same time as Djimon sent his fireworks forward, Volkan's wave of fire surged across the sands as well.

Crackling and hissing echoed between the pale stones as the orange lightning hit the wall of fire. It tore holes in the flickering mass, but still the flames kept coming.

Terror surged across Djimon's face as he realized what was about to happen. He dove back towards cover but the burning wave was moving too quickly.

A short cry rose but was abruptly cut off as the whole writhing mass of flames passed over him, leaving nothing but cinders blowing away on the warm winds.

The arena was dead quiet.

"How was that for entertainment?" Volkan's smug voice boomed into the silence. Striding to the middle of the circular field of sand, he spread his arms wide and turned in a slow circle. "This is what happens to anyone who dares to challenge my rule. You have witnessed them all. Seven brave fools who ended up in the ground or in slave collars because they were stupid enough to think that they could steal my throne." He turned so that he stared up at the other private balcony. "Strength and power, *that* is what a true leader exhibits."

King Aldrich gave him a small nod in acknowledgement. The other four princes wore expressions that varied from worried, to annoyed, to indifferent, to outright murderous. Next to them, leaning against the railing since there was no chair for him this time, was High Commander Anron. His sharp blue eyes gleamed in the sunlight as he watched the Prince of Fire and the deadly skills he had just displayed. I moved over to the stone railing and looked down at him as well.

Dust swirled in the air as a warm breeze blew through the arena. It made my hair flutter behind me so I tied up my long red curls with a piece of string.

"Seven fools have tried their luck and the rest bowed out before even setting foot on my sands," Volkan continued in a strong voice. "This marks the end of the tournament and there will be another fifteen years before you can–"

"Actually, sir…"

The whole crowd started in surprise as another voice dared to interrupt the Prince of Fire. Clothes rustled and leather creaked as everyone turned to stare at the small balcony that was directly above the place where the challengers checked in and got ready before the fight. Confusion rippled through the gathered audience as an elf with long red hair cleared his throat again. Erik. The elf who was in charge of organizing the tournament.

"Actually, sir," he called again. In the stunned silence his voice carried well even though it shook slightly with fear. "There is one more contestant scheduled for today."

Shock pulsed through the crowd.

"What?" Volkan glared at him. "Who?"

I leaped onto the stone railing. My tied-back hair shifted against black leather as I steadied myself and flashed him a wicked grin.

"Me."

CHAPTER 38

The whole arena turned to stare at me in shock. I stepped off the balcony railing. Wind rushed in my ears as I freefell through the air using the same move that Volkan always did. A cloud of sand rose up around me as I hit the ground and rolled forward to soften the impact. Coming to my feet, I strode straight towards the Prince of Fire.

"Erik, what is the meaning of this?" Volkan Flameshield snapped at the elf with long red hair still standing on the small balcony on the other side of the arena. "There are not supposed to be two matches in one day."

Erik flinched but stood his ground. "I'm sorry, sir. It's my mistake. I accidentally mixed them up and put both Djimon Skybreaker and Kenna on the slot for today, but I didn't realize it until just now."

Accidentally. That was one word for it, anyway. It wasn't as if the real reason was that I had blackmailed him into it. Well, not blackmailed per se. I had just blackmailed Viviane into owing me a favor when I realized that she was stealing, and then I'd had her steal an important document from Erik's satchel and then put it back after his meeting with Prince Volkan. And then I had just happened to solve that problem for Erik so that *he* would owe me a favor, and then I had called in that favor yesterday and had made him add me to the list of contestants and also had him make sure my fight happened today. But yes, let's go with *accidentally*.

"Are you telling me that there was an eighth challenger who had entered my competition that you failed to tell me about?" Volkan said, his voice dripping with threats.

Erik flinched back a step. "Uhm…"

"Volkan."

The crowd whirled towards the private balcony and stared at the King of Elves who had spoken up for the first time.

"We do have other things to do," King Aldrich continued, putting a slight emphasis on 'other things' in order to refer to the High Elf Commander currently standing two strides away from him. "We will not come back for a *second* final match. We are all here. If you are going to fight this match as well, then I would suggest doing it now. Otherwise, just declare the tournament finished."

"Oh, but how can the tournament be finished when there is one fighter left?" I challenged, my eyes locked on Volkan, as I closed the distance between us.

"Traitor," he growled at me before raising his voice. "You are not even a member of the Court of Fire, which means that you can't compete in this tournament."

"Am I not?" I lifted the gold collar around my throat, making it glint in the sun before letting it fall back down against my collarbones. "I'm your slave, aren't I? That means I'm your subject and therefore a member of this court."

He knew that I was right so he only narrowed his eyes at me as I came to a halt a few strides away.

"But you could always reschedule our match for another day." I made sure that my voice echoed between the sandstone walls as I locked eyes with Volkan. "If you're afraid to fight me now, that is."

A buzz went through the stunned audience. Volkan's yellow eyes flashed. I had trapped him in a fight he couldn't get out of and he knew it. It was within his rights to demand that we battled another day, but that would make him look weak. And it was for that exact reason that I had made sure the whole arena would be packed for this particular fight.

I had gotten Eilan to drink that scribe, Tristan, under the table at the party in the Court of Trees so that he would owe me a favor. To pay it off, he had forged that fake document about an attack plan that I had planted in Volkan's study for Anron to find. But that wasn't the only thing I'd had him make. He had also made some very official-looking flyers that informed people that the match last week had been pushed back a couple of hours.

That lean elf with light brown hair who had passed me in the corridor right before I set up Erik to be pickpocketed by Viviane, had been none other than Eilan in one of his shapeshifting forms. And the stack of papers he had been carrying had of course been those flyers that he had then proceeded to hand out throughout the city, leading to the poor attendance last week. All so that the arena would be filled beyond capacity today.

A vast portion of Volkan's court was here watching today. If he refused my challenge now in front of all these witnesses, he would be undoing everything, all the fear, that this tournament had helped him build. So he would have to fight me. Right here. Right now.

"No," Prince Volkan finally replied in a voice brimming

with poison. "No need to reschedule. It will be my pleasure to beat you."

I motioned towards my slave collar. "Then take this off." When he only stared me down, I let a smirk play over my lips. "I can't try to kill you with it on, remember?"

Spitting out a scoff, he stalked towards me. The whole arena held its breath as the Prince of Fire advanced on me, but I knew that he wouldn't attack before the fight was officially started so I simply stood there watching him.

He stopped barely a breath in front of me, but I refused to step back. Reaching out, his fingers curled around my golden collar. With a merciless tug, he forced me upwards.

"This was your plan all along, wasn't it?" he snarled in my face. "You only pretended to fall apart back in that breaking room so that I would bring you to this match. And that little fight with Evander in the corridor the other day, that was to truly sell the bit, I presume?"

"Yes, I knew that you would be passing through that corridor on your way back, so I told Evander to wait there and then we staged our little confrontation." Making no move to get him off me, I simply grinned up at him. "You can't imagine the relief that coursed through me when you made me that deal. I was afraid the staged argument had been a bit overkill, but it worked like a charm. Not only was I certain that you would be bringing me to this match, you also told me that you would let me choose my own clothes. Battling you in that fluttering golden dress would've been a pain, but now..." I cast a pointed look down at my shirt and pants made of dark leather. "It was at that moment I knew that the staged fight with Evander had been a good decision."

"And that night you came into my bedroom, demanding a fight that you thoroughly lost?"

"I needed to make you think that I had snapped completely. That I was close to breaking. And I needed to make you furious. To give you a push so that you would do something even worse so that I could pretend to break under the drastically increased pressure. Otherwise, you might have seen through my act."

Volkan tightened his fist around my collar and pulled me forward until he could whisper in my ear. "When I win, I won't kill you. A quick death is too good for a traitor like you. Instead, I will do everything I know you fear. I will burn you and beat you, I will have strangers fuck you, I will trap you in visions of your friends burning on endless loops until you are on your knees begging me for death." A whoosh of fire sped across the smooth surface of the collar, and then Volkan yanked it from my throat while still holding my gaze. "I will become your worst nightmare."

A warm breeze whirled around me, stroking my now empty neck like a gentle hand. After five weeks with a collar around my throat, the sudden absence felt as though I had gotten rid of a huge boulder I'd been dragging around. Rolling my neck, I sucked in a deep breath of air that smelled of warm sand and stone. And a trace of mint.

Taking a few steps back, I only flashed Volkan a cocky grin in reply.

Steel sang into the quiet arena as the Prince of Fire drew his curved sword and raised it to point straight at my chest. "So, you will fight me with your bare hands then, girl?"

Something whizzed through the air. I kept the grin on my face.

"Not exactly."

A second later, a gleaming sword and a sturdy dagger buried themselves point first in the sand next to me.

Snatching them up, I spun them a couple of times in my hands. The weight and feel of them were as familiar to me as my own arms. I cast a quick look to my right.

Two humans were leaning against the railing along the closest row of seats. With a bright smile on her face, Valerie gave me a cheerful wave while Theo chuckled and winked at me. I flashed them a grin.

The only reason that they had been in the Court of Shadows that morning when Volkan brought me there to taunt Mordren, was because I had written to Mordren in the traveling book after that lost fight in Volkan's bedroom and told him to figure out a way to get my weapons inside the arena so that I could fight properly. His answer had been 'by thief' so he had invited Valerie and Theo to get them on board. It had been sheer bad luck that they'd been there when Volkan arrived and realized what I truly feared.

Dropping into a fighting stance, I arched an eyebrow at him. "Well, shall we?"

He was silent for a few moments, glaring at me and trying to scare me into backing down. When it didn't work, he let a dangerous glint creep into his eyes.

"Let the match begin," he called in a strong voice.

I shot forward.

My biggest problem was that Volkan could use ranged attacks and I couldn't. So I had to force him into a close quarter battle before he could start throwing fireballs at my head. The fact that he had just announced that he wasn't actually planning on killing me helped my odds a bit too. Otherwise, he could've just burned me to a crisp from afar.

Metallic clanging filled the air as I slammed my sword into his defending one while also ramming my knife towards his side. He shoved my sword away and leaped back right before the second blade struck. Pressing the advantage, I jabbed my sword at his chest again before his feet had barely touched the ground. All those weeks training with Idra had really honed my skills.

Fire flared to life around Volkan, forcing me to stop my momentum to avoid getting my face burned. But the flame could do nothing against my blade. Steel cut through the shield of fire and sped towards Volkan. He yanked up his own sword and knocked mine aside before sending a pulse of flame in an effort to make me back up further. Heat washed over my chest and legs, but nothing caught fire.

From atop the otherwise empty balcony, Idra smiled slightly. The fire-resistant leathers she had lent me worked fantastically.

I snapped my gaze back to Volkan and swung my sword in a forceful attack at his side. He was still recovering from the surprise of realizing that unless he was prepared to turn me into a piece of charcoal, his flames were of little use, so he only managed to block the strike and move backwards without countering.

Twisting to the side, I feigned a strike with my left and then struck with my right.

The crowd sucked in a gasp of shock as my sword sliced through Volkan's tunic. A shallow wound appeared along his ribs. Red drops trickled down from it.

That seemed to snap Volkan out of the slightly sluggish surprise that had surrounded him since he realized that I had double-crossed him. With a snarl, he attacked. Silver glinted in the sunlight as his sword sped towards me. I ducked under it and jabbed my knife at his other side. The blade vibrated in my hand as he slammed his sword down on it to stop it. My arm shot downwards at the impact and I was momentarily out of position as Volkan's elbow smacked into my jaw.

Pain crackled through the side of my face as I stumbled aside, but I barely had time to gather my wits before a sword descended on me once more. Throwing myself backwards, I narrowly managed to avoid it.

Pyres flared to life in a circle all around me. And then the screaming started.

I kept my eyes on the Prince of Fire as the visions he forced me to see shrieked and thrashed against the poles when the flames devoured them. It was the exact same thing that he had shown me that final time in the breaking room. My worst nightmare. And he had no idea just how close he had gotten to actually breaking me with it. Only three things had saved me.

Firstly, Volkan could only affect my vision and my hearing. He could make me see my friends burning and make me hear them scream like dying animals, but he couldn't make me smell burning flesh. If he had been able to do that, I would have been on my knees begging him to stop. But without the sense of smell, I had a telltale detail that reminded me that it wasn't real.

Secondly, Volkan didn't know that Eilan was a shapeshifter, which meant that he didn't know that there was in fact no Julian Bladesinger. Volkan still believed that the one I truly loved was that blond warrior who had fought against him at the beginning of the tournament and who I had traded myself for. So when Volkan had forced me to watch as the skin melted off Julian's bones, he hadn't known that I was looking at a person who didn't actually exist.

And finally, I'm pretty good at shutting off all my emotions when the pain inside my heart becomes too unbearable. I'd done it once when I found out that my family had sold me into slavery, and after that, I had become fairly skilled at switching my feelings on and off at will.

And those were the only things that saved me.

Steel cut the air right in front of my chest. Leaning back, I evaded it while drawing my own sword in a wide arc. Volkan rammed his elbow into my forearm to stop the swing and then moved his own blade back towards me. But before he could get into position, I kicked at his hip.

He stumbled back a step and his attack fell short. I jabbed my knife at his side while defending from his other strike with my sword. Volkan sucked in a hiss as the blade grazed his skin. Twisting around, I slammed my sword towards him but he had let the first strike go through just so that I could make that move.

Pain shot up my arm as his sword cut through my leathers and split the skin underneath. Blood welled up in the wound but I yanked down my arm and sent another kick towards Volkan's hip. He saw that one coming and sidestepped, but it gave me the second I needed to get my guard back up.

Mordren had been right when he admonished me back in that cabin in the Court of Trees. This was a ridiculously dangerous plan. From the moment that I had decided to trade myself for Eilan all those weeks ago, I had already decided that I was going to challenge Prince Volkan to a fight in his own tournament. But I had known that it would be a race against time. If Volkan hadn't believed that I was in love with someone who didn't exist and if he had been able to affect my sense of smell, then he would have broken me that time when he showed me all my friends burning. Ridiculously, ridiculously dangerous.

As if on cue, the visions of my friends on those pyres

around me let out earsplitting screams of pain. I focused on the fact that the air around me still smelled of warm stone, sand, and a trace of mint.

Ignoring the flaming pyres that were only for my eyes, I instead advanced on Volkan again. He blocked my thrust but watched me through narrowed eyes. The fires eating away at the wooden poles and the people tied to them flared higher. Vocal cords broke as the visions screamed and thrashed like people possessed. I swung at Volkan's head.

In the blink of an eye, the burning faces around me disappeared.

Volkan yanked up his sword and parried my strike, but held it there as if to trap my blade. I rammed my knife towards his side instead. He leaped back.

While he was still airborne, he flashed me a triumphant grin. And then hundreds of Volkans shot out and landed on the sand around me. Since he couldn't distract me with a vision of my friends burning, he had gone for the one thing that he knew would work. Creating multiple visions of himself. If I didn't know which one was real, then I couldn't hit him. Or block his strikes.

Keeping my eyes on the Volkan that had been real when he leaped backwards, I flexed my fingers on the hilt of my blades.

"Are you sure you remember which one is me?" Volkan taunted, his voice coming from every side.

The mass of blond elves suddenly clustered together very quickly and then ran apart again. I flicked my gaze back and forth. There was no way I could have followed the real Volkan in that exchange so I held my weapons at the ready and turned in a slow circle instead.

Dark red and gold moved in the corner of my eye. I whirled around to find one of the Volkans charging me. Panic screamed inside me, but I forced myself to draw a deep breath. And then I let the sword hit.

It passed straight through me.

"Impressive," the army of Volkans said.

Another Prince of Fire attacked, and once more, I simply sucked in a breath and let the coming blade pass straight through me.

I could feel the annoyance rippling through the mass of Volkans. He was getting frustrated. Another shape leaped forward and swung at the same time as one behind me did the same.

Ignoring the one about to stab me in the back, I threw up my sword and blocked the one attacking from the front.

Metallic ringing filled the air as our blades clashed.

Genuine surprise flashed across Volkan's face when he realized that I had blocked the real him and not any of his incorporeal clones. In a show of strength, he kept pushing his sword towards me while I blocked it with my own.

"How did you know?" he growled at me while forcing me backwards.

I grinned up at him. "Magic."

And by 'magic' I of course meant peppermint-flavored water. After writing a quick note in the traveling book, it had been easy to stage the confrontation with Mordren and the others right outside the door to the stairwell. Getting Mordren riled up had been part of the script, but I had a feeling that he hadn't had to fake any of the fury, and then all we had to do was bring it to an almost fight that Ellyda would solve by throwing some water on the Prince of Fire since she was the only one who would be able to get away with it.

Even after the water had dried, Volkan's tunic smelled like

mint. And one of the senses that he couldn't affect was a person's sense of smell.

Rage flared to life in Volkan's eyes at my flippant response. Oh, he was getting angry now.

Flicking his wrist, he disentangled our blades and shoved me backwards. I kept my eyes on his real body as I straightened again and raised my sword once more. Fury burned like hungry flames behind Volkan's eyes.

He charged.

And so did all his shadow clones.

I swiped towards the real Volkan with my sword while blocking his own strike with my knife. Steel clashed as our blades met. It was followed by a snarl as my sword cut a deep wound in his upper arm.

He rammed his closed fist into my stomach.

Air exploded from my lungs as I staggered backwards from the blow. Something glinted above me and I threw up my knife to block it, but I was too late. Sharp pain shot through my shoulder blade as a sword cut through the leather, drawing blood. Sucking in a gasp between my teeth, I swung wide to force Volkan back but I had taken my eyes off him for a second and now I didn't know which one was the real one anymore.

Blood dripped down from the wound across my shoulder blade and the one along my arm while dull pain pounded through my ribs from the strike. From all around me, smug-looking Volkans stared me down.

I inhaled deeply, smelling the trace of mint in the air.

Two Volkans attacked at once. Twisting around, I raised my sword to block the one coming from my left while leaving my back completely unprotected for the other one.

Sunlight reflected off my sword as I slammed it towards the oncoming blade.

It passed straight through.

Due to the lack of resistance, I stumbled forward and barely managed to steady myself before I could topple over. I jerked upright and raised my sword but the fight was already over.

Cold steel bit into my throat from behind.

CHAPTER 39

My heart pounded against my ribs as a strong hand wrapped around my upper arm and yanked me back against a very solid chest. The curved sword at my throat pressed into my skin, forcing me to keep still against the body of a Volkan that was very much the real one.

Leaning forward over my shoulder, he hissed in my ear. "Oh, little Kenna, I am going to make your life a living hell from this day onwards. Remember what I told you before we started? I am going to become your worst nightmare and torture you in every way I know you fear until you are begging for me to kill you."

My sword was pointing inwards. I shifted it slightly but he was standing firmly out of reach behind me. Close. But not close enough. I swallowed against the wave of fear that coursed through me.

"Please," I whispered. "Don't. I'm sorry. Just tell me what you want and I will do it."

The army of Volkans had disappeared around us and the smell of peppermint on his shirt was suddenly making me nauseous. Or perhaps it was because I knew what was coming that I felt like I was about to throw up. My hands trembled as I lowered them slightly.

Worried faces looked down at me from the private balcony. Mordren, Eilan, Hadeon, and Ellyda had all climbed to their feet and were standing right at the stone railing. Next to them Prince Edric and Rayan flicked their gaze between me and King Aldrich, as if expecting him to do something about this. The King of Elves watched the scene below with a neutral expression on his face. Since he barely knew who I was, he had no reason to care about my fate.

The crowd that was packed together on the seats around the arena held their breath as they stared at us.

"What I want is for you to beg me for the sweet mercy of death," Volkan answered. I could hear the vicious smile in his voice as he pushed the edge of his sword harder against my throat. "Drop your weapons."

I shifted my sword hand. Fear and panic were screaming inside me. Screaming at me not to do this. But there was no other way.

So I drew in a shuddering breath.

And then I rammed the point of my sword right through my own chest.

A gasp ripped from my lips.

It was mirrored by a sharp intake of breath behind me.

Then Volkan coughed blood over my shoulder. His sword slipped from his fingers as his arms dropped down, hanging limply by his sides. Shock pulsed like forceful waves through the entire arena.

Blood ran down from the hole in my chest as I laughed. "You're so predictable. You've done this same move every time you've tried to break me. And do you know why?" A wet cough racked my body. "Because I left you an opening behind my back every single time in order to train you into doing exactly that. So I knew that if I left you the same opening now too, you would do it again."

Volkan tried to lift his arms as if to shove both me and the sword away so I pushed the blade farther in. Pain burned through me like wildfire and the knife slipped from my left hand. It thudded to the sand beside us. Focusing all my strength on the sword in my right hand, I kept it firmly buried in both of our chests as Volkan's body spasmed against me.

Giving up the futile attempt to get the sword out, he apparently decided to stall for time instead and pressed out, "You had planned to lose this fight from the start?"

"Yes, this was always the plan. While I trained you to always go for my back when I gave you an opening, I messed with your relationship with Anron just to buy myself some time and to keep any calamities at bay. But this was always my endgame because I knew I could never win against you in an actual fight. In terms of raw strength and magical power, I'm hopelessly outclassed against you. But strength is not the only way to win a fight. So I did what I always do. I blackmailed, manipulated, and schemed."

Another spray of red mist clouded the air above my shoulder as Volkan coughed again. "And now you just have to gloat."

"Yes. Because as soon as I draw out this sword, we have less than thirty seconds before you die. So if I'm going to gloat, it has to be now."

"If you pull out this sword, you will die too."

"Interesting point." I sucked in a shuddering breath before continuing. "During all those times when you tried to break me and I left you that opening to do exactly this, I was also able to accurately estimate where all your vital organs were located in relation to my own body. And you're right, if I had stuck to my original plan, there was a significant risk that I would accidentally hit one of my own organs while performing this move. But I was willing to risk it."

"So what changed?"

I could almost hear the wheels turning inside Volkan's head as he desperately tried to stall me in order to figure out a way out of this. The king and the princes and the High Elves were watching us as if they couldn't believe their eyes. It had only been less than a minute since I had shoved the sword through both our bodies, so I couldn't exactly blame them for not having snapped out of their shock yet. I didn't expect any of them to intervene, but still, I couldn't drag this out much longer. However, there was one more thing that I wanted Volkan to know before he died.

"I made a friend," I answered. "Did you know that Idra has extensive knowledge about anatomy? She was the one who showed me exactly where I needed to push the sword through to make sure that I lived and you didn't." A cold laugh dripped from my lips. "How does it feel to be betrayed by everyone you thought you could trust?"

Before Volkan could answer, I yanked out the sword. Wildfire pain tore through my body and set my every nerve on fire but I managed to keep a hold of my blade. Staggering a step away, I sucked in a desperate breath to steady myself. My hands still trembled slightly but I managed to turn around right as a heavy thud echoed behind me.

A pale cloud of dust rose into the air and drifted away on a gentle breeze as the Prince of Fire crashed down back first on the ground.

That broke the spell. Cries of shock filled the whole arena

around me, but I ignored them as I braced myself against the pain and crouched down over Volkan.

His chest was rising and falling in a ragged rhythm and a dark red stain was spreading across the sand around him. Grabbing the front of his tunic, I pulled him up a bit closer to me and placed the edge of my sword against his throat. His eyes were wild with pain and shock.

"This is for Mordren," I said, my voice a venomous whisper. "For Eilan and Hadeon and Ellyda. And for their parents. And this is for Idra." My fist tightened on the red fabric as I leaned a little closer. "But most of all, this is for me."

I slit his throat.

Fear surged in Volkan's yellow eyes but only a wet gurgling punctured the silence as he tried to breathe. The spray as I severed his artery hit me in the face, but I kept my grip on the collar of his tunic, staring into his eyes from only a breath away while his body convulsed under me.

Then it stilled.

The fear and pain on his face bled away and those fiery eyes that had looked at the world with so much hate and distrust glassed over.

I let him go.

The Prince of Fire hit the sand with a thud that seemed to echo between the pale stone walls. His eyes stared unseeing into the bright blue heavens.

Drawing in a deep breath, I finally straightened and turned to face the rest of the arena. Blood ran down my arm and chest and back, and a whole bunch of it that wasn't mine covered my face and hands.

Even small movements sent bursts of pain through my whole body but I raised my sword and pointed it at the gaping crowd while I turned in a slow circle.

"The Prince of Fire is dead." My voice cut through the silence and bounced around the stone structure. "Bow before your new ruler."

For a few moments, nothing happened.

Then Erik, the elf that I had coerced into making this fight possible, stepped forward on his small balcony and dropped down on one knee.

Leather creaked and fabric rustled as the rest of the arena scrambled to do the same.

Wicked satisfaction shone in my black manipulative heart as I watched the Court of Fire get down on their knees before me. The power and control I felt in that moment was unlike anything I had ever experienced before.

This had been worth it.

This had been so worth the risk.

Turning towards the private balcony, I was met with expressions that varied from giddiness to stunned disbelief. From the row of seats above me, Valerie and Theo waved enthusiastically. I winked at them before shifting my gaze to the royals above.

King Aldrich was staring at me with raised eyebrows, but when I met his gaze, he gave me a nod. My four friends from the Court of Shadows were looking at me with a mix of relief and gratitude, but so as to not draw attention to their involvement in this scheme, they stayed silent. I slid my gaze to the violet-eyed prince on the other end and drew in a deep breath.

It made pain stab like needles through my chest and stomach, and my breath hitched. Clearing my throat, I tried again.

"Oh, and Prince Rayan?" I called.

He started in surprise but moved a little closer to the railing.

I coughed blood onto my chest.

"I'm calling in that favor now."

A small laugh erupted from his chest as he shook his head in disbelief at what I had just accomplished, but then he inclined his head in acknowledgement of the debt and started towards the stairs.

The crowd were still on their knees, unsure of what to do now. So after picking up my knife and sheathing both of my blades, I seized the opportunity and strode towards the door set into the side of the arena. Every step sent a jolt of pain through my body, but this was too important a moment to show it. Steeling myself against the waves of agony rolling over me, I stalked away in a show of power. A trail of blood marked my path across the pale sand.

I managed to make it through the door and two steps into the hallway beyond before my legs gave out.

Barely able to catch myself, I slumped down on the floor and leaned my back against the wall. Hurried footsteps sounded in the corridor to my right.

A moment later, Idra appeared. Light from the burning torches painted her shining white hair with golden streaks. Prowling straight towards me, she assessed me with those strange black eyes of hers.

"You almost missed," she announced as she crouched down next to me.

I huffed out a laugh that made me cough more blood. "Yes, well, 'almost' being the operative word."

"If you hadn't moved your hand that final bit there at the end, you would've died too."

"That's why I moved my hand."

After draping my arm over her shoulder, she pushed us both upwards. A cry ripped from my throat. Idra let me have a moment to steady myself before she began moving us towards a room down the hall. A guard hovered awkwardly by the door.

"You," Idra snapped. "Find Prince Rayan and escort him here."

Armor clanked into the silence as he scrambled to carry out her orders. I stifled another moan as we limped down the red hallway.

"You know," Idra began as she cast me a glance from the corner of her eye. "I have been alive a long time. A very long time. But I don't think I've ever met anyone quite as crazy as you."

I laughed. It sent another burst of pain through me and I sucked in a gasp instead.

"Back in that training room, when you told me that you were going to make Prince Volkan take off your collar and that you were going to kill him, I thought you were crazy. But then when you explained exactly how you were going to do it, I *knew* that you were crazy. What would you have done if I hadn't shown you where to push your sword through?"

"Shoved it through my chest anyway and hoped for the best?"

As she paused to open the door, she turned and looked straight at me. I met her gaze. Understanding dawned in her dark eyes.

"Oh by all the demons in hell, you're serious, aren't you?"

"Yep."

"Bloody insane half-human spy," she muttered under her breath as she helped me across the threshold.

When we reached the desk halfway across the floor, she

transferred my weight to it so that I could lean against it and then she drew back. My hand shot out. She started in surprise as I wrapped my fingers around her wrist and pulled her back to me.

"What?" she asked, suspicion swirling in her eyes.

I held her gaze. And then I reached up and ripped the collar from her throat. Since Volkan was dead, the magic in the slave collar was already gone, but I knew that Idra still wasn't able to take it off herself. But in my hand, it came off easily, like any normal piece of jewelry.

Idra staggered backwards, her hand going to her neck. Disbelief flooded her eyes as she stared from my face to the open collar that I had dropped on the floor and then back again. Her scarred hand continued resting on her now empty throat.

"You..."

"I'm sorry it wasn't very ceremonious." I shrugged one shoulder. "But I figured you'd prefer speed to spectacle."

"I..." She continued staring at me, confusion and shock still bouncing across her features. "You just took it off. You're not going to try and make me some kind of deal? Enlist my services for the promise of freedom?"

"No," I answered simply.

"What if I just walk out that door right now and never return?"

"Then I wish you a truly wonderful life." I smiled at her. "And thank you, for your help."

Her mouth dropped open and she staggered back another step, but before she could say anything, the door burst open and four people poured across the threshold.

"I knew what you were going to do, but that was still the most reckless thing I have ever seen in my entire life,"

Mordren Darkbringer declared as he stalked across the threshold.

"He's right, Kenna," Eilan added as he followed him.

"You think she's reckless?" Hadeon chuckled and shook his head at me as he and Ellyda followed the other two into the room as well. "I think she's bloody terrifying. By all the spirits, Kenna, remind me never to get on your bad side."

While the other three stopped about halfway between the desk and the door, Mordren prowled straight up to me and took my chin in a gentle grip. I knew that my face was still covered in blood, but he didn't seem to mind as he turned it from side to side while he ran his eyes up and down my body as if to check just how badly injured I really was. I tried to push his hand away but I couldn't muster enough strength to accomplish more than a soft swat.

"I'm fine," I muttered.

"You're fine? You just fought a one-on-one battle against Volkan Flameshield with the intention of losing in order to trick him into a position from which you could run a sword *through your own body* and kill him in the process."

"Yeah, I know. I was there."

Still keeping his grip on my chin, he narrowed his eyes at me. "This was an insanely dangerous scheme."

"I'm pretty sure that you've forced me to admit that once already. Back in that cabin, remember?"

Mordren only stared back at me expectantly.

I blew out an exasperated sigh. "Fine. Yes, this was an insanely dangerous scheme. But it all worked out, didn't it?" A grin slid across my lips as I looked up at Mordren. "I killed the Prince of Fire without anyone being executed as a traitor and an assassin, and without anyone losing their court in the process. I'm fine. You're fine. And Volkan Flameshield is dead."

His silver eyes softened. "Yes, he is."

Leaning forward, he brushed his lips over mine in a gentle kiss. I wanted to rake my fingers through his hair but I couldn't manage to lift my arms anymore, so I only returned the kiss with a soft sigh. Afterwards, he didn't draw back but instead rested his forehead against mine. His eyes remained closed.

"Thank you," he breathed against my mouth.

"Yeah," I whispered back as I closed my eyes as well. "Thank you for what you did to make him heal my hand. I know what it cost you."

"It's what we do, isn't it? You and me. We take care of the people we lo–"

"Move aside," Prince Rayan ordered in his smooth voice as he swept across the threshold.

Mordren let out a soft laugh and stole one final kiss from my lips before retreating to give the Prince of Water room to reach me.

Rayan glided across the floor with confident steps until he was standing right in front of me. "Hmm."

"I hope that's a good 'hmm' and not a bad one," I said.

He peered down at me. "I seem to be spending a disproportionate amount of time repairing holes in your chest." His voice was supposed to be admonishing, but there was an amused twinkle in his violet eyes.

"At least this one isn't as life-threatening as the first one was."

"Barely." He held my gaze. "It's good that you just happened to be owed a favor by someone who is a skilled healer."

Just happened to. Right. As soon as I made my plan, I knew that I would need the help of a healer to survive it. So I had made sure that the Prince of Water owed me a favor right at the beginning of my scheme. If Rayan knew that that had always been my plan, he didn't seem very offended.

A warm feeling spread through my body as Prince Rayan started working his literal magic. I gave him a small smile before looking up at the other five people in the room.

Standing by the door, with shock still lingering on her features, was Idra. I wasn't sure what she was going to do now, but I knew that whatever it was, it would be her choice.

From a few strides in front of her, Hadeon was grinning widely at me, and even Ellyda's eyes were clear and focused as she gave me a nod. Next to them were the two black-haired brothers. Eilan smiled and shook his head while Mordren studied me as if he was seeing me for the first time in years. There was an intensity in his silver eyes that almost made me blush.

When I started this scheme, I had done it mostly for myself. To maneuver myself into power. But as I looked back at those five people that I really cared about, I was forced to admit that I had done it partly for them as well.

Because when life was crumbling around you and trying its best to bring you down as well, it truly was good to have friends.

CHAPTER 40

Brilliant white light glittered in the huge chandelier and cast thousands of tiny reflections on the pale marble walls. Wearing a black dress with metal shoulder plates, I was hard to miss in the gleaming white castle.

"She can't be crowned the Prince of Fire!" a nobleman protested.

A murmur of agreement spread through the left section of the sea of nobles. Dark shadows flickered around the edges of Mordren's sharp black suit as he slid his lethal gaze towards them, but they didn't back down.

"She's a woman," someone else called. "So she can't be a prince."

"And the princess of a court doesn't rule," the first one added.

"You are quite right," King Aldrich said.

Cold dread crawled up my spine as I turned to look at the King of Elves who was standing next to me on his white marble dais. The gathered crowd fell silent in anticipation.

Everyone of note had been invited to the coronation

ceremony. Edric, Rayan, and Iwdael stood with their spies and bodyguards around them while the nobles of their courts had gathered to form a colorful sea behind them.

Mordren, Eilan, Ellyda, and Hadeon stood in the center, at the front of the half-circle, with Valerie and Theo, while the noble elves and humans from the Court of Shadows were mixed in with the rest behind them. Even High Commander Anron and Captain Vendir were present, though they were at the back of the room, watching me with hostile eyes.

There was no sign of Idra, but Evander in his dark green suit was standing at the edge of the crowd. As the silence stretched on, he gave me what I think was supposed to be a brave nod.

No one dared to breathe while we waited for King Aldrich to continue. If he was going to denounce me and throw me out, there would be no way to salvage my reputation with all of these important people here to witness my downfall.

"Princess of Fire does indeed set the wrong tone since it is not the title of one who rules," the king said as his brown eyes slid to me. "I think Lady of Fire sounds much better." A small smile spread across his lips. "But it is up to you."

I blinked at him, and it took a second for his words to sink in. Then relief washed over me.

"I think Lady of Fire sounds perfect, my king," I replied with a grateful nod.

"Well then, Lady of Fire it is."

A buzz spread through the crowd. Half of it was excitement. The other half, disbelief. Sunlight fell in through the tall windows and illuminated the dark blue suit of a man who pushed himself towards the front.

"This is absurd," Lord Elmer Beaufort declared as he shook his fist in the air. "King Aldrich, please, you cannot crown that *girl* Prince or Lady or whatever of Fire. She is not even fully elven. She is half human, for gods' sake!"

Aldrich Spiritsinger tilted his head to the right, which made his long white hair ripple over his silver-trimmed robes. "So?"

"So someone who is half human cannot be allowed to rule an elven court! It is simply not done."

"Father." A human with short red hair the exact same shade as mine stepped forward and placed a hand on Lord Beaufort's arm before giving him a single shake of his head. "Don't." Elvin, my half-brother, shifted his gaze to me and the king and bowed at the waist. "King Aldrich. Lady Kenna. Please forgive the interruption."

Red flushed across Lord Elmer's face and he began stuttering protests, but his son was already pulling him back into the crowd. I stared after them in stunned silence.

"Anyone else who would like to question my judgement?" King Aldrich said in a tone that made it very clear that the only correct answer to that question was a resounding 'no'. "Good. Then let us proceed."

As if on some silent command, an elf wearing a long white robe emerged from the door behind the throne.

Another ripple went through the crowd.

A flash of nervous anticipation coursed through me as well when my gaze landed on the object in the elf's hands. He was cradling a small bowl made of white stone. Red flames burned inside it.

My heart was slamming against my ribs and I had to remind myself to keep breathing. I had never seen a prince being crowned before, but King Aldrich had explained what I was supposed to do with it before we had walked onto the podium.

In the thick silence, I could hear the faint crackling of the fire as the robed elf handed the white stone bowl to King Aldrich. The flames cast dancing shadows over his wise face as he turned towards me.

"Kenna," he began.

It was customary to address the person with their full name, but since I didn't actually have a last name, we had to make do with just my first name.

"Do you swear to lead your court with intelligence and strength, to defend it from enemies without and within, and to help protect our lands from anyone who wishes to do us harm?"

Keeping my chin raised, I met his gaze with steady eyes. "I so swear."

"Then claim your power and prove your faith."

King Aldrich held out the stone bowl. Taking a step forward, I reached out and placed my hands over his. He held my gaze for another few seconds before withdrawing, leaving the burning bowl entirely in my hands.

A sense of calm, of rightness, spread through my body as I looked into the flames. It was my power. My strength. My destiny. Calling me home.

With a smile drifting across my mouth, I raised the bowl to my lips and drank the fire without hesitation.

It tasted like honey and spices and it was thick, like molten lava, but at the same time light, like the flickering top of a candle. Warmth spread through my body. Starting in my throat, it flowed down into my chest and stomach, and from there out through the rest of my limbs. The smooth feeling was followed by sparkles. Like tiny fireworks going off all at once throughout my entire body.

Flames flared to life on my skin. They spread quickly until

every part of me was engulfed in fire. The bright flames even lifted my long red curls like a hand drawing its fingers through my hair. Then they retreated.

The warm and sparkly feeling inside me remained.

"Kenna has claimed her power and proven her faith in the old magic," King Aldrich boomed into the silent white hall as he took back the now empty bowl. "And the fire has accepted her."

Wonder and relief and giddiness the likes of which I had never experienced before washed over me as I looked back atced up the smiling king. His brown eyes glittered as he spoke up again.

"By the power of my crown, and with the blessing of the spirits, I name thee Kenna Firesoul, the Lady of Fire."

A deafening cheer erupted from the gathered audience. I swore that the loudest one sounded a lot like Valerie, but I was still in too much shock to turn and look at them. I knew that the princes were given a new last name when they claimed their title, but since I didn't even have one to begin with, I hadn't thought I'd be getting one now. But I had.

Kenna Firesoul.

My name.

I loved it. It felt as though it had always been my name and that it had just taken me until now to find it.

King Aldrich inclined his head and then motioned for me to rejoin the cheering ranks below. I bowed deeply, true gratitude on my face, before doing as he suggested. My black dress billowed behind me as I strode down from the dais and towards the small group in the middle of the semicircle.

A smile played over Mordren's lips as I stopped before him. He looked so much more like himself. During all those weeks when I'd been Volkan's slave, Mordren had constantly seemed on edge. Uncertain. Vulnerable in a way he hadn't been before. There was none of that now. Standing there in his sharp black suit, with a wicked glint in his eyes and a slight smirk on his face, he only looked confident. Powerful. Completely in control. It sent a pulse of heat through my body.

For a moment, we only watched each other. His intense gaze seared into me, and I wondered if his thoughts were heading in the same direction as mine. Then he inclined his head.

"My lady."

I replicated the gesture, all the way down to the slight smirk on my lips. "My prince."

"Has anyone ever told you that you are stunning when you scheme?"

"Briefly. But I might need to hear it again."

"We shall have to remedy that at your earliest possible convenience then."

"Indeed." The smug smile on my lips grew. "Tonight, I think."

"I look forward to it."

"Oh would you stop with the fancy wording already," Valerie blurted out as she stepped out between us. "I hate to be the bearer of obvious news, but this sexual tension here…" She flapped her hand between me and Mordren. "Can be felt from across the room."

Theo slapped her arm with the back of his hand. "Val!"

"What? You were all thinking it."

"That doesn't mean you need to say it."

"Bah," she huffed before casting a pointed glance at Eilan. "Someone had to."

A slight blush crept up the shapeshifter's cheeks, as if he'd been saying that earlier but hadn't expected Valerie to out him. He cleared his throat. "Well, she does have a point."

"Kenna," another voice cut in before Valerie could get started again.

We all turned to see Evander joining our small group. He was wearing a dark green suit that matched the color of his eyes and complemented his brown hair. There was a confidence to his movements as he walked. A small smile drifted over my lips. He looked so much better now that he wasn't wearing that awful golden slave collar around his neck.

"Congratulations on pulling all this off." Shaking his head, he stopped in front of me. "Though, I still wish you would've told me that your plan involved you shoving a sword through your own chest."

"I know, but it was safer for everyone if as few people as possible knew." I flashed him a smile. "But thanks for helping me set up that fake argument. You were really convincing."

Next to me, Mordren scoffed. "Well, that should not be too much of a surprise. He has a lot of experience with lying, has he not?"

"I'm right here," Evander retorted, his eyes locking on the Prince of Shadows. "And as far as I know, you have a lot of experience with lying too."

"Oh, far more than you could ever dream of." Mordren looked him up and down while dragging his tongue slightly over his teeth. Like a predator, sizing up his prey. For a moment, I thought he might be about to do something truly exasperating, but then he simply cocked his head. "At least you did not betray her this time."

To my surprise, Evander didn't cower before Mordren and the power that seemed to roll off him like black waves. Instead, he jutted out his chin and glared back at the

Darkbringer prince as if he was nothing more than an ordinary man.

"Neither did you," he said slowly, enunciating each word.

A cold and dangerous smile spread across Mordren's lips. Evander flinched as if in sudden pain. I opened my mouth to stop Evander's next words at the same time as Mordren started saying something as well, but before any of us could get so much as a syllable out, another voice rumbled through the air.

"Anyway," Hadeon butted in. "Congrats, Kenna. I can't believe you're actually a prince now. I mean, ruler... Whatever, you know what I mean."

That defused the tension and Evander took a couple of steps back. Mordren watched him with a slight smirk on his face.

"I can," Ellyda said before I could reply. She was wearing her casual clothes, brown pants tucked into high boots, and a loose shirt, as she always did. But her eyes were sharp and brimming with intelligence as she locked them on me. "But you won't have a very successful start if you keep dawdling here. We'll talk more later. Now go mingle."

I let out a surprised laugh but gave her a nod since I knew that she was right. With one final wink in Mordren's direction, which made him flex his hand while mischief swirled in his silver eyes, I set out to brave the sea of nobles waiting to speak with me. It was terrifying at first, but I soon fell into a rhythm where I moved through the crowd at a steady pace.

It was almost a bit jarring when the sea of glittering clothes thinned out and I was left stranded on the white floor somewhere at the back of the room. I was just about to turn back towards my friends when a smooth voice cut through the air.

"Kenna," High Commander Anron said as he closed the distance between us.

The urge to kneel grew stronger with each step, but I'd had more time to get used to it by now so it wasn't as overpowering as it had been the first few times I had met him. Captain Vendir swept calculating brown eyes across the room, as if checking for threats, while following his commander. I simply raised my eyebrows and let them come to me.

"My apologies," Anron said as they came to a halt a few steps in front of me. "Lady Kenna Firesoul."

I didn't miss the slight emphasis on my new title and last name, but decided to let it slide. "High Commander Anron. Captain Vendir."

Silence fell. He clearly wanted me to ask him why he had approached me, but I didn't want to give him that power so I remained quiet. Studying him with my eyebrows raised. Something dangerous flickered in his sharp blue eyes when it became apparent that I wasn't going to say anything.

"I just wanted to give you some advice," he said at last, his voice deceptively smooth.

"Oh?"

"Taking the crown is easy." A surge of power pulsed from him as he locked eyes with me. "Keeping it is the hard part. Especially when your enemies are more powerful than your allies."

"Oh, I think Lady Firesoul has a lot more allies than she has enemies."

Whipping my head around, I found an elf with shoulder-length white hair striding towards me. Idra. Surprise bounced around inside me as the lethal warrior came to a halt next to me and squared up against the High Elves. Her dark eyes gleamed with unspoken threats.

"And I think you will find that those allies are quite powerful too," she finished.

I hadn't seen her since I took that silver collar off her in the arena, and part of me had been certain that that was the last I would ever see of her. But now here she was, publicly backing me up against the High Elves.

"Indeed," a midnight voice said.

Warmth spread through my chest. I didn't even need to turn my head to know that Mordren and Eilan had taken up position on one side while Hadeon and Ellyda joined Idra on the other.

"Agreed," Theo announced as he and Valerie fell in beside me as well.

From the corner of my eye, I could see Evander edging closer to the two thieves. He stayed silent but gave me a nod.

"Is this supposed to scare me?" High Commander Anron scoffed and flicked a dismissive hand over our small group. "You are children, playing at an adult's game." A cold smile spread across his lips. "I am here on a diplomatic mission and I would never break that sacred trust. But *if* I were to come for you, trust me when I tell you that you would not stand a chance."

I returned his mocking smile. "That right?"

"Yes." Sharp blue eyes raked over my body as he looked me up and down. "Good luck with your rule… *Kenna*."

All around me, my friends took a step closer. Steady warmth spread through me in response to it and I flashed Anron a challenging grin.

He wasn't the first to try to take me down. A lot of other

people had gone up against me and I was still here. Besides, I wasn't alone anymore. And more importantly, this time I was the one in power.

A dangerous smile spread across his lips. And then the High Commander and his captain spun on their heels and strode away. I watched the sunlight glint off their polished bronze armor as they stalked out of the room. Power pulsed around them with every step. My new well of magic surged and sparkled inside me in response to it.

When I shoved that sword through Volkan Flameshield's chest, I had gotten rid of one enemy, but I had also created an even more dangerous one.

High Commander Anron would come for me. Of that, I had no doubt.

All I could do was hope that I'd be able to get the whole Court of Fire firmly under my control before the High Elves took their first shot.

BONUS SCENE

Do you want to know what Mordren was thinking during that shocking dinner with Volkan? Scan the QR code to download the **exclusive bonus scene** and read it from Mordren's perspective.

ACKNOWLEDGMENTS

Sometimes, the world really is trying its best to break you. To pull you under. To make you throw in the towel and scream "I quit!". Sometimes, it keeps throwing things at you that feel too big, too powerful, too insurmountable to handle. All in the hopes that you will drown. But look at you. You're still here. You're still alive. You have survived all of that. You are still surviving all of that. And every day you keep fighting. So if no one has told you this yet: well done.

As always, I would like to start by saying a huge thank you to my family and loved ones. Mom, Dad, Mark, thank you for the enthusiasm, love, and encouragement. I truly don't know what I would do without you. Lasse, Ann, Karolina, Axel, Martina, thank you for continuing to take such an interest in my books. It really means a lot.

Another group of people I would like to once again express my gratitude to is my wonderful team of beta readers: Alethea Graham, Luna Lucia Lawson, and Orsika Péter. Thank you for the time and effort you put into reading the book and providing helpful feedback. Your suggestions and encouragement truly make the book better.

To my amazing copy editor and proofreader Julia Gibbs, thank you for all the hard work you always put into making my books shine. Your language expertise and attention to detail is fantastic and makes me feel confident that I'm publishing the very best version of my books.

A huge thank you to Claire Holt, the incredible designer from Luminescence Covers, who made this absolutely gorgeous cover. Your talent for creating beautiful covers is out of this world and I'm so lucky that I get to work with you.

I am also very fortunate to have friends both close by and from all around the world. My friends, thank you for everything you've shared with me. Thank you for the laughs, the tears, the deep discussions, and the unforgettable memories. My life is a lot richer with you in it.

Before I go back to writing the next book, I would like to say thank you to you, the reader. Thank you for joining me and Kenna on this mission. If you have any questions or comments about the book, I would love to hear from you. You can find all the different ways of contacting me on my website, www.marionblackwood.com. There you can also sign up for my newsletter to receive updates about coming books. Lastly, if you liked this book and want to help me out so that I can continue writing, please consider leaving a review. It really does help tremendously. I hope you enjoyed the adventure!

Printed in Great Britain
by Amazon